The Diary of Dawn McWarlick

Nick Downs

ISBN: 979-8-218-58823-6

DEDICATION

To the restless spirits who inspired this tale,
And the brave souls who seek truth in the unknown.

To my family and friends,
For standing by me with strength and faith,
Even when the darkness closed in.

Thank you to my wife Jessica for all of your support.

And to you, the reader—
May this story ignite your curiosity,
Challenge your fears,
And remind you that truth often lingers
Just beyond the shadows.

May you tread carefully through these pages,

For every word is woven with reality,

And every mystery whispers echoes of the past.

CONTENTS

ACKNOWLEDGMENTS

I am deeply grateful to my wife, Jessica, for her endless love and support; to my son, Caleb, for inspiring me everyday; to my parents, Gary and Angela, for their constant belief in me; to my brother, Gary, and his wife, Terra, for always having my back; to my sister, Becky Norgaard, and her husband, Ben, for their unwavering encouragement; to Becky Campbell and Colette Magwire for being my biggest fans.

Thank you to my friends Luc and Tiffany Wittrock, Andrew and Angela Schwarz, Emily Timmons, Laura Krieser, Dale Williams, and Jacob Rothermund, for their friendship, laughter, and inspiration.

And finally, thank you to those who shared their paranormal experiences, your courage and openness made this book possible. Without each of you, this story would not have come to life.

THE DIARY OF: DAWN MCWARLICK

My name is Dawn McWarlick, and I began writing this diary when I was 14 years old. Now that I am older, I have taken the time to edit and rewrite my entries, seeking a clearer understanding of the events that have shaped my life.

I grew up near the city of Lincoln, in Lancaster County, Nebraska. Describing myself isn't easy because I often find it challenging to put my thoughts and experiences into words. This might be a good opportunity to let my imagination run wild. Despite this, I've never tried my hand at writing short stories or poetry. Keeping a diary, though, seems like a manageable task. More manageable than straightening my wavy brown hair. When my mother gave me a blank diary to jot down my thoughts, I anticipated that inspiration would strike and stories would unfold. Yet, over a year has passed, and these pages remain untouched. I feel a sense of guilt for not putting pen to paper-until now.

Every time I look intently into these empty pages, my mind draws blank, then at times they almost seem to come alive on their own. No matter how hard I put my heart into writing, nothing wants to come out. I often see my worlds through imagination. Pirates dock at bay or a child becoming courageous after slaying a monster, and yet I still continue to stare into the world of nonexistence. I have a dream of becoming a great writer. I have told many dreams and stories to my parents. They have always told me; I should write a book. My mother is my inspiration. She's a mystery novelist! Maybe one day, people will read her writings in bookstores, their fingers tracing the pages of stories brought to life by her imagination. I can't help but feel a sense of kinship with her, as if her words are extensions of my own thoughts. Since we share so many similarities, I find it easier to relate to her.

We both carry the quiet fear that others will judge our dreams—dismiss them as childish whims or unrealistic ambitions. And yet, we continue, compelled to bring our characters to life, to give their struggles meaning. We understand the loneliness of pouring our hearts into a world others might never fully see or appreciate. But it's not just fear that drives us; it's hope. Hope that one day, someone will pick up our stories and feel the same connection we feel while writing them.

Hope that our characters' adventures will resonate, their victories and heartbreaks touching lives far beyond our own.

In the end, it's not about the judgment or the risk of being ignored. It's about reaching that one person who truly understands. That's the dream worth chasing.

As eager as she gets every time I speak of my dreams or ideas, my mother would encourage me to push myself into writing something so exciting and creative. She likes to call it, "a glorious heaven". Mother could not wait any longer and gave me this diary of blank pages on my13th birthday. She once told me that I have better dreams than she does, and that I shall continue dreaming while I am still young.

The expansive plains of this dissected state, where I've spent my life, offer a wealth of resources for Nebraska's farming community. Here, farmers cultivate some of the finest produce and livestock in the nation, including apples, wheat, vineyards, corn, soy, beef, poultry, and pork, all commanding top markets. At least, that's my perspective. My mother often takes me to Nebraska City, where the juiciest apples burst with sourness the moment you take a bite. Just thinking about them makes my mouth water.

The seasons each bring their own character: breezy and chilly falls, painfully freezing winters, cool and sometimes warm springs, and scorching summers that make you long for winter's chill. As harvest approaches, I relish the opportunity to escape to the nearest farm and watch my "Uncle" David gather crops and roll hay in preparation for winter. I refer to him as Uncle David, though we're not related by blood. He's been a friend of my father's since they were kids.

The past three years have been hard on David during planting and harvesting. He and other farmers have suffered from horrible crop seasons due to droughts. There has been more rain this year, so I hope this will help crops grow faster and healthier. I know that would make David and other farmers much happier as well. At least beef and pork would remain in business! Then again, there needs to be plant life growing in order to keep the livestock healthy. Systematic agriculture, the growing and harvesting of plants and animals, is not really my best subject in discussions, so I will leave it alone for now. At least I learned big words from hanging around the farm. My father, on the other hand, believes hunting for your food is the best way of survival. "Men had been hunting for years before the technology of farming. If man did okay back then, man will be just fine today as we dine with our wine during our hunters feast!" My father can be so passionate at times.

My family and I, with me being an only child, reside not far into the countryside. Situated amidst woods southwest of Lincoln stands the imposing McWarlick Mansion. Friends and family have passed by our home unaware of its existence, concealed by the dense trees surrounding it. The woods maintain a cool summer atmosphere inside our home and mitigate the winter winds during harsh blizzards, allowing me to drift off into dreams while cozying up before the fireplace, humming "Greensleeves," I suppose I could call it a dream home compared to its size. This two-story house boasts four bedrooms, three bathrooms, a study, library, kitchen, dining room, master dining hall, father's trophy room displaying his hunting conquests, a vast attic, and numerous other chambers. Its dimensions are ample enough to accommodate another family of five, with a room to spare.

Little is known about the previous owners of this house. The previous owner, Martin Fernando, constructed it in 1898. His wife, whose name eludes me, contracted cholera. Martin tirelessly tended to her, rarely leaving her side except for trips to town for provisions. People from Lincoln seldom glanced at him, and encounters were brief when they occurred. Cholera was uncommon in Nebraska, but sadly, Mrs. Fernando succumbed to the illness at the young age of 21, her weakened immune system leading to a slow and agonizing demise.

Following her passing, Mr. Fernando withdrew from society, becoming a recluse even to his own brothers. Concerned after two weeks of silence, his older siblings visited the mansion, only to find it deserted, with Martin absent and everything left behind. Days stretched into weeks, weeks into months, and years passed with no sign or word from Martin Fernando. It was as though he had vanished into thin air, leaving no trace behind.

For as long as I can recall, I've harbored a desire to become a writer. Yet, whenever faced with a blank sheet of paper, I found myself uncertain of what to write. Occasionally, my mind would wander into a realm of emptiness when creativity eluded me. Though my imagination often flows freely, there are moments when I struggle to conjure a single thought, resorting to forcing myself to write anything, just to fill the void. I've made a promise to my mother that I will document every experience of my life within the pages of this book. Should anything ever befall me, I want others to know the joy I've found in my life.

This marks the beginning of my first diary. Until now, I hadn't considered the significance of recording the events of my life. However, I now understand the importance of preserving memories. Perhaps one day, in my older years, I'll look back and find amusement in revisiting my past. These entries may even become tales to share with future generations.

There are countless ideas and dreams swirling within me, yet life seems fleeting. Mother understood that I would cherish this gift. True to my word, I will faithfully document every experience within these pages and make the most of it. Perhaps a story will emerge in due time.

I shall never forget the advice my mother imparted to me when she gave me this diary: "Write what you see, not what you think!" It is a lesson I hold dear.

MAY 13

Dear Diary,

When I returned home from school today, I stepped into the main entry hall and heard my father's voice booming from another room. From what I could gather of his frantic words, he seemed to be fixating on something "Odd." Although I couldn't discern the exact nature of his conversation, it was evident he was speaking to my mother, yet he sounded terrified as he spoke, a sense of fear rather than anger. My father, typically composed, displayed an uncharacteristic demeanor, which left me perplexed.

Quietly, I closed the front doors behind me and traced his voice to investigate. Entering the dining room, I discovered my mother, visibly anxious, sitting deep in the couch, while my father paced the floor, gesturing wildly as if indicating multiple directions. His movements halted abruptly as he caught sight of me. My mother gasped, and my father immediately pointed an accusatory finger in my direction, his voice raised.

"Go to your room at once."

"What have I done?" I defended myself.

"Now." He demanded.

And so, I stormed out of the dining room, not bothering to close the door. I marched up the grand stairway to the second floor, hustled down the central hall, slammed the door, and stomped my feet halfway into my room. I didn't even bother to question why he was acting like this.

Why have I been sent to my room? What were my parents fighting about? My father has never sent me to my room for no apparent reason before. I couldn't help but wonder what they were talking about. So many things jumped out at me so quickly, I didn't know what to think either. Parents can be so secretive, but why?

I had no other choice but to walk over to my bed, upset. My head was full of questions by this time. I hugged my teddy bear, who always helped me feel better in almost any situation. I always turn to

Sorrows, my teddy bear, when I am feeling down, or just need someone to talk to. He's fairly old, but I have kept him since I was four years old. As I sat here on my bed, picking at Sorrows's soft fuzzy ears, I realized that neither of my parents asked how my day in school was today. Today was the last day of school and I didn't get the chance to tell them about my test score at the end of finals. Yet, I find it rather suspicious that the whole time I headed toward my bedroom, my parents did not continue their "odd" conversation. This might seem silly, but I hope my parents don't split up. They have never fought, well, around me they never did. Like I said before, parents can be so secretive.

I just heard a loud thud from outside my room. I believe the dining room door had slammed shut followed by heavy footsteps thumping up the stairs.

"You crazy son-of-a-bitch!" yelled my mother, before another door slammed shut. "I never want to hear such a bullshit story like that ever again," she sobbed loudly from behind her bedroom door, loud enough for my father to hear.

I opened my bedroom door, and sure enough, I heard my mother crying from the other side of her bedroom door. I assumed it was safe to leave my room and step outside. However, the moment I stepped foot out of my door, the floor creaked. Then, a loud crash followed by the sound of shattered glass came from behind her door. I hesitated to check up on her, fearing something might come flying at me. I pondered, what 'story' could my father have told her to make her so frustrated? Now was not the time to find out.

Knowing that my mother's room was currently unsafe, but relieved that she was alright, I chose to retreat down the central hall and return to the safety of my bedroom. The air was heavy with the smell of rum and tension, and I couldn't shake the sinking feeling that my father was intoxicated once more. The one uncertainty nagging at me was whether my father was alright.

Throughout the rest of the evening, which dragged on endlessly, I folded the clothing my mother had washed, dried, and stacked in my hamper for me to attend to. The smell of fresh, clean cotton and detergent enveloped me, evoking memories of a meadow teeming with flowers on a crisp summer's evening. It is quite the opposite now. The weather outside is hot and muggy, and I can smell my father's cherry tobacco as he puffs it from his old pipe downstairs in the trophy room. The scent seeps through the doors and the aged floorboards of this house. Ugh... I wish he would at least smoke outside. Unfortunately, my wish is not granted. My father only smokes in the trophy room, so I often know where he is, while my mother must be cooking dinner at this time.

After putting away all my clothing, I glanced at the clock hanging above my mahogany wood dresser. It read six-thirty-five. I had been in my room for more than two hours. Time had certainly flown by quickly, yet dinner was running a little late. The sun was nearly setting, and the air had grown cooler. The crickets had started chirping, and I was definitely hungry. When a lady is hungry, she can become rather feisty, aggravated, cranky, and even a tad demon-like. What can I say? Us ladies have a strong affection for our food.

Finally, it was ten minutes to seven when my mother called me for dinner. I descended the stairs into the kitchen and seated myself at the table. I noticed a shift in my mother's emotions, although she was deliberately ignoring my father, who seemed to have made an effort to freshen up in an attempt to rid himself of the aroma of hard liquor. Disregarding their childish behavior, I helped myself to the large, juicy ham roast, corn on the cob with warm butter, tender green beans, and topped it all off with a slice of fresh, hot maple and cinnamon apple pie for dessert. No more demon-like Dawn.

As I indulged in the moment, stuffing my face, there was silence among us. It felt a bit eerie. I sat at the table, observing my father eagerly devouring the ham roast, which was a bit noisy and annoying, almost to the point of drooling. On the other hand, Mother sat gracefully, taking smaller bites of her food. Although it may not have been significant, the sinister expression on her face sent shivers down my spine. Even the simple act of reaching for another serving of tea across the table made me uneasy. When I caught my mother staring directly at me, it felt as though there was no soul within her. Despite my attempts to ignore her gaze, it was rather amusing to watch her stab her fork into the green beans repeatedly, as if she were stabbing someone in the heart, over and over again.

Did I do something wrong? Were her actions directed towards me? My mother shifted her gaze briefly to my father, then back to me with a glare. I had the impression that I could read her mind, telling me that she was angry with father, although it was obvious. I believe that women have this ability among themselves to convey what is on our minds without explicitly saying it. It's a form of special communication that men simply do not possess.

I remember about a year ago when I came home from the park and suddenly had the impression that my mother was communicating with me just by looking into my eyes. She had that innocent look on her face, with a reddish blush and a smirk, yet she was trying to suppress her grin. I could almost hear her voice in my head saying, "Go look at your father." Raising an eyebrow, I thought, "Where is he?" She rolled her eyes and glanced to her left, then quickly back at me. I tried to stifle my laughter. "You didn't?" I wondered to myself. Walking past her into the kitchen, I stepped into one of the funniest moments of my life. My father was at the kitchen sink, looking startled as he saw me come in. His face was covered in purple goo. I had never laughed so hard in my life.

"It's not funny," he cried. "The damn pie just blew up on me." Father clearly doesn't understand that it's almost impossible to bake a mulberry pie. His face had been stained purple from the mulberries for three days. Now, mother has a cute nickname for him, which changed from 'sweetie-pie' to 'mulberry-pie'.

The rest of the night was peaceful. Father went to bed early to sober up from his evening drinking. He's not an alcoholic; the only time he drinks is when he is socializing with guests or on holidays. But tonight, he seemed uptight about something. I'm not really sure if I want to know what had him so bothered, which caused him to drink like that. Mother on the other hand stayed up reading a book. She often immerses herself in a completely different world when it comes to her mysteries or spooky stories.

I wouldn't say that tonight had been boring or anything, but rather mysterious. I wonder what happened between my parents or my father before I came home from school today. I should start getting ready for bed. It's a quarter to ten, and I want to start my morning early. It saddens me that I never got the chance to tell my parents how my last day in school went today. Oh well, there's always tomorrow.

Coincidentally, following my previous entry, my bedroom door opened. It was my mother. She entered quietly and walked over to my nightstand, picking up my teddy bear Sorrows before sitting next to me.

"What a night, huh?" she asked.

"Yeah, I suppose," I replied, but I couldn't help but think, "I found it rather 'odd'."

Mother sighed. "So, how was your last day in school?" Finally, I had the chance to talk to her.

"I passed my final test in science and scored the highest in the class today," I told her.

"That's great, dear," she cheered. "I'm so proud of you; I knew you could do it." I knew what she said was true. My mother and I both spent nights studying for that test.

"What about your English essay? How did that go?" she inquired.

I sighed.

"What's wrong? You couldn't have..."

"No," I interrupted. "The teacher was proud of the work and effort I put into my report, but he deducted five points for using too many sophisticated words," I continued. "Plus, he 'questioned' if it was even me who wrote the report."

"Don't let it get to you so much! He's just jealous that he's not as smart as you are," she said, smiling at me with pride in her eyes.

"I wasn't sure if he was being smart, but he said the way I wrote my essay, I could teach the class a thing or two about the Roman Empire, as if I've lived it!"

"And yet he deducted five points?"

"Yes, he said he had to pull out a dictionary to find the definitions of more than eleven words. I guess he became rather annoyed." I continued, "I didn't have the heart to tell him that my mother was the one who taught me my vocabulary better than my English teacher could." I said sarcastically.

Mother leaned over me and gave me a tight hug that seemed to last forever. "I'm so proud of you!" She reminded me again.

I was worried that her happiness would go away once I asked, "Mom, can I talk to you about something? It's been on my mind since I got home." At that moment, I feared I had erred, akin to moving my final piece in a critical game of chess, leading to my downfall.

"Of course, dear. What is it?" It seemed too late; I might have already landed myself in checkmate. I really didn't want to wipe the smile off her face, but I had to inquire.

"What were you and dad arguing about this afternoon?" I was mistaken; her smile remained unchanged. She rolled her eyes and chuckled.

"You wouldn't believe it yourself if I told you," she remarked. "You know your father as well as I do." I envisioned my opponent resigning the game by tossing down his king. She continued, "Every Friday, he's at the pub, drinking his week of hard work away, socializing with his coworkers." She paused, placing my teddy bear Sorrows between us. "And to think he would tell me such an 'odd' story."

There was that word again…

"I shouldn't be telling you this," she paused again, glancing around the room to ensure the coast was clear. "At first, I thought it was a joke," she whispered. "But when I caught the scent of rum, I just knew he was drunk with stories. I won't trouble you with it any longer. The past is behind us now, and I'll leave it at that."

"No, please," I begged her for more information.

Mother raised both her eyebrows and sighed. She hugged my teddy bear and placed it on my lap.

"It's late, dear," she continued. "It's something that might give me nightmares tonight. Don't stay up too late tonight, okay?"

I agreed and gave my mother a kiss goodnight, hugging her tightly again. I will never forget the scent of her lilac perfume and the softness of her hair. I have always envied the vibrant redness and silky, rose-petal softness of her hair. It's so curly and full of life, unlike my brown, pulled-back, wavy hair. Watching her walk away to the door, I could almost imagine how beautiful I would look if I had her redness and curls. She slowly closed the door, saying "Goodnight."

Tonight, I will finish this entry with the remembrance of my mother, Amethyst McWarlick, for her kindness and love.

Goodnight.

MAY 14

I awoke from a bad dream, unable to recall any specific details. All I could remember was that it was unpleasant. You know those dreams where you can't remember anything but you notice your heart racing? That's how I felt this morning. I was hot and sweaty, and I needed to take a shower. Getting out of bed, I stumbled over to my dresser to choose some clean clothes. It didn't take me long to decide what to wear for the day. I kept telling myself, "Today is going to be a good day." I just hoped both Mother and Father had forgotten about last night. They usually never argue. They're a good couple, Mom and Dad. Still, I didn't want to dwell on their argument. Today was still going to be a good day.

Father, Mother, and I are heading to the meadows today. What a perfect way to start a beautiful Saturday morning! I want to relax in the sun a bit at the park in the meadows. Maybe do a little bit of reading or perhaps continue writing my daily experiences here in my diary? Last night, all I could do was write, write, and write. I don't know what it was, but it was the first time I've ever really put so much effort into my writing. Time flies by, but sometimes I get lost in what I'm writing and don't realize the time. I have a good memory, but my spelling and grammar need work. What can I say? I'm only 14 years old, and nobody's perfect. I know that when I grow up and look back at these pages, I'll laugh. I'm new to this diary writing thing. Mother was right when she gave me this diary book of empty pages. "It's hard to start writing. Once you start writing, it's even harder to stop," she said. I glanced over at the clock on the wall and noticed it was nine forty. Good! I have plenty of time to get ready. I must put this diary down for now and prepare for my day.

I stepped into my bathroom, turned on the hot water, undressed, closed the shower curtain, and scrubbed myself from head to toe. I didn't want to rush because the water felt nice and hot. Even though I showered longer than I had planned, I regretted leaving my womanly chambers. I got out and rinsed off the soap and toweled off.

Just then, I had a vision or a flashback of some sort. Mentally, I pictured someone in my room last night. It was dark, and I couldn't get a good look at him or her. I shook it out of my head and continued grooming myself.

As I stood at my bathroom mirror to brush my hair, I noticed something out of the ordinary. Looking back at my own reflection, I saw a red handprint on the left side of my breast. It startled me for a moment, but I didn't remember being hit or grabbed there that would have caused it. For sure, I would have remembered if someone had fondled me or something, but that was not the case. The moment I touched it, it faded away. I thought of how unusual it was to be there, but again, I did not recall anyone groping or even touching me. It did not feel like an irritation or burn either. Oh well, it could have been just my imagination or my own hand since I was under hot water just moments before.

Just as I started to clean up after myself, I began to feel a little unease. I felt as if someone was watching me. The bathroom door was closed and locked, but I felt someone standing in the doorway. Another vision came to me. A dark, shadowy figure stood at the foot of my bed. It tilted its head to look up across the bed at me, its fiery red eyes burning. I then got chills down my spine. I couldn't remember anything else from there at that moment. Again, I shook it off then continued on getting ready for the day.

After drying and brushing my hair, I began to get dressed when I caught a whiff of what seemed like maple, bacon, and eggs. Once I had dressed myself, I heard a knock at my bedroom door. I answered it, and to my surprise, it was my father.

"Did you sleep well last night?" he asked. I found it strange that he would ask, so I questioned why he wanted to know.

"I heard you moaning overnight," he explained, "so I assumed you were having a bad dream. I came to check on you and asked if you were alright. You then rolled over and looked up at me, saying you were 'okay.'"

I told him how I woke up startled this morning but couldn't recall the dream. I also mentioned, "I don't remember you coming into my room at all."

He shrugged his shoulders, hugged me, and said, "Everything will be okay." I didn't fully understand what he meant by that, but it was comforting to know that he was there checking up on me.

After breakfast, Mother was waiting for me in the entry hall. Father was outside, waiting while puffing on his pipe. He normally doesn't smoke inside the house unless he is in the trophy room. There, he doesn't consider it part of the house; he thinks of it as his home away from home. It's his place to get away from everything and anyone, just sitting and puffing away while staring at his prized kills from his hunting explorations mounted on every wall. My father spends a lot of time in his trophy room, or what Mother calls it, his study, reading. Most of the books he reads in there are about "Expedition Exploration" information or "Adventure Wildlife." A few other books in his collection are ones Mother had written, which are his favorites.

I guess with Mothers writing skills and Father's reading abilities, that's where I come in as the daughter who best describes them both: my mother the writer and my father who enjoys reading but cannot write a single paragraph if his life depended on it. One time he tried, and that upset Mother; she thought she was either being mocked or he was trying to be competitive, and she is not one to back down from a challenge, even against her writing. His short story about a hardworking monkey and a stubborn housewife donkey that lived in the mountains was what set her off. Since then, he never attempted to write another story again.

Mother wore her best dress to the meadows, which was my favorite. The dress was a brightly colored sundress covered with pink roses printed all around it. The bottom of it was laced with silky white trimming she added for extra flair. It was a dress she made a couple of years ago, and every six months or so, she adds more to the design. Father thinks she should just go out and get a new one, but mother agrees with the idea of shopping and buying another dress. This dress, on the other hand, was something she favored the most. She started making it, and will continue creating it. She says someday it will look lovely for me to wear once I am old enough to fit into it. I agree!

I watched my father push Mother on the swing. Her long red hair waved with a gentle breeze. I would have died to have hair like hers. Her red and pure hair reminded me of a fairy or a princess from a storybook. The joy and comfort of watching both of my parents happy together made me daydream if I will ever meet a man who would make me as happy as she was. Although they have their moments, who doesn't?

I wanted to forget about last night. Something has been compelling me to know exactly what it was all about. Seeing my mother so happy at that moment showed me that she had already forgiven him, still, I couldn't help it. Mother has always told me stories of their past to laugh at and sad times she and Father shared.

Now that I think about it, I am certain she will tell me sooner or later. Maybe then was not the time to start asking questions while they were so happy at that moment. I think I understand why she may have either forgiven him or forgotten about it. She scares easily, and what Father had told her could have done more than frightened her. "Forgive and forget," my mother always told me. If my mother has something on her mind, she will either speak her opinions, whether it hurts your feelings or not, or ignore the subject and act like nothing happened. That might not be a healthy way of doing things her way, but she tends to bottle up her emotions often.

We had a wonderful picnic in the meadows of glorious, bright-colored flowers. The wind blew soft white dandelion seeds through the air, resembling a winter landscape trapped in a glass dome. The cool, fresh spring air danced lightly across my skin, carrying with it the sweet aroma of blooming flowers and newly sprouted leaves. I imagined fairies dancing all around as the children from the park chased and danced along with them, while Pan played his hypnotizing melody.

A unicorn lowered its head to take a drink from the flowing stream; an elf kissed his bride as many others cheered in celebration of their tradition; a rainbow curved and arched, bowed and bent in several impossibly imagined ways as nymphs slid up and down the bow, landing in a pool of sparkling glitter, while a knight in shining armor passed on his white steed in search of his one true love.

Okay, that was a little too much. Let me get back to the real world!

It was a lovely moment watching my parents holding each other, smiling and laughing, talking about this and that, until Father started feeding Mother strawberries as she giggled from his flirtatious intentions. It sent awkward shivers across my body. I didn't know whether to hurl or to get up and run off screaming in horror. But all I could do was sit there on the blanket holding a ham sandwich with a sour look on my face as if I had been sucking on a lemon. It did not take much to lower the heat, but the look I gave them made my mother laugh with amusement and pushed my father away from her in denial. Father wasn't pleased. He leaned forward to kiss her; she pulled back, teasing him. He leaned even closer; she pushed him back again, giggling. As he tried to make another attempt, Mother quickly cocked her head forward and gave him a quick kiss, smiled, and said, "I love you, dear, but not tonight."

Father pouted. Mother and I both laughed. She loved every moment of taunting him and watching him pout about it. I wasn't sure, by the look on Father's face, if he was either disappointed or furious. No matter, Mother and I kept laughing at him as we high-fived each other.

"Oh, THAT DOES IT!" Father yelled, leaping towards us and tackling both Mother and me, tickling us until we both cried out of breath.

After our afternoon in the meadow, we packed away our picnic. I grabbed my diary, Mother gathered the flowers Father had picked for her, and then we started to head back home.

The sun was setting, and the air became cooler. The breeze grew slightly stronger as thick, dark gray clouds started to build up over the horizon. Mother walked ahead of me and looked up.

"Damn it!" she called out. "It's about to rain," she said as she hurried us along.

I took a deep breath through my nose. It was a pleasant, earthy scent of wet soil and plants moving and kicking around in the air, which became prominent. I learned about the scent of petrichor in school, and I love the nostalgic feeling it evokes when I smell it. It meant Mother was perhaps right; it could rain at any moment.

"Nah, it's not going to rain," Father said bluntly. "Knowing these storms in Nebraska, all it is going to do is head directly east and pass us from the south. That storm is several miles away, and we will make it home just fine. We won't even notice the clouds once we get home," he said, then pointed down the path into the woods leading home. "Heck, there is plenty of time to walk through these woods and savor the moments of nature. Don't let some clouds spoil this evening while the sun is still out." He took a deep breath in, exhaled, and smiled. "Doesn't that air smell nice? Come now, there is no need to get your bonnet in a tangle about it." I had no idea what that meant. By the look on Mother's face, she looked insulted. We then continued to walk into the woods directly down the trail leading home.

Along the trail, fog started to seep from between the trees and over our path. I thought nothing of it at first but kept walking anyway. Father halted us. He decided to take a different route than the one we had initially taken. Mother was a little uneasy with the idea because she wanted to get home before rainfall, and taking the other route would get us home later.

"This is a shortcut," Father lied.

"No, we are going home down this path," Mother demanded. "I'm telling you, if we do not hurry—"

"We are going RIGHT NOW!" Father yelled, interrupting.

"TODD!" Mother scolded Father. There was a short pause, then she continued, "Why are you insisting this is a shortcut? I have taken this path for the past couple of years, and this is the way home. There is little time left before it begins to..." Mother's speech was interrupted by a loud clash of thunder, which made all three of us flinch. "rain," she said last.

"Please, Amethyst!" Father begged.

Mother and I both looked at one another, knowing Father was wrong. She sighed and then suggested, "Follow your father, dear." And so we did. We had been following an unfamiliar trail for little over half an hour. We would have been home probably twenty minutes earlier if we had stayed on our usual route.

The fog became thicker, and the rolling thunder grew closer by the minute. After a short while, the fog became so thick in the woods that we could hardly see the path ahead of us. Only a few trees and bushes in front of us were visible. I tried not to worry. Mother was too angry to even care or speak to correct Father's mishap. Usually, fog settles in the air, but something out of the ordinary caught both Mother's and my attention. As for what seemed to be the path we had been traveling, the fog appeared to be breathing in and out, shifting forward and backward along the path, creating the illusion that the trail was alive and about to swallow us whole. At that moment, Father came to a startling halt. He looked as if he had seen a ghost.

"Not again," he said under his breath. The look of terror in his eyes sent goosebumps down my arms. I turned away from him to look at Mother and gave her a concerned glance.

"Mom," I whispered. "I have a bad feeling."

While rolling her eyes, Mother slowly turned to look at Father. Then, her eyes widened as she looked past him in the same direction he was facing.I didn't want to look. I was too afraid something would reach out and grab me. Just then, a loud clash of thunder roared through the air. I clasped my hands over my ears from the loud sound and closed my eyes tightly. After shielding my ears, I opened my eyes and saw both of them still standing in the same position, looking in the same direction. Neither one of them flinched from the clash. noticed that after the roaring echo, everything was silent; completely silent. No birds sang, no crickets chirped, nor did any small animals rustle in the leaves. It was as if time had stood still.

Then, all of a sudden!

"Dawn..." a whisper called out to me from within the thick fog.

"MOM!" I screamed. Then, the world started to move again, slowly returning to its normal pace. Mother quickly turned to me, directing her attention toward me, and then jabbed her elbow into Father's side. He let out a rough puff of air, and as mist formed from his breath, an eerie suspicion crept over me. It disappeared as quickly as it appeared.

"Ouch!" he yelped as he gasped for air. Father rested a hand against his side and turned with a grin.

"Don't start, you," Mother replied. "The last thing I need from you is to give both Dawn and I the spooks."

I was a bit confused at the time. I had just seen Mother look as terrified as Father did while gazing into the foggy path. Had she not just shown fear, or was I more focused on the environment around me? I've heard of someone's imagination taking over, but that wasn't very pleasant.

"That hurts," he replied, trying to hold back the pain in his ribs from Mother's jab. "Why did you do that?"

"Serves you right for trying to scare us like that," she replied.

"Dad, let's just get home," I said as I continued ahead of them, slowly.

I noticed no one was following, so I stopped and looked at my father. Once again, his gaze was fixed deeper down the trail. I had no idea what he was looking at or thinking. Besides a couple of birds fluttering from tree to tree, there was nothing there. I followed his stare; he was fixed on something.

"Dad," I called. "What's going on?" I had to ask. I was not about to take another step forward unless I was sure of what he was up to. I was not about to fall into one of his tricks, if that was indeed what he was doing. I knew the fog and thunder were strange, but his behavior was very unusual, especially on an unfamiliar path that might not lead us back home. I thought we were lost.

"I am okay, really. I'm ready!" he lied again. "Let's go home, shall we?" That was the best idea from him I had heard all afternoon.

Just then, I heard another voice whispering behind me. It was the same voice I had heard just moments before, but I couldn't quite make out what it was saying because the wind had picked up, and the sound of the leaves drowned out the voice.

"Is that her?" said the voice.

"Yes, yes... That is her," said another voice.

I could not see anyone, but I could hear a short conversation from within the woods. Mother and Father had not seemed to notice or respond to the voices.

"It's her!" a girl's voice exclaimed. "It is, it is her," the voice repeated.

Another voice, this one sounding like a boy, asked, "What is she doing here?"

The two voices sounded like children, but as I searched high and low, I saw no one. The wind stopped abruptly, and an unsettling silence fell over everything.

I spun around, startled to find myself face-to-face with my father. His intense gaze pierced into my eyes, sending shivers down my spine. Unease gripped me, but behind his stare, I felt as though I understood his unspoken question: Did you hear them too? To be honest, I didn't want to remember what I had heard. Did I hear it? I must have. But my confusion and fear left me doubting myself. Maybe my imagination was taking over. All I wanted now was to get home.

Mother pushed forward, causing a disturbance between my father's gaze and mine. After breaking eye contact, the fear vanished, and I felt calm as if nothing had happened. My mother marched ahead, with my father walking beside me. As we continued along the path, I couldn't help but ponder: Was that a father-daughter bonding moment? If it was, it certainly occurred in a peculiar manner.

The slower father walked, the longer it felt to get home. I noticed several times that my father slowed down, looked around, and then caught up to us, only to slow down again and peer around a bush or behind a tree to check if anyone or anything was lurking around. I didn't know what it was that seemed to bother him, but his actions appeared to worry mother. Her eyes followed his every move, and she would raise an eyebrow or roll her eyes every time he made a sudden stop. He shifted his head from right to left, looked back, turned, and continued walking, then repeated the process. This continued for a while.

"I'm beginning to worry about you again, Dad," I said.

"You can never be too careful," he whispered. "Thieves!" He paused, then continued, "You never can tell. There just might be a thief hiding nearby." It was something in his voice that told me thieves were the least of his worries. I knew he was hiding something, but I ignored it for the time being because thankfully I saw the mansion down the hill. It was about time we made it home.

The moment we stepped through the front door, Father instantly stretched out his arms and yawned. "I'm bushed," he said, avoiding a conflicted conversation with Mother. She looked as if she were about to start questioning him about his actions. He quickly stormed out of the entryway and into the trophy room to take a nap. I don't like going into that room very much with all the dead animal heads mounted on the walls and the stuffed prize kills standing in every corner, which still looked lively. Every time I go in there, I get the impression their eyes follow my every move.

I distinctly recall a time, I assure you, when I entered the trophy room one night, the giant stuffed bear across the room and the wild boar head over the fireplace watched me in curiosity as I entered. In the left corner of my eye, I thought I saw the bear slowly crouching down toward me. When I turned to face the bear, it seemed as if it had suddenly stood back up into its original position. I don't remember exactly why I went into the room, but I recall being frightened and sneaking my way out. I reached the door, turned the knob to open it, when I heard something from behind me—a grunting sound. I looked over to the wild boar above the fireplace; its stare was fixed across the room. I looked over to the fox next to Father's desk; it was still motionless with its jaw shut. I was foolish enough to stay in the room to investigate the sound and pondered which animal my father might have forgotten to kill. I heard the grunt again. Stupidly, I followed the sound. Looking around, I couldn't seem to find the source of the grunts until I came upon the backside of Father's auburn leather couch, positioned in the middle of the room and angled from the fireplace. The grunts became louder and louder as I approached it. I was expecting a wild animal of some sort to leap out at me, though I felt completely unable to run out of there. I felt even more foolish when I peeked over from the backside of the couch and found my father snoring away as he slept. Still to this day, it bothers me to even think about going into the trophy room.

Later, after dinner, Mother entered my bedroom where I had already begun writing in my diary. She settled beside me and once again placed my teddy bear Sorrows between us. Leaning closer, she kissed my head and shared a brief conversation about today's events in the woods. Suddenly, the sound of pouring rain pounded against the house

and streaked down my window. Both Mother and I turned our attention
to my window. The room flickered with light several times as lightning
struck, followed by the rumble of thunder.

"I guess your father was right!" she said. "We did make it home
hours before the storm hit."

"I'm worried, do you think the storm will get worse?" I said.

"I am sure all will be just fine," she comforted me. "It is just a
small storm that should soon pass."

"Mom," I asked, "may I ask you something about Dad?"

Mother stood up and kissed my forehead. "Maybe we should
talk about it tomorrow?" she interrupted. "Your father has not been
himself tonight, and I don't want to be up all night over something that
just may be nothing at all. You know how your father is, paranoid over
spilled milk, thinking the world will come to an end." We laughed.
"Seriously, it is nothing to worry about." She smiled at me, dimmed my
lights, and wished me sweet dreams. I don't think sweet dreams are
what I would call them. Dreams of forgetfulness and confusion are
what they seem to be these past couple of nights.

As soon as Mother stepped out of my room, closing the door
behind her, I started to brainstorm. I knew that neither Mother nor
Father would tell me everything I wanted to know about what had been
going on. What were they fighting about? I assume that maybe they
have a diary or a journal where they've written about it. Maybe
somehow I could sneak a peek to get the answers? I'm not sure if
Father has one, but I think Mother still writes in hers. But where would
it be? The only way I will discover anything about yesterday is by
searching their bedroom for one. My thoughts went back to when we
walked through the woods. Who were those voices that had been
speaking? Had Mother and Father both heard them? They didn't seem
to pay any attention to them at the time. And why would these voices
want to know who I was? All in all, I guess I'm now the one saying that
today was rather "odd."

MAY 15

Sunday, the most boring day of the entire week, next to Monday. Although the days together make it seem longer than any other days of the week. By Wednesday, every other day seems to fly by so quickly that it ends up being just any other boring old Sunday all over again. But this Sunday was different. Mother and I both worked outside in the gardens. As often as I got to help, it was lovely to see all the hard work Mother had put into making her gardens come to life. Flowers scattered, blooming, all around; vines hanging from every corner of the back courtyard walls; butterflies and hummingbirds fluttering their wings just to get a taste of nectar; sun beaming through the leaves of the bushes and trees while pollen danced in the air like fairies seemed to make the garden more fairy-tale-like every day. And the center of attention to her "garden of heaven" was the life source of it all: the stone dragon fountain spouting fresh water from its mouth.

My mother's garden is an eternal heaven of peace on Earth, with trees, flowers, bushes, and stone paths that curve and turn like a small maze. Everything there is calm and peaceful. Sometimes I find myself wanting to take only a few moments to relax and get out of the house as often as possible, seeking a change of atmosphere, only to realize later that I have been out there for several hours without even noticing. The sound of trickling water from the fountain and the scent of lilies, roses, and daffodils just make my heart more at ease. Sometimes I step out into the garden to clear my thoughts or to study for my homework during the school season. The cool spring breeze and the warm sun beaming upon my face give me the feeling of being settled, planted, like a flower. I would live in Mother's beautiful garden and breathe life every day if I could. There's nothing like the freshness of crisp air to wake you up in the mornings.

There was something, however, about Mother's garden that had a hint of disturbance. Not every garden has its good without evil. I don't know what it is exactly, but sometimes I have experienced the sensation of feeling a presence without the sense of being watched. It's like an unspoken acknowledgment that someone or something is nearby, yet without any direct awareness of their attention. It's as if there's an invisible companion sharing the space with me, their existence subtly perceived through a heightened awareness of my surroundings. I might feel a gentle shift in the atmosphere, an unexplained warmth or chill, or simply an intuitive understanding that I'm not alone, even though there is no visible evidence of another's presence. It's a curious blend of familiarity and mystery, like sensing the echo of another's energy lingering in the air, silently affirming their existence without intruding upon my conscious perception.

I worry that this mansion keeps trying to crawl up my spine, driving me crazy. I mostly shake them off. Cold spots, mysterious drafts, rasping noises in the walls are usual goings-on. I'm not sure how old this place is, but it certainly seems to settle every now and then. Perhaps it's nothing, but the gardens, with their eerie comfort, appear too mystical to me.

I've always been fascinated by the myths and legends of dragons. The dragon fountain is my favorite structure in the gardens. It's a stone-walled round pool with a dragon standing in the center of a stone dome, clutching its claws around a crystal ball as water spouts from its mouth. It's the spot where I enjoy spending most of my time in the gardens, especially when thorn vines weave and wrap around the entire fountain and the roses are in full bloom.

I remember when I was nine years old, sitting along the fountain wall, enjoying a moment to myself. I was just sitting there, thinking about little things, nothing too important to remember at the moment, but I was left with the impression that the statue could talk to me. I know this sounds ridiculous, but I was nine. It wasn't that I didn't believe in imaginary friends; this was something different. I felt something there. I don't know; maybe I'm just crazy? Back then, I didn't know what to think of it and shook it out of my mind. I don't know how to explain it, but one time I caught myself answering questions that no one had asked. I remember saying, "They are lovely! Mother and I worked our green thumbs to the bone." For a sudden moment, I felt a little embarrassed for talking to myself. Thankfully, no one was around to have noticed. I wasn't crazy. I wasn't losing my marbles. I also know I wasn't hearing voices in my head either. It was just one of those strange spur-of-the-moment occurrences that made no sense to me. I shrugged my shoulders and laughed. Who was I kidding? Myself? It may have been my imagination, but it didn't really matter anyway. It's my little garden secret, best kept to myself.

Mother made a picnic today just for the two of us. Nothing beats a ladies' afternoon under the shade, away from father. She and I usually have picnics in the gardens every weekend. It's always nice to have mother-daughter time once in a while. A red and black checkered blanket was spread out along the grass in a small opening surrounded by bushes and flowers. She made a pitcher of freshly squeezed lemonade, ham sandwiches left over from the other night, fresh-cut potato salad with mustard, and a bowl of sweet, juicy red strawberries grown in a garden within the gardens.

As I listened to my mother speak about her day, I watched her gestures as well. The way she calmly waved her hands showed her true calmness, serenity, and purity. She tried to keep a smile as she spoke. She has always had the most glorious smile I have ever seen on another person. Something about her smile always made me feel safe. As she and I hid away in our heaven, nothing could have ruined that perfect moment under the shades in our own personal fairytale world.

After our picnic, I went back to the fountain to try and draw it on an empty page in this diary. I was in the mood to be creative and give myself a little bit of a challenge. I may not be a great artist, but I try to draw what I see. The dragon fountain is rather old. According to what my parents have told me, it's over a hundred years old and was once the center of an abbey courtyard before the house was built over it. Abbeys are very rare in the United States, let alone in Nebraska. I don't think it's of any importance to get into any of its history since I don't know much about it other than that. Whoever built this house before my parents moved in sure did like the fountain enough to keep it as the only foundation that remains of the old ruins of the abbey.

*** * * ***

Later this evening, my parents and I sat at the table for dinner. I didn't eat too much; I was still full from the big lunch mother made for our picnic. My father was in a cheerful mood, which surprised both my mother and I. The smile he gave us indicated that it was alright to ask,

"What's on your mind, dear?" asked Mother. She knew father was eager to start a conversation but he was never good at opening speeches.

"Well!" my father bellowed. "It's funny that you ask," he continued with a huge grin upon his face. "Today I got to thinking!"

"That's a first," she joked.

Father paused for a moment, then continued. "Anyway... I got to thinking that maybe we could spend a weekend this summer up in the mountains and go camping?"

That was actually a good idea, I thought. I looked over at my mother, and she seemed interested in the thought as well. It was obvious that mother had no objections. We hadn't been camping in several years. Just the thought of it all brought back memories. The crisp, burning aroma of logs under roasting marshmallows, smothered over a chocolate sliver on a honey-baked graham cracker, stuck in my nose.

"Eight hours away in the mountains, huh?" asked Mother. "I could really use some fresh air away from these farmlands. Maybe we should go, Todd?" she continued, her voice tinged with hope. "This just might be one of the best things I've heard you say in the past few days. Finally, a chance to leave the house far away before I go insane."

"Then it's agreed!" exclaimed Todd, my father. "We shall pack our things and then take our leave the weekend of the 27th."

It was amusing to hear those words from Mother. If she had not been reading my mind, then she and I are just too alike. I really need to get out of the house for a change. Don't get me wrong; I am always out in the gardens or taking walks out to the park. I love the outdoors. Hiking in the mountains is peaceful; dancing under waterfalls is pure and spiritual, and watching the sun rise over the mountain horizon is unbelievable. Just thinking about it more and more makes me want to start packing now and just head out the door, no questions asked. I know the 27th is not that far off, but I can hardly wait. I'm beginning to feel like this mansion is draining my very life away. I need a recharge.

* * * *

Something strange just happened. As frightened as I am at this moment, I will try to write this the best I can as I struggle to keep my pen straight. It started as I had just finished writing my latest entry. I walked across my bedroom and placed my diary on top of my dresser. As I began to change into my nightgown, I heard a noise coming from outside my window. At first, I couldn't quite make sense of it. I ignored it, assuming it was just raccoons. I soon heard it again, this time more distinctly. I was certain it wasn't a raccoon; it was the faint sound of a child laughing. I slowly walked back across my room to peer outside over the windowsill. The window was partially open. I pushed it halfway open and peered down into the gardens to check if anyone was outside. The night breeze passed through my window, giving me a slight chill. I shook it off and covered myself with my robe. In a whisper, I called down from the windowsill. I didn't want to speak too loudly, fearing my parents would hear me.

"Hello?" I called out. "Is anybody out there?" As I turned away from the window, I heard the laughter of a boy.

"Come find me," spoke an unfamiliar voice. "I'm over here!" he laughed again.

It startled me, but I didn't hesitate to investigate. If some kid was playing in our yard late at night, I was ready to hunt them down and chuck them out over the brick wall, leaving them in the dark woods that surround my home. Why would anyone be out in these woods at night? Especially at this hour. I glanced at the clock above my dresser. It read 11:32.

"In the garden. Come find me!" The voice invited me to play.

I was far from wanting to play any sort of hide-and-seek with a stranger, no matter how old they may be. As foolish as I felt, I still went out to investigate. I slowly crept past my parents' room, across the hallway, down the stairs, and through the kitchen leading to the doorway heading out into the backyard gardens. I opened a drawer of a short table next to the back door to retrieve a flashlight. I unlocked the door. The night's chilled air quickly breezed past me as I pushed open the back door and stepped outside. It was quiet... A little too quiet. The eerie tension lingered throughout my body as I stepped further into the gardens, searching for a mysterious child on the night of a full moon. "What am I thinking?" screamed and echoed in the back of my mind. But I am stubborn, so I pressed on. The full moon's light gleamed ahead of me. I stepped further and further in, leaving the back door open.

"Hello?" I called out. "Is there anyone out here?" There was no answer. I thought to myself, who was I kidding?

I walked far enough from the house up to the dragon fountain. At that moment, I didn't feel safe. I looked around quietly, asking who was outside, but still got no answer. For a brief moment, to my right, I thought I saw somcone rush past and leap out from around the greenhouse toward the backside of the shed. By then, I hoped my eyes were playing tricks on me. I saw movement again, this time from the shed back to the greenhouse, only a few feet apart from each building.

I quickly chased after the trespasser. I arrived at the back end of the greenhouse. It was a dead end. No one was there. Again, I saw movement from behind me and suddenly chased after it back towards the fountain where, once again, no one was in sight. I stood there, trying to catch my breath.

From a distance within the woods, from the other side of the garden walls, coyotes cried and howled to one another. They yipped, barked, and howled for some time. Then they stopped. It was quiet again. I took a deep breath and thought to give up and head back inside. I slowly turned and shined my flashlight forward. I noticed a short, slender figure standing before me. I turned and ran as fast as I could back towards the open door into the house. I tripped over a vine, scraping my knee. I rolled onto my back and saw no one. I quickly picked myself back up and ran inside, closing the door behind me and locking it tight.

I checked and rechecked to make sure the doorknob and deadbolt were both locked. My heart raced faster than my adrenaline. I was terrified! Who was in our yard? Did I see someone, or was my mind playing tricks on me? I couldn't have imagined it. Could I? I know what I had done was very risky and dangerous. I didn't know what I was thinking. It seemed as if my mind had taken over my body in search of a ghost of non-existence. Maybe I was tired and only saw what my... What am I talking about? My actions were just plain stupid. I could not help but wonder who would be outside in our yard. I had to face the facts. I was facing reality, not a dream or imagination. I know what I saw, and someone was out there. Breathing heavily, my back against the door, I waited. No intruder tried to get in. All was quiet again.

I started to walk back upstairs to my bedroom. My flashlight started to flicker the moment I got to the foot of the stairs before climbing up. I smacked the end of the flashlight multiple times, causing it to flicker more until it suddenly beamed and stayed on. Suddenly, I heard a creaking sound from atop the stairs. A door slowly opened. My flashlight again flickered on and off.

"Hello?" I whispered, fear creeping into my voice. I got no response. "Mom? Dad?" Still no response.

I was no longer feeling up to investigating. I feared someone had broken into the house from upstairs by climbing through a window. I had no choice but to investigate anyway. When I arrived at the top of the stairs, I shined the flashlight down the long, dark hallway towards my room. I noticed something out of the ordinary. Quickly, I stepped back and saw a short, dark, shadow-like figure peeking around the corner from my bedroom door.

"Who... Who's there?" I demanded, my voice trembling with worry. The figure slowly drifted backward into my room, out of sight. It seemed to have taunted me to follow. "Shit!" was the only word that slipped out of my mouth. Slowly, step by step, I walked towards the door.

Shielding myself with the flashlight in case something came lunging out at me, I peeked into my room. I heard footsteps rushing from behind me. I swung my arm to attack, but no one was there. Just then, the flashlight went out, and my bedroom door slammed shut hard. All I could do then was stand there alone in the dark emptiness of the hallway, terrified, breathing heavily. I tried to calm myself by holding my breath. I listened to my heart beat loudly. I exhaled as my heart slowed. I took a deep breath to hold my breath again. I listened, my heart slowing even more. Again, I exhaled and then took another deep breath and held it. I held my breath a little longer, listening all around me. My heart beat slower and slower until all was quiet.

Then, all of a sudden, I heard someone exhale in front of me. I gasped for air to scream but fell backwards, tripping over my own feet to the floor, bumping my head hard. I heard a loud thud and then saw a bright flash of white light in my eyes. The flashlight kicked back on and beamed into my face. In pain, I grabbed the light and waved it all about as I stood back up. As soon as I faced my bedroom door, knocking could be heard from the otherside. I reached for the doorknob. The knocking stopped. I stepped inside. Shining the flashlight into my bedroom, there was no one in sight.

Again, I heard a knock, knock, knock. It came from my closet door. As I slowly approached my closet, the soft creaking of the wood flooring beneath my feet echoed through the room. Each step seemed to amplify the tension in the air. The dim light of the flashlight cast eerie shadows across the polished wooden surface, highlighting every knot and grain in the floorboards. A faint scent of pine lingered in the air, mingling with the musty odor emanating from the closet. The floor felt cool and smooth beneath my toes, a stark contrast to the rising anxiety that pulsed through my veins. With each step, the floorboards whispered tales of years gone by, adding to the surreal atmosphere of the moment.

The mysterious knocking continued. I reached out to grab hold of the doorknob. My fingers brushed against the metal, sending a shiver through my entire being. I could feel the knob vibrate as the knocking persisted. I raised my flashlight, ready to strike at the intruder from the other side. Suddenly, the doorknob started to rattle and shake violently, as if someone were trying to get out. I grasped the knob, twisted, and pulled with all my strength, wrenching the door wide open. I swung downward with force, striking and dislodging some of my clothes from the hangers. In an instant, the knocking ceased, plunging the room into an eerie silence. I stood there in shock. No one was in the closet. How could that be? I was certain that someone was in there. I was confused. I still am as to how any of it could have been possible. How? The blood in my body rushed rapidly through my veins. I started to feel light-headed and dizzy from the blood rush to my head. I needed to collect myself.

Tonight has been the strangest and most unusually terrifying night I have ever experienced. In all my 14 years of life, I have never been so scared. I took a few deep breaths, cautiously trying to calm down. I wanted to run out of my room and sleep anywhere but here, in my bedroom. The more I thought about it, the more I figured there had to be a good explanation for all of it. Perhaps sleepwalking or something out of the ordinary; I doubted it was a night terror. I have heard about those, and I do not believe it was that.

After the events of the evening, I climbed onto my bed, clutching my diary, determined to capture everything while it was fresh in my mind. The dim glow of the flashlight cast shadows on the pages as I wrote down every detail I could remember. Sleep felt impossible;

my mind raced with lingering thoughts, and my heart still pounded from the fear.

Despite my exhaustion, I could barely keep my eyes open. Yet, I knew rest would elude me. With a resigned sigh, I decided to set my diary aside and sit on my bed, waiting for sleep to come naturally.

For reasons I can't fully explain, I left the closet door open—a small, irrational comfort against the unease creeping through the room.

MAY 19

Oh, sweet diary! It's been a few days since my last entry, and things have been a bit overwhelming. These past few days have brought a lot of stress, and I've spent much of the time alone, trying to sort through my thoughts and make sense of what's happening.

I'm not sure how to explain it, but I've been questioning what's real and what isn't. Part of me wonders if I'm just imagining things, but I can't ignore how shaken I still feel from the "occurrence."

I want to get everything down while it's still fresh in my mind. These past few days have been strange, and I'll do my best to describe it all. Let me start from the beginning.

May 16th

My window was cracked open a little. I woke up to the early summer morning air carrying a crisp, invigorating scent. It was a delicate blend of fresh-cut grass, blooming flowers, and a hint of dew. The subtle fragrance of wildflowers mixed with the earthy aroma of damp soil, creating a refreshing and rejuvenating atmosphere. The cool breeze brought with it a touch of sweetness, reminiscent of ripening fruits and the promise of a warm, sun-filled day ahead.

I noticed my closet door was closed. I guessed that maybe Mother had come in earlier this morning to hang up my clean clothes. I went over to open my window and found my father down below, digging a fresh hole to plant a new tree. Despite the seemingly hard work, he appeared cheerful.

"Someone's in a good mood today!" I said.

Father stopped what he was doing and looked up at me. "Well, good morning, Dawn!" he continued and asked, "Did you sleep in this morning?"

"Yeah," I replied, glancing at my clock, which read ten-thirty-five. "I have been really tired lately."

I usually wake up between seven and eight, but last night was a long one. Father dropped his shovel, wiped the sweat from his forehead, and placed his fists on his hips.

"Did you stay up late last night?" he asked. This time, he didn't look as cheerful as before. "I mean, were you out in the garden last night?"

I smiled at him and pulled my hair back from my face. "Yes," I responded honestly. "I'm sorry if I woke you up."

"No, you didn't," he said softly. "Your mother found the back door unlocked though."

"Wait, how can that be?" I gasped, confused. "I double-locked it when I came back inside."

"Well, I don't know what to tell you. Luckily, the coyotes didn't get into the house," he continued. "When I stepped outside to get a shovel from the shed, I found four large, deep claw marks on the outside of the back door. I discovered them when I was coming back into the house."

I continued to listen.

"The strange thing is that the markings were dug really deep. It's hard to believe that a coyote could have done it. The claw marks are about half an inch deep and two of my fingers wide from one another," he said, raising three of his fingers to provide a better description.

"I was positive that I double-locked that door," I affirmed.

I ran downstairs to investigate the door myself.

There it was, just as my father described. At the bottom of the back side of the door were four long, deep claw marks, just as Father described. The sight of it made me feel sick to my stomach. I wondered if they had already been there before I went out into the garden the night before.

Father's theory may have been correct. Those markings looked too large and too deep to be made by a coyote. They're even too large to be made by a wolf, for that matter.

Later that afternoon, I decided to go for a walk to the meadows. I'm happy to be out of school for the next few months. With vacation just around the corner, I'm relieved to have the time to spend with my parents.

As I headed to the meadows, I decided to pick some flowers. I thought that bringing some home and arranging them in a vase might liven things up a bit. It's nice to get out of the house every once in a while, and I needed the time alone.

An hour later, I was resting, lying down in the open meadows, surrounded by blooming flowers while birds sang their songs. It was warm and peaceful, with not a single person around to bother me. Every woman needs her fantasy life of relaxation now and then to dream. One day, we may rule the world.

Once it started to get late, I gathered my things and headed home. I didn't want to leave, and I could have stayed much longer, but my mother never liked me being out in the woods after dark. I understand why. Personally, I have never enjoyed strolling through the woods in the dark. Who does?

The more I dilly-dallied, the sooner the sun would set. While taking my time, breathing the palliative air, and walking across the meadow towards the path leading home, I could smell the scent of rain. It was the usual aroma of wet dirt and tree bark, otherwise known as the fragrance of Mother Earth's perfume. I love that smell.

At times like this, I wish I had bought that bottle of perfume called "Thunderstorm" from a seller in town. However, at the time, I had spent my money on a birthday gift for my mother. I think she would have liked that fragrance too. After all, Lincoln is the city of trees; you can smell them almost anywhere you go.

As I was following the path home, the air became still and cold. The sensation was eerie, a chill creeping down my spine as I observed my breath materialize in wispy clouds, a tangible reminder of the frigid air enveloping me. The once vibrant flowers I had picked now bore a ghostly sheen of frost, their delicate petals stiffened and coated in an icy veneer. It was as if a sinister presence lingered in the air, casting a sinister aura over the serene landscape. A sense of unease settled in, sending shivers through me despite the warmth I attempted to summon.

As I stood there, transfixed by the frost-kissed flowers and the misty tendrils of my breath, an unsettling thought wormed its way into my mind. What unseen force had caused this sudden change in the atmosphere? Was there something lurking in the shadows, unseen yet palpably present? The once-familiar path now felt like a sinister labyrinth, each step forward fraught with a sense of foreboding. I quickened my pace, eager to escape the eerie grip that seemed to tighten with every passing moment. Yet, no matter how fast I walked, the feeling of being watched persisted, a silent specter haunting my every move. I hurried along the path, my heart pounded in my chest, matching the rhythm of my hurried footsteps. The woods around me seemed to close in, the branches reaching out like gnarled fingers, casting elongated shadows that danced in the dim light. Every rustle of leaves, every creak of a branch, sent a jolt of fear through me, amplifying the sense of impending danger.

With each passing moment, the feeling of being watched intensified, a cold sweat breaking out on my brow despite the warmth of the air. I dared not glance back, afraid of what I might see lurking in the darkness behind me. My mind raced with thoughts of unseen threats and hidden dangers, the hairs on the back of my neck standing on end.

Just then, I realized where I was. A familiar tree stump marked my path, the same one my father had shown us the other day. This was where he had acted so suspiciously. The memory sent a chill down my spine, but I tried to ignore it and continued on my way, now in a bit more of a hurry. The unsettling feeling of being watched grew stronger, and the shadows seemed to stretch longer as the light faded. My footsteps quickened as I pushed the disturbing memory aside, focusing on getting home as fast as possible.

Suddenly, I came to a stop, trembling uncontrollably with fear and feeling insecure and overwhelmed by uncertainty. I suspected something was very wrong. Then I began to hear something seemingly ordinary—a low rustling sound followed by whispering. The voices were faint, and I couldn't quite make out what was being said. One voice after another drowned out the next, their tones growing louder and louder. The trees, the ground, and soon, my whole world started to spin around me. I was surrounded by children's laughter, but it was not joyful. It was filled with hatred and maliciousness. I didn't know what to do? Then, the world around me came to a screeching halt.

A shadowy apparition moved with a light, sweeping motion before me. I could not get a good look at who or what it might be. The apparition rotated in half circles, twirling and diving with a rapid, whirling motion. It made its way closer to me. Then, for a moment, I felt an overwhelming sense of calm. The dark apparition stood in front of me briefly, as if examining me. I didn't speak or move. I became nervous. I didn't know what it would do.

Its hollow eyes seemed to pierce through my soul, sending shivers down my spine. I felt an icy breath on my neck, and the air around me grew colder with each passing second. The figure's form wavered, flickering like a dying candle, yet its gaze remained steady and unblinking.hen, with a soft breeze, it dissipated like smoke blowing in the wind, fading out of existence. Shadows seemed to crawl out from its presence, stretching toward me as if trying to pull me within the darkness around us. My heart pounded loudly in the eerie silence, and a cold sweat broke out on my forehead. The longer it stared at me, the more paralyzed I became, unable to tear my eyes away from whatever it was. Then, just as suddenly as it had appeared, it dissipated into thin air, leaving me in the oppressive stillness in the woods.

I heard the whispers again. This time, I could hear them more clearly. While other sounds were still drowned out by the din, I managed to stay focused on the much louder voices.

"Go back," one whispered, a chilling command slicing through the air.

"No, please stay," another voice pleaded, its desperation tinged with a sense of foreboding. "If you value your.."

"If you go further, he will find you." A third voice interrupted and warned.

"No, no, you must not go," echoed yet another, a sense of urgency palpable in its tone.

"Go. Now." The final voice trailed off, leaving an ominous silence in its wake, urging a retreat into the shadows.

I searched around but could find no one in sight. I was afraid to move, yet afraid to stay. I knew that if I left and ran back to the meadows, it would be dark, and I might not find my way back for some time. The voices started to fade out.

"He is coming."

"Don't go."

"Run. He's going to find you."

So, I ran as fast as I could in the opposite direction, away from the meadows. My heart was racing, and my legs kept moving. Before I knew it, I found myself pressed against the outside of the front door to my house. It stood before me, solid and secure, closed but unlocked. I quickly entered inside and leaned to block the door. Leaning there in the entry hall, I gasped for air, my lungs straining for every breath. My heart thudded painfully against my chest, a relentless drumbeat echoing in the silence of the house. The exertion of my flight left my legs trembling, a fiery ache spreading through them with each passing moment.

I stood frozen in that moment, feeling the weight of exhaustion and fear bearing down upon me. The mere thought of moving seemed an insurmountable task, as if my body had become anchored to the spot by the weight of my apprehension.

Summoning every ounce of willpower, I attempted to steady my ragged breaths and calm the tumultuous storm raging within me. Rationalizing that it was merely my imagination running wild seemed to offer a faint glimmer of solace amidst the chaos. With each measured breath, I sought to regain control over my trembling limbs, preparing myself to confront whatever awaited me beyond the safety of the front door.

I remained silent during dinner. I wasn't about to interrupt the good conversation my parents were having over something they might dismiss as made-up. But was it truly made up? I've ventured into those woods dozens of times and never encountered such a phenomenon before. Could I have imagined everything—the voices, the apparitions?

Is it possible to misinterpret something as more significant than it really is? Whatever the explanation might be, it seemed undeniable rather than illusory.

I ate as much as I could and did what I had to do to make myself feel better. I excused myself from the table and went to my room for the remainder of the night to pray. I've addressed my prayers to God, asking for forgiveness if I had committed any sins. I am so frightened right now. I don't know if I will ever want to go back into those woods alone again. I'm going to crawl into bed early tonight and wait until I fall asleep, though I worry if I will be able to.

MAY 17

My Aunt Emily and my cousin Dean (the 9-year-old brat) came to visit. Since my uncle Eugene's death, my aunt has not shared any friendly companionship with friends or family. She hardly communicates with us these days. Dean, fortunately, remembers his father, who died when he was six years old. I'm not sure if he gets it from his mother, but he doesn't talk much either. He's notorious for following you everywhere you go. However, I will give him credit for being a curious little guy.

My Uncle Eugene's death was not a pleasant one. I don't think any death is pleasant, but he died in a horrible manner. My aunt and uncle were not a poor couple. They owned a farm in Dorchester, Nebraska, raising cattle and tending crops until tragedy befell my uncle.

My Uncle Eugene and a friend went hunting near his farm. It was a day like any other, as he embarked on his solitary pursuit of deer amidst the tranquil embrace of the wilderness. With every step, he treaded carefully. But fate had other plans. As he crossed a fallen log, his foot found an unsteady perch, and in a heart-stopping moment, he lost his balance. And then, in a sudden flash of agony, the deafening roar of his rifle shattered the silence, a cruel reminder of his dire predicament. The bullet whizzed past him. He was lucky. Until he took another step and fell off a cliff. In that fleeting moment of impact, life and death converged in a tragic ballet, as my uncle's journey came to a tragic end. His body lay broken amidst the jagged rocks, a somber testament to the unforgiving nature of the wild. And so, amidst the serenity of the forest he loved, my uncle met his untimely demise, a victim of circumstance and the cruel whims of fate. But his spirit lives on, a silent guardian of the wilderness he once called home.

My father had suggested I take Dean to the park, which was not a bad idea. The park is opposite from the meadows, which meant I would not have to take that creepy trail. To be honest, I wasn't too comfortable walking into those woods anyways, even early in the morning. I thought of taking my time and waiting until noon to go anywhere. All I really wanted was just to stay home and relax. An afternoon with Dean would surely annoy me, but he has nobody else to spend time with besides his mom.

As soon as we got to the park, Dean ran off into an open patch of flowers to catch bugs. A few times when he jumped to try and catch a butterfly, he'd tumble to the ground after missing it. I sat on a bench for a while, watching him. I thought about how lonely he must be after losing his father and not having any siblings. He's just a poor boy with no good social skills. He talks, I'll give him some credit, but he often walks away when other kids try to play with him. He's a bit strange to be honest.

A young woman approached the bench and sat next to me. She had cute, straight black hair cut to the bottom of her ears, brown eyes, and busty breasts. Noticeably bigger than mine. Her clothing was a different story. She wore a loose-fitting velvet dressing gown that looked like a negligee. I thought it was a little late for Halloween, but she looked good in it.

"Lovely day, isn't it?" she said.

"Yes... Yes, it is," I answered.

She sat close to me with her hands clasped in her lap. She seemed to be mesmerized by Dean, her attention completely absorbed by his presence. Dean had been approached by another child. He stood there, just staring at the child. He neither moved nor spoke, his stillness unsettling. I wanted to call out to Dean to let him know it was okay to respond, but, as I mentioned before, he lacks communication skills. The sorrow of his silence weighed heavily on me.

"Is that your son?" the woman asked.

"Good God, no," I replied. "That's my cousin Dean."

"He's not very talkative, is he?"

"No, not really. I mean, he will talk to his relatives, but it's a long story. His father..."

"I understand," she interrupted. "Leon's father left me the day we made love for the first time."

A voice screamed in the back of my head, "*Why is she telling me this?*" I couldn't figure out where this lady was going with her story, but I was certain we were not on the same page.

"We had been dating for two years, seeing each other every day. We were inseparable," she continued. The sky was flooded with stars, resembling a sea of ethereal entities drifting through the celestial realm above. Gavin and I used to come here, to this very park, every weekend late at night to gaze upon the heavens and count as many wishes as we saw shooting across the sky." She sighed and bowed her head. "We were in love, or at least I was. I knew I was ready. Ready for anything, until I spoke of a wish I wish I hadn't." Her voice changed, as if she were about to cry.

"You don't have to tell me if you don't want to," I said. I should have begged her not to continue.

"If you don't mind me telling you," she sniffed, "it makes me feel better to talk about it."

"I don't mind," I lied. I hate depressing circumstances, especially those that are not my own.

"He heard my whispering wish, and he leaned over to kiss me. Romantically, he kissed me all the way down to my breast and started taking off my clothing."

I raised an eyebrow in shock and thought, "Why are you telling me this?" She then laid a hand on my knee.

"We were naked and full of joy. I had felt as if I had been kicked in the gut, but I knew it was love! He spread my legs and took his long, hot, hard organ, and entered me with an upward and downward motion." She stopped. Thank God. "Sigh... I am so sorry," she paused. "But after that night, I never heard from him again. Nine months later, Leon was born without a father to care for him."

"How, um, how old is he?" I asked, my voice cracking slightly as I nervously fiddled with the edge of my sleeve.

"Seven," came the reply, the word hanging in the air awkwardly, as if she wasn't quite sure of the answer herself.

"So, uh, just out of curiosity, how old are you?" I asked, raising an eyebrow in exaggerated interest.

"Please don't judge me," she said cautiously, her voice barely above a whisper. "But, sigh… I'm now twenty-one years old."

I gasped in shock. "You were the same age as I am now?"

"Take my advice, don't fall in love until you are twenty," she laughed.

"You sound just like my mother," I laughed too.

"I'm Tanis Krieser. It was a pleasure meeting you!"

I shook her hand. "Dawn McWarlick. Nice meeting you too."

Tanis looked at me in shock. Her eyes opened wide and her jaw dropped. She looked as if she had seen a ghost.

"Are you okay?" I asked.

She turned to look at her son, who had managed to get Dean motivated by running around, tossing a ball back and forth.

"I'm sorry," she said. "Any connections to the McWarlick Mansion out there in those woods?"

"Yes, that's where I live."

Her attitude changed quickly, shifting from shock to excitement.

"Oh wow! I'm talking to a legend!" she bellowed.

"I'm sorry?"

"Gavin used to tell me stories about that place. He said it was housing spirits or something. I was told that no one lived there."

I knew she had to be mistaken. "What did you hear?" I demanded.

"Oh, it's nothing. I know for sure he was feeding me a bunch of bullshit. That much is certain."

"Look, it's getting late. We should be going," I said.

Tanis walked over to where Leon and Dean were playing and calmly told them that it was time to go. Following her lead, I did the same for Dean, and we began to head home.

"I hope to see you again soon, Dawn!" Tanis yelled. "We should get together sometime. I don't have many friends, and you seem like a nice person."

"Sure, I'll be back in a couple of days." I hollered back.

"Okay, we'll be here!" she smiled and waved.

We said our goodbyes, as did Leon and Dean.

Today, I made a new friend.

Walking down the path, Dean had been more energetic than ever. He was in a more cheerful mood than before. Not only did he make a new friend, but he got the chance to play and run around. Though he was acting a bit strange. We were almost home when he came to a complete stop. He ducked down to lower himself to the ground like an animal about to pounce on its prey.

A squirrel darted out from behind a bush, prompting Dean to chase after it. He leaped out from behind a rock, hurdled over a log, and pounced towards the terrified critter as it escaped. Afterward, Dean picked himself up from the ground and brushed himself off.

"Oh, man..." he complained.

Dean then became completely silent for a moment, though it didn't make a difference. His behavior changed dramatically. He transformed from an extinct raging predator from the Mesozoic period into a curious, inquisitive nine-year-old. I couldn't quite tell what he was looking at. He became shy and bashful, as he does when meeting new people. And then it happened.

"Hello! My name is Dean. What's yours?" he said, breaking the silence.

All I could think was, what had gotten into him now? It's not like him to talk to himself.

"Nice to meet you," he said, bowing. "I'm nine. How old are you?" he continued. "Really? That makes you two years older than Dawn." He then pointed at me.

"Uh... Dean? We should be going..." I stopped as I noticed something bounce off my shoe. I bent down and picked it up. It was a medallion of some kind—a small piece of metal with a memorial image or inscription engraved on one side and smooth on the other. A long, narrow blue strap made of some kind of material secured the object. It was a woman's choker necklace, I believe. I couldn't make out the design too well; it looked like several letters jammed together to form some kind of foreign symbol.

Dean laughed.

"What's so funny?" I asked, putting the necklace in my pocket.

"Nothing," he lied.

"You're up to something, kid," I said, hoping to get a better answer out of him.

"Whatever..."

"Kids will be kids," I muttered. I demanded that we leave at once to get home in time for dinner. Dean agreed, his eyes darting nervously around, and followed me as I took the lead.

"Bye, Theodosia. I hope to see you again soon," he called out, his voice echoing eerily as he ran to catch up with me.

I wasn't about to ask what that was all about. He might have just been playing a game with me. Whatever it was, I wasn't having fun.

∗ ∗ ∗ ∗

Aunt Emily and Dean stayed for dinner. Mother had made another large meal, enough to feed more than the five of us. Sipping her wine, Emily asked, "How was your day?" Dean, who had been slouching in his chair, sat up straight and reached over the table to help himself to another bread roll. He grinned.

"I met a new friend today!" he said.

Emily was astonished. She set aside her wine glass, cupped her hands together, and rested her chin upon them. "That's wonderful, dear," she cheered, her eyes sparkling with delight.

I haven't seen my aunt this happy in a long while. It was as if the news had lifted a weight off her shoulders, bringing a rare and genuine smile to her face.

"I hope you had a great time at the park with Dawn," she said, winking at me as if to say, "Thank you!"

"I bid wav a gwap twim wiff her," Dean attempted to say with his mouth full of bread. He swallowed and corrected himself. "Sorry. Yes, I did have a great time with her today." He paused to swallow again, drank from his cup, gulped, and continued, "And then I met Theodosia!"

"Two new friends? Wow, I'm so happy for you, son!" my aunt

exclaimed, her voice brimming with genuine excitement.

"Well, if it wasn't for Dawn, I would have never met Leon," he explained. "I was playing with this boy named Leon. We had fun until his mother came and said they had to go. Then we left. I was running after a squirrel and fell. This tall, pretty girl helped me up and asked if I was okay. She was a nice girl." He paused, then slowly turned his head towards me and said, "Then we talked about Dawn."

By this time, I was feeling uneasy. "Go on," I urged.

"She didn't say much about you, except..." He paused, letting the silence stretch uncomfortably. "You don't show her any attention."

"Attention?" I cried in shock. "There was no indication that anyone had been around!"

My parents looked at me in confusion. I didn't know what else to say. Consumed by a mix of disbelief and concern, I wasn't about to accuse Dean of lying, but maybe there was a good explanation for all of this.

Then Dean laughed. "She said all you have to do is expect it to happen, and she will tell you her secrets," he whispered. "If you hear something, call out to her. Don't be afraid of her."

I had no clue what he was talking about. This nine-year-old was good at playing head games. Though his words made me nervous, I had no choice but to change the subject.

Later, my mother, father, and I said our goodbyes to Aunt Emily and Dean. My mother hugged her sister tightly, not wanting to let her go. Who knows when we will see them again? They know they are always more than welcome to visit.

Dean ran toward me with his arms wide open and wrapped me in a hug. "She's waiting for you," he whispered in my ear.

"Who?" I asked.

"Her, the girl in the woods," he replied. "She said she will meet you in the same spot."

I figured he was talking about Tanis, the girl we had met at the park earlier. He turned and followed his mother as they stepped outside. We waved goodbye and watched them walk down the path into the woods toward the meadows. As they disappeared into the shadows, a chill ran down my spine. The woods seemed darker, and an unsettling silence filled the air.

Father closed and locked the doors, stretched, yawned, and said he was going to bed. As he slowly stumbled up the stairs, Mother approached me. The entryway was now empty except for the two of us. She stood between the dining room door with her arms crossed, leaning against the doorway. She raised an eyebrow and smiled.

"So, who's Theodosia?" she asked.

"I don't know. I've never met her," I replied.

"I thought Dean had said..."

"It's strange. I don't know what he was doing," I interrupted. For some reason, I figured now was the best time to tell her everything that had been happening over the past few days.

"I have all night if you wish to talk about it," she said, as if she had read my mind.

I told my mother everything, from the beginning: the voices below my window, the dark figure in the garden, the figure in the hallway, and the knocking on my closet door. She gestured for me to follow her into the dining room.

I sat on the blue fabric couch while my mother set a silver tray on the coffee table in front of us. She was silent as she poured a cup of warm tea for each of us, then she sat next to me on the couch. The whole time felt like an eternity had passed, and my heart raced as my mind swarmed with ideas about what she was thinking about all that I had just divulged to her.

Finally, she turned to me with that comforting motherly smile. I wasn't sure if this was going to be what I needed to hear or not.

"It must have been a dream," she assumed.

Yup, there it was.

"No, no. I was aware of everything that was happening to me, Mother," I told her. "Everything was clear to me. A whole day had gone by, and I never dozed off to sleep. Like this afternoon, for example, or when..." Something stopped me from telling her about the voices I heard that afternoon when we all came back from the meadows.

Anger boiled beneath my skin as I struggled to believe what I was seeing: my mother, covering her mouth and giggling beside me. She thought this was a joke, a farce, something to laugh about?

"What's so funny?" I demanded. "It's all true, Mother. I have no reason to lie to you about any of this."

"Well?" she asked.

"Well, what?" I replied as she tipped her tea and took a sip.

"You didn't tell me about Theodosia yet," she said, setting her teacup on the table.

Dean's behavior had changed from that of a completely shy child to that of an energetic and spirited one. While I had yet to figure out what was behind his actions or the reason for his sudden change, it hadn't really bothered me all that much. So, I tried to explain the incident to her in the best manner I could.

"He seemed to be talking to someone who wasn't really there. I wonder if he was maybe talking to himself?. It wasn't like him to do something like that," I said.

"You saw no one?" she asked.

"Correct," I continued. "It was odd for him to behave like that."

"Odd is a silly word to use to describe an experience like that," she replied.

I was familiar with her example of "odd" in the sense of my father's behavior. Nevertheless, I was going to move on.

"He was having a conversation with someone who didn't exist."

"Oh my..." she said, then broke out into laughter again. "Do you remember when you were five years old, and your father was angry with you when the picture frame he had built for your grandmother's birthday somehow broke?"

I then realized what had been going on. I felt utterly foolish, yet relieved. I had forgotten about Modus Vivendi, my childhood imaginary best friend. So, Theodosia must be Dean's imaginary friend he just made up—or should I say, met?

I remember—I used to blame a lot of my troubles on Modus Vivendi. I guess in a way, I kind of miss him. My parents have been so upset with me that they demanded I stop with my imagination nonsense and get rid of Modus Vivendi. They insisted that I never speak of him again.

Mother kissed me goodnight and walked across the hall to her bedroom. Why didn't I think of it before? A lonely child seeking a safety net, a best friend, and finding it in a new imaginary friend.

Despite the fact that nothing was solved during the earlier part of the conversation with my mother about what was happening to me, I felt some relief. Her modest words afforded me some much-needed slumber that I had not had in a long time that night.

MAY 18

3:15 A.M.

I awoke to the sound of creaky hinges. Sitting up in bed, I noticed that my closet door was closed, even though I distinctly remembered leaving it open before falling asleep several hours earlier. Feeling uneasy, I decided I didn't want to stay in my room any longer. I grabbed my pillow and headed downstairs to sleep on the couch. Just then, I heard another creaking sound. Looking up, I saw the closet door slowly opening in front of me. A chilling breeze swept through the room.

The room suddenly became freezing cold. I could see my breath as chills ran down my spine. Clutching my pillow tightly in an attempt to shield myself from the cold, I felt my teeth begin to chatter. Closing my eyes, I took a deep breath and whispered to myself, "Please don't open. Please don't open..."

And when I opened my eyes, there it was—my closet door wide open. I heard a breathing sound next to me. Summoning every bit of courage, I turned to face the sound head-on, but there was nothing there. I exhaled and took a deep breath of fresh air, not realizing I had been holding my breath. Slowly, I turned back towards the closet. There, in the deep darkness, I saw a pair of fiery red eyes staring at me.

I wanted to scream, but my voice was gone. Fearless, I was not. My arms and legs were stiff, my jaw clenched tightly, and my palms started to sweat. My body shook uncontrollably. I felt as if fate itself had abandoned me.

I quickly pulled myself together and hurled my pillow into the closet. To my surprise, the pillow went right through the apparition, confirming it wasn't a physical presence. The ghostly figure was clear and undeniable. I knew I wasn't dreaming. It made no sound or movement, but its stare followed my every move. It watched me as I crawled out of bed, its eyes tracing each step I took toward the hallway.

I slowly turned the doorknob, and the fiery red eyes widened. I forced the door open and ran out as fast as I could.

As I ran in terror, the hallway seemed to stretch endlessly before me. Each step felt like an eternity, the walls closing in around me as if the house itself were alive and trying to trap me. Shadows danced menacingly in the dim light, and the air grew thicker, making it harder to breathe. My heart raced with each frantic step, and the sound of my own footsteps echoed eerily, amplifying my fear. It felt like the end of the hallway would never come, as if I were caught in a nightmarish loop with no escape in sight. I could almost sense the ghostly presence behind me, its malevolent stare piercing through the darkness. Every shadow seemed to hide its form, every creak of the old house echoed with its silent pursuit. My breath came in ragged gasps as I pushed myself to go faster, desperate to outrun the relentless specter that haunted me. Finally, I reached the top of the stairs and stopped, gasping for breath.

The sound of someone humming caught my attention. I slowly turned around, realizing the eerie rhythm was drifting from my bedroom, sending shivers down my spine. The unfamiliar tone lingered in my mind, haunting me. I didn't bother closing my door. So, I continued down the stairs and entered the living room. I couldn't tell if the humming had stopped or if it was just stuck in my head. I even found myself humming the tune. My body trembled with fear. All I could do was curl into a ball on the couch and cry with my head between my knees, watching the internal conditions of the environment decompose around me.

I didn't sleep at all that night. My mind was consumed by the persistent humming, replaying endlessly like a broken record. It sounded like a child humming—a girl, perhaps? I was no longer sure of anything. I desperately needed an answer to what was happening. As I struggled to stay awake, my eyelids grew heavy, and sleepiness began to overtake me.

12:00 P.M.

Waking up at noon was not what I had planned. I had the urge to sleep longer, but several mysteries prevented me from doing so. Sitting idly in the living room did not calm me. I wasn't even hungry; my appetite was long gone. I didn't feel like bathing or changing my clothes. Only one thing came to mind that seemed like it would bring some relief: fresh air. Maybe some sun in my eyes would do the trick. I wanted to take a walk, hoping it would calm me down a bit and help me work up an appetite. As restless as I was, I feared I might soon go crazy. What is this house doing to me? I feel like my soul is being drained from my body. I need to get out of this house before I pull all the hair out of my head.

I asked my mother if she could bring me a pair of clean clothes. She was confused, but I told her I would explain later. I wanted to dress in the living room. There was no way I was going back into my room right now, even in broad daylight. The only time I will go back there is when I need to get my diary or when I feel safe again.

A warm breeze blew into the main hall as I opened the front door. Closing the door behind me, I stepped down off the stairway and caught the scent of my father's tobacco as he puffed his life away again. This time, it didn't bother me. In fact, I thought I could have used a drag or two myself.

Stepping away from the house, the warmth of the afternoon sun showering upon me, I felt a fleeting sense of freedom and ease. Despite the tension knotting my muscles, I hoped they wouldn't cramp. A shoulder rub would have been perfect, or even a day at the spa to rejuvenate my skin, but I knew those were distant fantasies. The sense of dread still lingered, reminding me that true relaxation was out of reach.

I ended up walking to the park. I sat on a bench, leaned back and closed my eyes, and just listened. Dogs barking, birds singing, children laughing, and the soothing sound of the river flowing behind me is all I cared for. It was nice and peaceful. I finally felt relaxed with the sun beaming down upon my face. For the moment, I didn't have to worry about dark shadows creeping from every corner, waiting to trap me and suck the very life from my body like a parasite. I might be exaggerating; I'm sure it's just stress playing with my mind.

For a moment, I did think about home. I couldn't help but wonder what it was that frightened me so much. I forced my mind to stray off track and absorb the elements around me. I wanted nothing to hold me back. Forgetting about home and my family, I stretched out and yawned. Feeling relaxed and free was all I wanted. Keeping my eyes closed, I dozed off.

I opened my eyes when I realized everything had become silent. The park was empty; no dogs barked, no birds sang, no children laughed. I tried to take advantage of the silence but wondered where everyone had gone. As I stood up to look around, I noticed that nothing around me was casting shadows from the sun. Thick, dark clouds were forming above me, filling me with a sense of caution.

A flash of light tore across the dark sky, followed by a loud clash of thunder that startled me. Terror gripped me as the thunder lambasted through the trees, trailing off into the distance like a thousand drums being hit simultaneously. I figured this was a good, albeit uncomfortable, time to head home before the rain started.

Sleep must have overtaken me. I felt well-rested but was unsure how long I had been asleep. Another streak of lightning rippled across the sky, illuminating the area around me. I stopped, preparing for another loud crash of thunder... but nothing happened. Then, the torn sound of the blistering crash caught me off guard, causing me to jolt forward.

Then came the downpour. Rain smacked hard against my skin, feeling like bee stings and lashes hitting every inch of me. Rushed and desperate for cover, I ran into the woods to shelter myself as best as I could until I got home.

Walking deeper into the woods, I thought the rain might have stopped. I could still hear the echo of rolling thunder in the distance and the sound of rain pouring down over the trees, yet I could neither see nor feel a single drop. The only evidence was the muggy odor of wet dirt. Everything around me was dry—the ground, trees, rocks, and even my clothes were now dry.

Another crash of thunder startled me. It was all coming back to me; I felt like I had been here before, like déjà vu. I looked around, searching for something familiar, trying to recall the path I had taken. I didn't want to be alone. My head started spinning, my ears began to ring, and then I dropped to my knees. I realized I was on the path where I had heard those strange phantom voices while walking home with my parents. Then, all of a sudden…

"Dawn!" Someone was calling my name. It was an unfamiliar female voice, soft and quiet, as if whispering from a far distance…

"Hello?" I asked, hoping not to get an answer. "Is anyone there?"

"It's been a while!" the voice replied.

"Who are you? Show yourself," I demanded.

"I'm sorry," she spoke. "I didn't mean to frighten you. It is silly of me to hide."

I turned around, and to my surprise, there stood a little girl with long, straight hair hanging over her white nightgown. As her hair swayed in the breeze, I noticed strands of white and natural brown that created a faint aura around her upper body. Her gown seemed to softly glow, adding to the eerie atmosphere that suggested I might be facing a ghost.

Her bright, mirthful blue eyes stared into mine. The pupils of her eyes were white, pure, and untarnished, without a hint of sin. I felt a sense of unease. I had no emotional response—no fear, terror, horror, happiness, or sorrow. It was almost as if she were an angel.

"Do not be afraid," a voice said. Her lips did not move; it was as if she had spoken to me through mental processes—telepathy. Her pale face cracked a smile, adding an eerie aura to the encounter.

"I can see your thoughts," she said softly. "You must be aware. Please focus on what I tell you." Her words echoed strangely in the silence, adding to the eerie atmosphere that surrounded us.

I was listening, yet perplexed. She continued speaking, her voice steady yet somehow unsettling in its calmness.

"You are exposed to the evil of one who is marked by mental deficiency. You will face a moment during the first phase of the moon in its first quarter when you must deny yourself in judgment. The prayer wishing harm upon someone has cursed a place where three reside. A place tied to your birthplace, condemning you to exile."

Not entirely sure what she meant by all of that, but her warning was stuck in my head. For some strange reason, I knew I would never forget them. But what did she mean by, "It's been awhile?"

"Who are you?" I asked.

She started to drift away. I hurriedly chased after her, but was abruptly pushed back by a chilling gust of wind, as if an unseen force was keeping me from reaching her.

"Do not go back," she warned me. "The parasite of evil is execrable. It will find you. Do not go back." Her threat carried a tone of hatred and malicious bitterness. I listened to her advice with a mixture of fear and understanding, holding no grudge against her warning. Suddenly, another clash of thunder startled me.

I awoke and found myself on the bench in the park. Looking around, I saw no one nearby. The trees were swaying violently in the wind, and dark clouds loomed overhead, signaling that a storm had just begun.

Did I have a bad dream? It seemed so real, though. I didn't

want to question myself anymore as a raindrop fell upon my head. Quickly, I rushed into the woods to get home. The storm picked up, and I hurried as fast as I could to reach safety. The rain fell hard, and the wind slowed me down. Fatigue began to catch up with me.

I slowed down. The wind was pushing me back even stronger.

The fear of giving up felt like it could blow me over. Suddenly, I became lightheaded, with the constant pounding roaring in my ears, mixed with thunder and wind, while my blood flowed rapidly to my head. Images of my dream flooded my mind like flashbacks. My gut cramped, and sickness spread through my body. I couldn't focus straight; I had to stop. But then...

Everything went black.

MAY 20

I woke up in my bed, frightened and confused. As I regain my senses, I notice that I'm dressed in my nightgown. A sharp pain pulses through my head, and I realize I have a terrible headache. It feels as though I've been struck by a blunt object. The disorientation adds to my anxiety, making it difficult to piece together what happened. The room is dimly lit, shadows dancing on the walls, adding to the surreal and unsettling atmosphere. I try to recall the events of the previous night, but my memory is hazy, fragments slipping through my grasp. The lingering fear gnaws at me, and I can't shake the feeling that something is terribly wrong.

I got out of bed to get dressed. As I walked to the mirror on the wall, I caught sight of blood on my legs and between my thighs. The shock overwhelmed me, and I fell to my knees, halfway sitting on the floor, crying as I stared at my reflection. There were no cuts or visible injuries, but when I felt around, more blood rushed from between my legs. A blood-curdling scream escaped my lips, filling the room with my terror and confusion. The horror of the situation consumed me, and my mind raced with questions and fears. What had happened to me? How did I end up in this state? The answers seemed just out of reach, shrouded in the darkness of my fractured memory.

Mother stopped herself at my door. I saw terror in her eyes, likely reflecting the fear in mine.

"Oh my God!" she exclaimed. "My baby girl's a woman!" she said, her face lighting up with joy. I stopped crying as confusion slowly took over the terror in my body.

"I'm dying, Mother," I said very seriously.

"No, you're not," she bellowed. "It's called menstruation, a period. Every woman goes through it and lives."

What... What?" I sobbed.

She continued to explain, reaffirming her support. "It's a process only women go through. It's a painful experience that causes a periodic flow of blood from the uterus, known as a period," she said, her explanation clear and precise.

"Periodical pain? You mean it happens more than once?" I asked, adding unintentional sarcasm to my question.

"Correct. It recurs approximately every twenty-eight days until you reach your forties," she explained.

"You're almost due, aren't you?" I said sarcastically, questioning her statement.

"In another fifteen years," she lied, "when a man and a woman have sexual intercourse..."

"I know, I know how babies are made. We've had this talk before," I reassured her, though the full details were a bit unsettling for me at this time. I filled in the blanks on my own.

"You're still too young to meet boys, but we can talk about that some other time," she said with motherly concern, as she walked out the door. "Of course, there's always masturbation!"

"Mother!" I exclaimed in shock, but she had already gone out the door!

Mother returned with a pail of wet hot towels. She rushed me into the washroom so I could clean myself. It took me a little while, The blood had seeped down, staining my inner thighs with dark red streaks. I was a mess. Washing my naked self-off, I used nearly half a bar of soap. The warmth and moisture from the towels mixed with the blood, creating a reddish tint that clung stubbornly to my skin.

"Does it usually take this long to clean up after every period?" I asked.

"No, if you watch yourself and keep tending to your needs, you never have to worry," she explained. "You think that's bad? Try getting it out of your clothing."

"I see." While washing behind the bathtub curtains, I heard my mother stepping out and closing the door behind her. Her voice was muffled as she spoke from the other side.

"I'll be right back, dear. I need to get the bleach," she said.

"Okay, Mother," I replied.

The door opened and then closed. Mother must have already brought back the bleach and my gown.

"That was fast!" I said. I got no reply. I thought nothing of it at first until I heard, "Dawn," she whispered.

"Mom?"

I pulled back the curtains and found nobody in the room. On the floor were little puddles of water, like footprints, leading to the door. The room became colder, and I could feel the water I was sitting in drop in temperature. My body shivered, and my skin faded to a light bluish color. Cold breath slipped between my lips as I sat there, quiet and inert.

THUD! THUD!

I heard knocking coming from the door. My eyes slowly scanned the room as I waited, my heartbeat racing, my mind wondering what was going to happen next. A deep, heavy voice called out from the other side of the door.

"Dawn," it said, the voice chilling and otherworldly. "Decent?" it asked, the word echoing ominously through the cold air.

My hearing had gone faint. The door slowly creaked open, and to my surprise, my mother stood there, ready to save me, flooding me with relief.

Pulled from the dryer, Mother wrapped hot sheets and blankets around me. I might have been suffering from hypothermia; my body was dangerously cold, and I shivered uncontrollably. She then brought me hot chicken noodle soup to help warm me up from the inside. She was clearly concerned.

"You're sick," she admitted. "You need to get some rest. You were caught in last night's storm."

"So, it wasn't a dream," I realized aloud. "How could I have been in one place and then, next, here?" I asked, bewildered.

"Do you remember what happened?" asked Mother, her voice tinged with concern.

"I fell asleep at the park," I told her. "I had this strange dream again."

"Again?" She looked at me, puzzled.

"Deja vu, it seemed like. Kind of like a recurring dream," I explained.

"Then what?" she asked, urging me to continue.

I proceeded to tell her about my dream.

"That would be a strange dream," said Mother.

"Then I woke up in the park as if nothing ever happened. I started to run home as it began to rain. Then..." I paused.

"Dawn?" Mother tried to interrupt.

I sighed. "Everything went blank from there. I don't remember how I got home. I just woke up in my bed."

"I'm sorry!" She sat next to me on my bed as I lay there motionless, the blankets wrapped tightly around me, almost preventing me from moving.

"A storm was coming, and you had yet to return home. Your father and I started to worry. So, he went looking for you. He got in his truck and drove into the woods, knowing you were at the park. He stopped to examine a body in the middle of the path. He was even more terrified when he discovered it was you."

She started to cry, overcome with fear and relief.

"You were lying on the ground. He feared you were dead. A tree branch fell and knocked you out cold," she added.

That explained the bad headache. I felt the top of my head. It stung, and I had a large lump that hurt to touch.

I took in her words, processing the shock of what she had just revealed. The memory of the stormy night started to piece together in my mind: the darkness, the rain, and now the painful evidence on my head.

"I can't believe it," I murmured, my voice barely audible. "I had no idea."

Mother reached out and gently touched my shoulder, her own tears mixing with mine. "We were so scared," she whispered. "But your father found you, brought you home. We took care of you all night."

I nodded, feeling a mix of gratitude and disbelief. The weight of what could have happened settled heavily on my chest, and I hugged my mother tightly, thankful for her presence and for being safe at home.

"When he arrived home, he carried you in his arms, soaking wet. I panicked, so he demanded that I leave and calm down in the dining room. I refused and ran into your room with him to prepare towels to dry you off with. He laid you on your bed and left to get more blankets to warm you up with. I undressed you..." She stopped.

"What's wrong?" I asked, alarmed by the seriousness in her expression.

She took a deep breath and looked me in the eyes, her own filled with concern. "I noticed a cold, red indent of a handprint on your left breast."

I gasped, the gravity of her words sinking in.

"Do you know anything about it? Or remember anything about it?" she asked..

"No," I lied. I didn't really know how to explain it myself, nor was I about to admit that I too had seen this marking. Terror gripped me as I contemplated what it could mean.

"I was scared to think..." she continued, her voice faltering. "Have you been attacked in any way?"

"No," I said honestly, or at least that I know of.

"Well, I saw it plain as day. When your father returned to your room, I showed him."

"You SHOWED HIM MY BREASTS?" I yelled, shocked and angry.

"Calm down. I had to. If you had been attacked, I needed to rule out any other possibilities. I thought maybe he did it by mistake carrying you home," she explained, her voice pleading for understanding. She paused again, gathering her thoughts.

"Did he do it by mistake?" I asked, my voice tinged with concern and confusion.

"Well," she chuckled nervously. "When I showed him, the marking was already gone. He didn't get to see it. He knows nothing about it."

There was a knock at my door. My father walked in, his head bowed and his hands twisting his hat nervously. I wasn't sure if he was going to cry or hug me. Instead, he spoke.

"How ya feeling?"

"She may have hypothermia," Mother jumped in. "I called a doctor."

"I brought you some medicine," he said, handing it to Mother.

"It was just what I needed. My head was killing me." Mother broke open the seal and fed me two caps full of the purple liquid. To be honest, it wasn't that bad tasting, but some food would have helped it go down easier. I was starving and thirsty, I told them.

"Look, Amethyst, before you go to fix her something to eat, there is something you both should know," he said nervously.

Mother sat back down, concern etched on her face.

"Dad?" I asked.

"On my way to town, I drove past the park. The tornado destroyed everything in its path," he explained gravely.

"A tornado?" I yelled!

"The park is gone. Rumor has it that a body had been found dead."

Mother gasped. "Who was it?"

"People were talking. It was Miss..." He paused. My father looked down at me with tears in his eyes, silently conveying who it was without saying the name, assuming I knew who he meant. Finally, he nodded.

"Tanis is dead?" I asked, tears streaming down my face, filled with sorrow.

Both of my parents looked at me, startled and confused. I felt as though I had said something wrong. My father slowly sat on the bed next to me, and then my mother sat down unsteadily, almost as if she had lost her strength. She remained still, like a motionless statue of clay.

"How do you know about Tanis?" Mother asked.

"Dawn," Father interrupted, "Tanis has been dead for more than seven years. She died giving birth."

"She died of a broken heart, all alone in this world," Mother said.

"Miss Krieser, Tanis's mother, took her grandson to the park before the storm hit. When a search party went out looking for her, they found her. She was..."

"Todd, that's enough," Mother bellowed.

"Well, Leon was safe. He's with his grandfather now. Are you okay, Dawn?" my father asked, concerned.

"I want to be alone," I said.

My parents slowly left the room without saying a word. In a soft voice, I murmured to myself, "I'm sorry, Tanis. I didn't know."

I sat there, feeling the heaviness of the moment settle around me. The memory of Tanis and the unanswered questions filled my thoughts. Deep down, I wished I had known her better, understood more about her life. I lay down in my bed to rest for a bit.

* * * *

I had another dream.

I was lying on a grassy patch somewhere in the garden. A warm light shone down on me, casting a spotlight. I sat up and looked around. Everything was dark. All I could see were the dark outlines of the greenhouse, shed, and dragon fountain. The sun shone above, but its surroundings were black. Everything looked like a set for a play or an extravagant design for a theatrical act.

I stood up and began to move around. The spotlight from the sun followed my every step. I looked around, trying to see if there was an audience, but I was certain that I was alone in my backyard.

It was warm. No wind blew, and no other sounds were made. Everything was silent. I walked a short distance and came upon the greenhouse. It was covered with thorny vines. I noticed that the shed and the fountain were also bound with vines.

I approached the fountain and discovered a single rose that had blossomed from a vine hanging over the well wall. It was not its natural color of red. Instead, this rose was blue. Then I felt another presence with me. I turned around and saw a young boy.

"My feet hurt, Mommy," he said. "My feet hurt really bad."

The boy walked toward me with open arms. As I stepped back, I noticed that thorns pierced his feet in every way possible. A trail of blood was left behind him as he walked closer. I could see his eyes—bright blue with pupils dilated white. His hair was a similar brown and white mixture, identical to the apparition I had seen in the woods.

The vines quickly came to life and wrapped themselves around the child's legs. He cried in pain. Blood oozed as the vines pierced him, tightening their grip. He stopped moving and looked up at me, tears streaming down his face.

"My feet hurt, Mommy," he repeated.

I was overwhelmed with pity for him, paralyzed by my inability to act. The scene grew more terrifying as the vines tightened their grip, causing him to cry out more in agony. Blood flowed freely from his wounds, pooling on the ground around him. Despite my desperate desire to help, I remained powerless, haunted by the sight of his suffering and the chilling realization that there was nothing I could do to save him. Then the light vanished. All I could see were his blue eyes and the faint outlines of his white hair. I heard an evil chuckle from behind me. Turning around, I saw the same child, but his features had transformed. His eyes blazed red like fire. His body started to fade out of sight, like an apparition dissipating, leaving only his fiery eyes fixed on me. His voice deepened into a dark, ominous tone.

"What did I ever do to you?" he laughed, his voice echoing through the yard. The spotlight shone on me again, now with a vibrant redness like blood. I felt a tightness wrapping around me, piercing thorns into my body. The vines had a hold of me.

"What have I done to deserve this?" he continued. "I will not let you hurt us anymore."

The vines grasped tighter. I could feel my bones popping, on the verge of snapping or shattering. I couldn't breathe or speak. Just as I thought I would be crushed under their relentless grip, I woke up.

Gasping for air, I bolted upright, drenched in sweat. My heart pounded against my chest as I tried to steady my breathing. The vividness of the dream lingered, and the terror felt all too real. I glanced around my room, reassuring myself that I was safe. But the image of the boy's fiery eyes and the sinister laughter echoed in my mind, leaving me shaken and unable to shake the feeling that the nightmare was far from over.

"Amethyst?" my father's voice called from a distance, startling me.

"What is it now, dear?" my mother asked, walking towards my bedroom.

"Have you seen my journal?"

Mother opened my bedroom door and sighed, "It's in the second drawer of your nightstand."

Then she stepped into my room, walked across the floor, and stood at the foot of my bed. Her expression was welcoming. I knew she was checking on me and the condition I was in.

"How are you feeling?" she asked.

"A little better," I said.

"Here, it's late. You should have something to eat."

She walked over to my nightstand, where a silver tray lay. Mother must have set it there some time ago while I was asleep. I was still cold and a little hungry.

"What time is it?" I asked.

"Nine-thirty," she answered. "You should eat something to keep your temperature up."

"Found it!" Father yelled from his room.

Mother shook her head. She seemed more concerned about my health than anything else in the world at that moment. I knew she would rather be by my side, taking care of me, than tending to even her loving husband's needs. I suppose any loving mother would do the same for their child. She had always been protective of me and didn't care what my father was doing. I ate the soup and drank all of my tea. Bean soup, my favorite.

I heard a shuffling sound as Mother flipped a deck of cards in front of me, gesturing for me to play.

"Want to learn how to play 21?" she asked.

"21?" I replied.

She taught me how to play 21, a card game with a standard deck of 52 cards. Here's how it works: The dealer gives each player two cards. One card is dealt face down so your opponent cannot see it, and the other card is dealt face up so both players can see their score.

Players then look at their cards to calculate their points. Kings, Queens, and Jacks are worth ten points each. Aces can be worth either one or eleven points, whichever is more advantageous. The other cards are worth their face value (two through ten).

The objective is to score as close to 21 points as possible without exceeding it. If a player's total exceeds 21, they "bust" and lose that round. The player with 21 points or the closest to it without going over wins the round. If both players have the same score, it's a tie. The dealer (the person dealing the cards) must "hold" at seventeen points or higher. This means they stop drawing cards once they reach or exceed seventeen points.

It's a popular game for gambling and can be quite competitive, Mother explained.

So, Mother and I gambled with pennies. I had the upper hand in cash, being up two dollars and three cents, until she wiped my stash clean. She was good at this game, but I was determined to play more and beat her at it soon enough.

"My mother and I used to play this game all the time when I was your age," she said. "I would save up as much money as I could and never spend a dime, just so I could play with her. We played for a dollar."

"I bet you were good at it, huh?" I said.

Mother sighed. "I had beginner's luck for a while. I would lose just enough to earn back all my spending. Day after day, I would work to earn a few dollars just to play and try to gamble to win her money," she continued. "I think that was a lesson to never gamble, but then it was a lesson taught to save money for the things you cherish the most."

"How much did you win?"

"In a two-week period of playing one-dollar bets, I lost two hundred dollars."

"Oh my!"

"About three months later, on my fifteenth birthday, she gave me back my two hundred dollars and doubled that with another two hundred dollars as a gift. I felt rich with four hundred dollars. She taught me an important lesson. I saved it to this very day. Every earning I made, I'd save."

After our final round, she gathered all of the cards, kissed my forehead, and told me goodnight. She promised that we would play again, then left my room, taking the cards with her.

It struck me. Father asked about the whereabouts of his journal. Mother told him it was on the second shelf of his nightstand. Now that I know where it is, I can somehow get to it and try to solve a mystery. If he had written anything about the reason mother and he were fighting, I could maybe uncover the secret of his "odd" experience.

I had forgotten all about it until now. There are some things that I want to know. All these strange happenings may be linked to his behavior as well. Whenever I discuss odd happenings with Mother, she becomes nervous and changes the subject, and the same happens with Father's suspicions too. I need to get to his journal and find out what happened on May 13th. I don't know if I will find what I am looking for, and I might get into trouble if I get caught. Mother taught me how to gamble, so I have to take risks. It's worth a try.

MAY 21

I woke up feeling well-rested this morning after spending the entire day in bed yesterday. I got up early, around seven-thirty, but my legs felt a bit weak. I hadn't walked around to stretch, nor had I felt very motivated to do so. The only thing on my mind was eating; I was starving. I stumbled out of bed and made my way to the kitchen. The smell of fresh coffee filled the air, instantly lifting my spirits. I brewed a pot, savoring the rich aroma, and poured myself a steaming cup. As I took my first sip, I felt a warm sense of comfort.

My stomach growled loudly, reminding me of my hunger. A bowl of fresh fruit caught my eye, so I grabbed it along with some yogurt and granola. I made myself a hearty breakfast, piling the granola on top of the yogurt and adding a generous portion of fruit. I sat down at the kitchen table and dug into my meal. The sweet, juicy fruit combined perfectly with the creamy yogurt and crunchy granola, satisfying my hunger and brightening my mood. As I ate, I felt my energy slowly returning.

After finishing my breakfast, I decided it was time to stretch my legs and get moving. I put on some comfortable clothes and stepped outside. Mother met me in the hallway and asked if I would like to help her out in the garden. She mentioned that some green-thumb work would be beneficial for my health. I was ready to start my day. My head was still sore, but I could tolerate it for now, as I'm not one to give up easily.

I couldn't help but occasionally glance between the greenhouse and the shed. I tried to focus on planting flower buds, but images from my dream kept resurfacing like a bad flashback. It was a little chilly outside this early in the morning, but by noon, I was sure it would warm up.

After a while, I became bored and walked into the alley between the shed and the greenhouse to look around. I had a feeling about something that had become more than a bother, more like something calling out for attention. However, I noticed the vines along the shed needed to be cut down.

Light shone through the plastic covering of the greenhouse, revealing no shadows or darkness. The alley was well-lit, which allowed me to clearly see the moss and vines that had grown and twisted along the gray brick of the shed. As one of the chores that was to be done in the garden, I pulled out the clippers and started to cut down the vines. I thought it would be an easy job, but the vines twisted and curled deep into cracks, making them hard to pull out. Next to me was a heap of thorns and vines that needed to be burned.

Mother had started a fire pit, burning leaves and vines from her cuttings. As I picked up vines from my work, I noticed an engraving on a loose brick in the shed wall. I ripped and pulled out some vines around it, examining the symbol closely. It was the same foreign-like symbol that was also marked on the pendant I had found in the woods.

The engraving was about half the size of my hand. I dug my fingers into the seam around the brick and wiggled it out. When I finally removed it, I discovered a small wooden box with the same symbol in the center of its indentation. Within the channel of the indentation, two wedge-shaped gears were visible—one at the top and one at the bottom, as if a center cog was missing.

"A clue," I said to myself.

I tried to pry it open with as much force as I could muster, but soon gave up, not wanting to break it. I had some thoughts about what the box might hold. The gears suggested that it might be a music box of some kind. Then I considered whether the pendant I found in the woods might be the key to opening that box.

Just then, Mother called for me, "Dawn, come here quick. Come see this."

I put the box back into the hole in the wall and placed the brick where I found it. I will come back for it later. I guessed whatever she wanted was important, so the box would have to wait.

Mother waved quickly for me to hurry. She looked surprised. I stood next to her, facing the fountain. I gasped in shock at her surprise. Her voice trembled as she spoke.

"That wasn't there before," she said.

I looked to see what she had been pointing at: a rose. Not of the natural rose red, but a shrub vine with a sharp, prickly stem and a fragrant blue flower.

"Do you think it means something?" I asked.

"Well, don't let your dreams get to you," she added, sounding unsure. "I don't know what to make of it. I've never seen a blue rose before."

"Neither have I," I replied, feeling equally confused. It was a mystery to us, seeing something that could be considered a rare occurrence.

Mother had gone inside without saying anything. After she left, I couldn't help but admire the blue rose. Wet with moisture, a drop fell from one of its petals and landed on the ground. I then realized the moisture wasn't water. As it fell from the blue flower, the liquid spread into a small damp spot of red fluid. It was blood.

I couldn't just walk away and dismiss it. I wanted my mother to take a look at it, but before I could call her, the blood transformed into vapor. I knew that shouldn't be possible. I was absolutely certain it had been blood. As it evaporated into a mysterious mist, it left a brown blood stain on the brick ground.

I ended up walking away, trying to dismiss it from my mind. All I wanted was to rest. My eyes had played tricks on me, and I had heard things I wished I hadn't. My mind seemed to be in a completely different world. So much for my spontaneous life.

As I walked into the house, all I could do was laugh. It was my father who once told me, "God's favorite music is laughter." Laughing always helped me feel better.

"I guess laughter really is the best medicine," I mused to myself, recalling my father's wisdom. "Even in the weirdest moments, it's good to find humor." I chuckled softly, feeling the tension easing. "Maybe I just need a good night's sleep," I thought aloud.

Later, I was told not to go anywhere.

My parents wanted me to rest and take things easy for a while. They were going to the market and asked me to watch over the house while they were gone. House-sitting isn't that hard of a task, so I didn't mind.

I stood before the entry hall window, watching them get into my father's truck. I could still smell the tobacco burning in his pipe.

"Take care of yourself," my mother called out as they drove off.

"I will," I replied, waving goodbye.

I lingered at the window for a moment, the faint aroma of my father's tobacco lingering in the air, a comforting reminder of his presence. As their truck disappeared through the woods, I turned back into the house, feeling a sense of responsibility settling over me as I prepared to keep watch until their return.

I walked into the kitchen, driven by hunger. Since last night's soup and a scant breakfast this morning, I hadn't eaten. Spotting leftover pasta, I quickly filled a plate, poured a tall glass of milk, and added a slice of cheesecake. It was clear—I was famished.

Then the grandfather clock in the entry hall started to chime. My parents had only been gone for half an hour. I quickly ran into the entry hall to look out the window, but they had not returned. At the eighth and final chime, it dawned on me.

I sprinted up the stairs, down the central hall, and opened my parents' bedroom door. Stopping abruptly, I stood there, breathing heavily, overwhelmed with a strong sense of desire. My father's journal!

There it was, atop his nightstand. I couldn't help but ponder what secrets lay within those pages. As I laid my hands on it, a wave of guilt crept up behind me. I stepped away, leaving the journal in its rightful place. With a sigh, I turned away from it.

Just then, a sharp pressure gripped my left breast, causing my heart to skip a beat. Another wave of pain surged through me, and I instinctively pressed against my chest, trying to alleviate the force. I tried to pull it off, but there was an unseen force in front of me. It felt as though someone or something was clutching my heart. With determination, I reached forward and grabbed the journal. Suddenly, as quickly as it had started, the pressure vanished.

"What was that all about?" I asked myself aloud.

There, within the grasp of my hands, was the leather-covered journal with the assortment of small print in red ink: Todd McWarlick. I flipped through the pages until I came across a familiar date: May 13.

THE ODD

(These are the pages from my fathers Journal)

MAY 13

My nerves are almost shot. I've been living through the reality of my relentless dreams, and it's overwhelming. It's so odd, and I've tried to explain it to Amethyst, but she refuses to listen. She called me harsh names—"a bumbling drunk son-of-a-bitch." Honestly, I can't blame her. I understand why she thinks I'm a liar. She says I'm always telling tall tales. But no, I am certain that what happened to me was not make-believe. My emotions and fear have been pumping rapidly through my veins. I don't know what else to do.

I've had another dream. Four nights have gone by, and I have hardly had any sleep. These dreams repeat themselves, and I never bother writing them down in this journal. But those red eyes haunt me to this day. I only pray that my only child, Dawn, never finds out about this. I've asked my wife to never speak of it to her. I don't want my child to think of her father as a madman.

I left work to meet up with the guys at the pub. We had spent the day recovering and placing orders from railroad shipments. An afternoon of drinking away our stress and welcoming the weekend was our usual routine for our monthly get-together. I admit I had a bit too much to drink, so I decided to sober up and let the guys catch up to me. Before long, I noticed the time. I hadn't had a drink for more than an hour by then and knew that Dawn would be home from her last day of school. I figured I should leave so I could talk to her about how her day went. I was more interested in that than in drinking.

The guys understood what I had to do. I told Harry, my work partner, that I didn't need a ride home. I wanted to walk home to sober up since the house wasn't far and the weather was nice. I reached the woods, and by then, I was fully aware of my surroundings. My buzz had faded.

Not too far down the road, I came across a stranger. He wore a dark cloak that hooded his head, and he had long black hair that hung over his shoulders. He approached and greeted me with his name. A foreign name, I'm sure. Unfortunately, I can't recall it exactly.

The stranger's face bore a stigma, the look of disgrace. It was hard to tell if he was young or old. He wasn't someone I would welcome in the dark. What happened next was horrifying.

"I have a purpose in mind that involves you," he intoned, his voice a chilling blend of menace and allure, resonating from deep within his chest. His eyes, gleaming with a sinister light, bore into mine as he continued, "Your soul, a rare and precious essence, will be of particular use to me."

He continued talking about some curse that had been placed upon my home. I didn't believe him, but who would do such a thing, and why? Either he was drunk and stupid or I had a lot more to drink than I thought. I tried to move on my way, but some invisible force held me in place, rendering me powerless. Then, from behind him, a black mist began to materialize. It grew thicker and more menacing, shifting and swirling as if it were alive, pulsating with a bad energy. The mist seemed to whisper dark secrets and ancient curses, none of which I could understand.

The mysterious stranger warned, "If you fail to perform this sacrifice, I will condemn you to a realm of extreme wretchedness and horror."

I still could not move. Though I wanted to strike him, I felt as if I were bound by an invisible power.

"Sacrifice the child to me as an offering. Give me your most valued woman and child in exchange for your soul," he demanded.

I disagreed with him, which only seemed to anger him further. The black mist rose from behind me and struck me in the head, right between my eyes. There was no physical pain, but instead, I felt a wave of dark, sorrowful emotions coursing through my body.He laughed, his eyes beginning to burn bright red, as if they were engulfed in flames.

Had he stolen my soul? Fear gripped me as I struggled against the invisible bonds that held me in place, the weight of dread settling heavily upon my chest.

I must stop here. I never want to remember this again. I had no other choice but to do as he demanded. Why did I have to kill them? What have I done? The weight of guilt and horror pressed down on me, filling my mind with anguish. Now, I wish I had let Harry take me home. Please, God, save me. I prayed, desperate for deliverance from the nightmare gripping my soul.

I tried to tell Amethyst in hopes of making myself feel better and hoping it was only a dream. Her expressing her opinion didn't help. Tears ran down her face; I knew she was terrified. She slapped me across the face just for telling her.

"You asshole!" she yelled. "How dare you speak of death as if it were a pleasant thing! Don't you ever tell me that you're going to kill yourself."

I knew she was angry and hurt, but killing myself was the first, dumbest, thought that could get me out of this nightmare. I wondered, was I going too far? Should I calm down and rethink some of my thoughts? Should I have not told her?

"I hate you!" she cried.

"Don't you find it rather odd that..."

"It was only a dream, Todd... It was only a fucking dream."

Dawn walked into the room, her eyes scanning the chaos that surrounded us. I felt a surge of frustration and pointed towards the door, yelling, "Why can't you ever knock? Can't you see we're in the middle of something important?"

She paused, taken aback by my outburst, her face a mixture of confusion and hurt. "I didn't realize," she stammered, her voice trembling slightly. "I just got home from school."

"Go to your room at once." I shouted.

"Why? What did I ever do?" she defended herself.

I barked back at her. Before I knew it, she was gone. Amethyst was even more pissed at me now. She scolded me about why I did that and how I could have handled the situation better. She explained how I could have stopped it all at once and could have greeted her instead. But no, I had to take the easy route. She ended the conversation by storming out of the room.

"You crazy son of a bitch," she yelled, slamming our bedroom door. "I don't ever want to hear such a fucked-up, bullshit story like that again."

For some reason, I didn't care anymore. We didn't talk for the rest of the night. Even at dinner, Amethyst and Dawn both kept to themselves. I wanted to ask Dawn how her day was, but I was more worried that she was still mad at me for sending her to her room for no reason. So, I kept to myself as well.

I don't know what to do.

"Stop acting like you give a shit. You're worthless," echoed a voice in the back of my mind.

(I noticed scribbling written under the text. I tried to write what I could make of it.)

"Please, God, help me."

"God cannot help you."

I feel sick. I hear voices in my head.

"We are of many voices. We are all one. We are..."

I still see that demon in my mind.

"We are, and always will be, many."

All of a sudden, my whole body felt calm and relaxed. I wasn't stressed anymore. The voices and images had gone away. It was clear to me what I had to do. I have to...

(The rest of the page was ripped out.)

* * * *

The floor in the hallway creaked. Someone was coming. I closed the book and placed it back where I had found it. I turned and froze. The bedroom door was slowly creaking open.

"Mom?" I called. No answer. "Dad?" Still no answer.

The hinges squeaked, echoing through the silent house as the door slowly creaked open all the way and stopped. My heart pounded in my chest, racing as if I had just run a mile. With a deep breath, I slowly approached the door, each step heavy with dread. The hallway stretched out before me, shrouded in shadows. I prayed neither of my parents would be standing there, waiting for me. To my relief the hallway was empty. There was no one to be seen.

I stepped back around the corner of my parents' bedroom door when I noticed my door across the hall had opened. The hinges squeaked too, just like before. Someone was in my room. Blood rushed to my head, and I felt like I was going to faint. A loud ringing echoed through my head, disorienting me. I tried to focus, gripping the doorframe to steady myself. Now was not the time to black out, I told myself, fighting against the overwhelming sense of dread that filled the air.

"Hello?" I whispered, the sound barely escaping my lips. Still, no one answered, and the silence that followed only heightened the eerie atmosphere.

I could hear footsteps coming from downstairs, echoing faintly through the entry hall. A door closed—a soft click that I recognized as the kitchen door just below where I stood. Then another door closed, possibly the storeroom in the kitchen, followed by a loud thud. My heart skipped a beat. Someone was in the cellar.

Stepping out into the central hall to investigate, I was only a few feet from my door when I caught a movement in the corner of my eye. I turned and saw the little boy from the garden, peering down over the railing. A chill ran down my spine, sending shivers through me as I stood there, awestruck by the unexpected sight.

I moved towards him, slowing my breathing, determined not to alert him until I was certain whether he was real or a figment of my fears. As I got closer, I extended my hand, intending to touch him, when suddenly I stepped on a loose floorboard. The floor creaked loudly beneath me, breaking the eerie silence.

The little boy turned and stared at me with his bright, empty blue eyes. It felt as though he were peering straight through me, freezing me in place. Without breaking his gaze, he slowly turned his head and glanced down the stairs. Step by step, he descended, each footfall creaking in the silence. The creaking echoed through the stillness, each sound stretching the silence and amplifying the sense of unease that hung heavy in the air.

I stood rooted to the spot, unable to move or even breathe, as he reached the bottom of the stairs and swiftly disappeared around the corner into the kitchen. There was no sound of a door closing this time, only the eerie silence that followed his vanishing footsteps. I then gasped for air. I hesitated for a moment, my instincts warring with my curiosity and fear, but ultimately, I summoned the courage to follow him into the kitchen.

The kitchen lighting was dim, almost a dark gray hue. Moonlight filtered in, casting slow-moving rays across the floor—shadows that belonged to the little boy. He reached the store room door and glanced back at me. The wall behind him was shrouded in darkness, his bright blue eyes the only visible feature.

As the door creaked open, he disappeared into the store room. I hurried after him, but before I could react, the door slammed shut. I rushed to turn the knob, but a strong force gripped it, preventing me from twisting it open. I pushed with all my strength, but the door remained stubbornly closed. It was as if someone or something was holding it shut, refusing to let me in.

"Theodosia!" a boy's voice cried urgently. "Hurry, get out!"

"Help me, Shelton!" a girl replied, her voice strained. "He won't let go of my arm."

There was nothing I could do. The door refused to open. I banged on it desperately, trying to get their attention.

"Let me in!" I called out frantically.

"No, you have to try. Reach for my hand," said Shelton urgently. "Reach out to me—I'll hold the door open."

"It hurts," she replied, her voice strained with pain.

"Grab my hand, Theodosia... That's it! There you go!"

"Shelton...!"

"I've got you. Pull!"

For a moment, everything fell silent around me. The tension hung heavy in the air as I pressed my ear against the door, straining to listen for any sound beyond. I could hear faint breathing from the other side of the door.

"Are you okay?" Shelton asked, sobbing. Someone was breathing heavily on the other side of the door, their ragged breaths audible through the wood. My worry deepened as I realized someone else was in distress.

"I'm bleeding," Theodosia answered, her voice crackling with sadness.

A loud thud inside the room, followed by a deep, menacing laughter, forced me to instinctively step back in fear.

"No! Let her go!" cried Shelton, his voice filled with anger and fear, echoing through the tense silence.

"Shelton, HELP!" Theodosia screamed, her voice strained and gasping, as if someone were choking her. I pounded even harder on the door.

"Open the door!" I pleaded. I had a feeling things were about to get much worse than I could ever imagine.

I stepped back to prepare for a forceful push, hoping to break through the stubborn door. Despite my effort, nothing happened; the door still did not budge. Determined, I tried another forceful push. This time, I lost my footing and slipped, causing me to fall hard to the floor. Groaning, I stood up and pressed my ear against the door once more. Inside, I could hear the sharp sound of glass breaking, accompanied by the clattering of various objects crashing to the floor and shattering into pieces.

A loud, heavy thud slammed against the backside of the door, knocking me off balance and causing me to fall to the floor again. As I regained my senses, I noticed the small fingers of one of the children slipping between the floor and the door, desperately grasping onto the bottom edge. Something from the otherside was attempting to pry the child off the door. Tug after tug, I could hear the child pleading for help, their voice growing more desperate with each pull. With a final, desperate tug, their fingers slipped back inside. The child cried out in blood-curdling agony.

"Let her go!" Shelton cried out.

Then, I heard the sickening sound of a body smashing into the door. The impact was so intense that it forced me to pick myself up off the floor, where I had been knocked down moments before. My heart pounded in my chest as blood began to ooze from underneath the door, forming a dark, sinister pool on the floor.

I took a step back, my entire body shaking uncontrollably. My mind raced, trying to piece together the horrifying scene that must have unfolded on the other side of the door. I feared the worst, unable to comprehend the full extent of the horror that awaited me.

"Theodosia? Shelton?" I called out through the door, my voice trembling. There was no response.

The storeroom door slowly creaked open, revealing a harrowing scene. A bright light shone down upon a little boy covered in blood, kneeling beside a little girl lying in a puddle of blood. She was unmistakably dead. Shelton was crying in grief, his sobs echoing through the room. He looked up at me, his tear-filled eyes locking onto mine with a look of profound sorrow. Behind him, a dark shadow began to rise, taking shape into the figure of a cloaked being.

"No!" I screamed, my voice cracking with desperation. "Stay away from him!"

The cloaked shadow turned to face me, its fiery red eyes glowing with malice. As it shifted its shape, it grew more human-like, and its face began to come into focus. A chilling familiarity washed over me—it looked as if I had seen him before. From its own form, the shadow raised an arm and conjured a sinister, swirling mist. With a swift and ruthless gesture, it enveloped the little boy in the mist, as if some unseen force was consuming him alive. Witnessing each agonizing moment, I screamed in terror, my voice reverberating through the room.

Panicked, I turned to run, but a powerful force knocked me down. It felt as if I had collided with an invisible wall. Dazed, I looked up and locked eyes with my father, who was standing over me. The last thing I remember was blackness surrounding me, consuming my vision, until there was nothing left but an overwhelming void.

MAY 22

I awoke to the sight of my mother sitting beside me on my bed. I lay there, stiff and unwilling to move. She reached over to my nightstand and picked up a cup. Steam rose gently from the cup, curling in the air like tendrils of a ghostly presence.

"Good morning," she whispered softly, her voice a soothing balm to my groggy state. The warmth of the steam contrasted with the chill that had settled in the room overnight.

I struggled to shake off the remnants of sleep, my mind still clouded with the vivid dreams that had plagued me throughout the night. The familiar comfort of my mother's presence was a welcome reprieve from the unsettling visions that had danced behind my closed eyelids.

"Here, drink this," she said, handing me the cup. The aroma of chamomile and honey wafted up, promising calm and comfort. As I sipped the warm tea, the stiffness in my body began to ease, and the tension in my mind started to melt away. I started to feel like going back to sleep.

In that moment, with the steam rising and my mother's reassuring presence beside me, the world outside my bedroom faded into the background. As I handed the empty cup back to her, she gently stroked my hair, a familiar gesture meant to calm me, as she always did. I wasn't in the mood for much talking.

"Last night..." she began, her voice trailing off with concern.

"I just want to be alone," I interrupted, my voice barely above a whisper. I couldn't bring myself to relive the night's events just yet.

Mother sighed, her expression weary, as if she already knew the weight of my thoughts. It was difficult to talk about anything in that moment. I was overwhelmed—too much had happened, and my emotions were tangled in a way I couldn't unravel.

In other words, hysteria. But who am I kidding? I'm hardly the one to diagnose my own problems.

My mother, always the anchor in my stormy seas, continued to stroke my hair, her touch a silent promise of support. Despite her attempts to reassure me, I couldn't shake the feeling of dread that clung to me like a second skin. The room felt smaller, the air thicker, as if my anxiety had a physical presence.

"I know it's hard," she finally said, her voice breaking the silence. "But we'll get through this together."

I nodded, not trusting myself to speak. The truth was, I didn't know how to explain the terror that had seized me, the sense of something lurking just beyond the edge of perception. It was easier to stay silent, to hope that, in time, the fear would ebb away. For now, all I could do was hold on to the small comfort of my mother's presence and hope that, eventually, the darkness would lift.

Leaning forward again, this time to kiss my forehead, she smiled. To be honest, I didn't really want to be alone; I wanted her to stay for a while. She got up and headed toward the door.

"You looked as if you had seen a ghost," she said.

"Well," I replied, "I don't know what I saw."

"Would I believe you if you told me?"

"I don't know."

"Get some rest. We can talk about it tomorrow."

She then walked out the door, closing it halfway. I looked at my clock; it was one-fifteen in the afternoon. I found my diary and wrote down everything that had happened last night and today. Other than that, all I wanted to do was rest and gather myself together. Perhaps it would be better to hold off on any activities until tomorrow. I know Mother will listen.

I took a long nap, and when I woke up, Father came into my room with dinner. I always enjoy it when he cooks. Tonight, he brought a plate of steak, baked potato, and corn on the cob. The lemonade was perfectly balanced with sweet and sour, just the way I like it, with plenty of sugar.

By the time Father brought dinner, it was six-thirty-five, and I was still feeling tired. He stayed in my room for a while, clearly wanting to talk. I was a little uneasy after reading his journal, but I tried not to let any signs of suspicion show.

"Are you excited about the camping trip?" Father asked.

"Yeah, I'm just tired these past few days. I'm sure I'll feel better by then," I said.

"Your mother told me you're a woman now. Congratulations."

"Thank you, I guess?"

"Well," he yawned, stretching his arms, "I'd best let you get your beauty sleep."

"Goodnight, Father," I said, watching as he opened the door.

Just as he was about to leave, he turned back to me. "If you're feeling better tomorrow, how would you like to go fishing with me at the lake in Pawnee?"

I smiled at the thought, feeling a sense of excitement. "I would love to!"

Well, what do you know—he actually wants to take me fishing with him. I had never been invited on any of his hunting expeditions before. Maybe it's because he knows I don't like causing harm to animals. But it's time I grew up and faced the outdoors.

"Here, I got this for you," he said, reaching into his back pocket. He unfolded a greenish-gray ball cap that had a print of a dark-colored blackmouth bass above the bill.

I can't believe I'm saying this, but the ugly fish was kind of cute. He put it on my head, and it fit perfectly.

"Thank you. I love it!" I told him honestly.

"I'm glad you do!." He said blushing.

That was the first time I had ever seen my father blush. It was a good feeling, finally getting the chance to spend time with him. We never got to do this. Now that his little girl was finally a woman, he could show me what it's like to survive and hunt in the outdoors. I couldn't wait.

"Goodnight, Dawn," he said, closing the door halfway as he left. "We're getting up bright and early."

I turned to my diary, feeling a mix of excitement and contentment as I penned my final thoughts for the day.

MAY 23

It was the beginning of a new day in Nebraska. The air was humid, carrying a damp heaviness that clung to everything. A small sliver of light peeked over the hills, but darkness still enveloped the landscape. The raspy cries of frogs and the high-pitched chirps of crickets echoed across the lake. Despite the humidity, the atmosphere was perfect for a fishing day with my father. When we reached an open area along the lake, my father kneeled down and whispered, "Look, Dawn," he pointed. "A six-point buck."

We watched in silence, captivated by the deer's presence. The stillness of the moment was broken only by the gentle ripple of the water as the deer drank. My father and I exchanged a glance, a shared appreciation for the beauty of nature.

After a few moments, the deer lifted its head, ears twitching as if sensing our presence. It stood motionless for a heartbeat before turning and disappearing silently into the underbrush. We remained still, listening to the fading sounds of its retreat.

"That was incredible," I whispered.

My father nodded, a proud smile on his face. "Nature has a way of surprising us," he said softly. "Now, let's get to our fishing spot before the sun gets too high."

We made our way down to the lake, the early morning light slowly growing stronger. The water was calm, a perfect mirror reflecting the sky above. We set up our fishing gear, the familiar routine bringing a sense of comfort and anticipation. As we cast our lines into the water, the peacefulness of the lake surrounded us, and I couldn't help but feel grateful for this moment with my father.

"I really wish I had a rifle to take down that deer back there," I said, breaking the silence. "Mount that baby right on the wall in your trophy room." I lied.

"I couldn't be prouder of you right now." my father said with a smile. "We haven't been here long, but already your primal hunting instincts are kicking in."

"What are primal hunting instincts?" I asked.

"Let me put it this way," my father replied. "Primal hunting is when a mature individual develops the predator instinct necessary for survival by killing and eating an animal. For thousands of years, humans have hunted to protect and feed their families."

A lot more was said, but I'll leave out the gory details. I think I've explained enough. However, I did learn a lot about fishing as well. I learned that primal hunting involves all sorts of "game" hunting, as my father puts it. Hunters wear clothing to blend into their environment and the elements of nature so that game such as deer, moose, bears, ducks, and other animals aren't able to see them.

My father handed me a fishing pole and expertly tied a lure onto the end of my line. The lure, shaped like a wooden jig, was designed to mimic a sharp metal hook, creating an enticing appearance for the fish. He demonstrated how to fish with it, showing me the right technique for casting and retrieving.

With a nod of understanding, I cast my line into the lake, watching as the lure plopped into the water with a satisfying splash. My father then pulled out his own fishing pole and cast his line a bit farther away from mine to avoid any tangles. The lines arced gracefully through the air before settling into the calm lake, where we both waited in anticipation.

By the time my father had reeled in his line to cast out into the lake a second time, I had managed to catch a fish. He was pleased to see that I had caught something. The underwater creature thrashed and pulled, trying to break free, making it feel as if I might be pulled in myself. I forced myself to stay steady and strong. Meanwhile, my father instructed me to "reel and feed, reel and feed." After a short while of battling with the fish, I finally managed to pull it out of the water.

"Beginners' luck," my father chuckled, a playful grin spreading across his face as he looked at my catch.

I caught an ugly-looking fish with smooth, slimy skin and hardly any scales. It wiggled wildly, swinging back and forth like someone hanging from a noose. The cold-blooded creature, which my father identified as a catfish, was clearly not happy. My father demonstrated how to unhook the fish while I held it, his hands steady and practiced. Watching the catfish's gills open and close was strangely unsettling, almost creepy.

The croaking sound the fish made was eerily uncomfortable. Its deep, guttural noise reverberated through the air, creating an unsettling sensation. The sound, coming from a creature with such an alien appearance, was oddly discordant and disconcerting, adding an extra layer of discomfort to the already strange experience of handling the catfish.

The catfish was as long as my arm, from my shoulder to the tip of my middle finger. I was thrilled with my catch and eager to cook it right away. However, as I was handling the fish, I accidentally dropped it onto the ground after getting pricked by a thorn on its fin. Though I didn't bleed, the sting from the thorn made my hand itch intensely.

I found a pair of gloves in the tackle box and put them on; their worn leather fit snugly over my hands. I bent over to pick up the fish that had been lying motionless on the ground for a little while. I could feel the slight chill of its body through the gloves. Not long after I held it, the fish jolted and began flipping about continuously. Trying to avoid getting pricked again by its sharp fins, I unfortunately dropped the fish on the ground once more. It flopped around wildly, making it even harder to regain control without getting hurt.

Suddenly, without warning, there was a loud *SMACK* as my father swung a mallet, striking the fish's slimy head and stunning it instantly. The fish lay still, its body twitching slightly as the shock set in. My father glanced at me, his expression a mix of determination and relief.

"That should keep it from flopping around," he said.

I quickly grabbed hold of the lifeless catfish, its weight heavier than I anticipated. With a firm grip, I lifted it and tossed it into a bucket that was already half full of lake water. The fish landed with a splash, its body sinking into the cool, clear water. The bucket rocked slightly from the impact, but the fish remained submerged, its once thrashing movements now stilled.

I grabbed my fishing pole to cast out another lure. Oddly enough, I struggled to cast it out into the lake. Apparently, I let go of the cast too early, causing my hook and lure to snag onto something behind me. Annoyed, I turned around to see what had happened. To my surprise, the lure had hooked onto an old, weathered tree stump partially buried in the ground.

The stump was covered in moss and vines, making it look like it had been there for ages. I carefully approached it, trying to free my line without damaging it. As I got closer, I noticed something unusual about the stump. There were strange markings carved into the wood, almost like ancient symbols. My curiosity piqued, and I wondered what story this old stump might hold and how it had ended up in this seemingly forgotten corner of the lake. I sighed and carefully began untangling the line, hoping I wouldn't damage the lure or the tree. As I worked, I couldn't shake the feeling that my day of fishing was off to an unusual start.

As I was trying to unhook the lure from a small stone that was wedged in a crack on the top of the stump, I noticed something unusual. The stone seemed oddly out of place, almost as if it had been intentionally positioned there. Curious, I leaned in closer and saw that the stump was covered in strange, intricate carvings. They appeared ancient, worn down by time, but still faintly visible. The discovery sent a rush of adrenaline through me. What could these carvings mean? Had I stumbled upon something significant? As I freed the lure, I decided to investigate further, feeling an inexplicable pull to uncover the secrets hidden within the stump.

I pulled the stone out from the crack of the stump. It was the size of a domino game piece, yet heavier. As I examined it, I noticed a familiar rune symbol. It resembled the symbol I had discovered on the box in the garden at home, but this one had a more intricate design.

The foreign letter engraved into the stone was captivating. I couldn't shake the feeling that my imagination wanted to believe I had stumbled upon something significant, something powerful. I can only hope the symbol means good fortune.

After a long day of fishing with my father, we drove back into Lincoln. We pulled into the gravel parking lot of the new local ice cream hotspot. Since it first opened last month, this charming little place has become my favorite spot. It's a cute, quaint house situated right across the street from the popular chicken restaurant. Now, sitting outside the ice cream shop, I savored the creamy flavor of my favorite ice cream while thinking about our day's adventure. The cool spring evening was filled with the distant laughter of children playing. Spending time with my parents in and around Pioneers Park always felt special, creating cherished memories that I knew I would hold onto forever.

Next, he drove all the way across Lincoln just to indulge in a couple of Tasties with cheese and a bucket of onion chips from his favorite "In and Out" restaurant.

The "In and Out" restaurant was a local legend, known for its mouth-watering food and friendly atmosphere. Nestled in a bustling part of town, it was always busy, filled with the chatter of satisfied customers and the irresistible aroma of grilled meats and fried delights.

As he parked and walked in, he was greeted by the familiar sights and sounds: the sizzling grill, the clatter of plates, and the friendly staff who knew him by name. He placed his order, watching as the cooks expertly assembled his Tasties with cheese and filled a large bucket with freshly fried onion chips. Taking his first bite, he savored the perfect blend of flavors and textures—the tender, flavorful beef and seasonings, the gooey, melted cheese, the tangy mustard and pickle, and

the satisfying crunch of the onion chips on the side. It was a moment
of pure bliss, a reward well worth the drive across town. My mouth is
watering just writing about it. As for me, I, too, enjoyed every single
bite of those delicious loose meat sandwiches.

Once we got home, my father proudly unloaded the fish. With a
gleam of satisfaction in his eyes, he carried the bucket of fish into the
kitchen, ready to filet them. There was no way I was going to stick
around to help with the gutting; the mere thought made me queasy. My
mother, on the other hand, couldn't even bear to look at the fish unless
they were safely behind aquarium glass. She wouldn't touch them, eat
them, or even consider keeping one as a pet. Her distaste extended to
birds as well. I've always wondered why she's so terrified of them.

After all, today was a better day. I've been feeling better too,
despite the bloating and cramping. I'll live. I went to bed early this
evening and figured I'd write in my diary about today's fishing
experience. The anticipation of a catch kept me on my toes, and when I
finally reeled in my first fish, I couldn't help but smile. I look forward to
my next fishing trip with my father, hoping it will be just as enjoyable.
For now, though, I'll cherish the memories of today and let them soothe
me to sleep.

Oh! I almost forgot.

I pulled the rune symbol rock out of my pocket, having
forgotten I took it. Maybe it's a bad luck stone? Nah, probably not. I
actually had a good day today, so maybe it's a good luck charm?
Although, I wouldn't necessarily call it a charm. I'm sure I could find
more information about it if I look in the family library. But for now, I
am going to sleep.

MAY 24

There comes a time in everyone's life when you wake up in the morning and know you've woken up on the wrong side of the bed. That's how my day started. I wasn't looking for trouble, but sometimes it finds you regardless of your efforts to avoid it. Despite my attempts to take it easy and maintain a positive outlook, everything seemed to go wrong. It felt like the universe had conspired against me, and no matter what I did, I couldn't catch a break. Some days, you just fall, and there's nothing you can do but pick yourself up and try again.

For starters, my hair was a mess the moment I got out of bed. I stumbled to the washroom to brush it, hoping to tame the wild strands. Just my luck—the brush got hopelessly tangled in my hair, and no matter how hard I tried, I couldn't get it out. In a fit of frustration, I decided to cut it out. Big mistake. I was so upset that I didn't pay attention to what I was doing and ended up cutting more than three inches off my hair just to remove the brush. I stood there, staring at a handful of hair and an uneven hairstyle that looked like my head had been attacked by a weed trimmer. My hair was now a jagged mess, with random short sections sticking out in all directions. The morning had barely started, and I already felt defeated.

Thankfully, if it hadn't been for my mother stepping in to cut and even out the sides of my hair, I might have gone insane and butchered it all off myself, probably making it look even worse. As she worked on my hair, I was distracted by the relentless cramps that were bothering me so much I didn't even think to thank her for her help.

After she finished, I went into the closet to grab my shampoo and conditioner and headed to the washroom to take a shower. It's not wise to walk around people knowing I smelled like a fish. It's rude in its own humorous way. The hot water and familiar scent of my shampoo were a small comfort, helping me feel a bit more human again after the chaotic start to my day.

The "hot" water in the shower was disappointingly cold, and

the water pressure was pathetically low. It was far from soothing. To make matters worse, the conditioner I applied to my hair smelled off—an odd mix of burning wax and coconuts. As I stood there, puzzled by the strange texture oozing between my fingers, I decided to investigate.

I picked up the bottle, and to my horror, discovered it was not conditioner at all. It was suntan lotion. Just great! Now my scalp would get a nice tan. Ugh. I felt a mix of frustration and embarrassment as I rinsed out the lotion. Ugh, could this morning get any worse?

After finally washing it all out, I confronted my mother about the suntan lotion. She said that she forgot to replace the conditioner bottle.

"Mom," I began, trying to keep my frustration in check, "why was there suntan lotion in the shower instead of conditioner?"

She looked up at me, a hint of surprise on her face, and then a sheepish smile crept across her lips. "Oh dear, I must have forgotten to replace the conditioner bottle," she admitted. "I was using the suntan lotion the other day and must have left it there by mistake."

I sighed, rubbing my temple. "Well, it smelled awful and was a nightmare to wash out. Plus, the shower water was freezing."

Mom's smile turned apologetic. "I'm sorry, honey. I'll make sure to replace it right away and check on the water heater too. How about I make you some breakfast to make up for it?"

Mother soon handed me a bottle of her conditioner, a sincere look of apology on her face. I thanked her and headed back to my washroom for another shower. The moment I stepped back under the spray, I sighed in disappointment—the water was still cold, and the pressure was as low as before.

Shivering, I applied the conditioner, trying to be quick but thorough. The cold water made the process agonizingly slow, and the weak pressure meant it took even longer to rinse out all the product.

Each icy droplet felt like a tiny, relentless pinprick against my skin.

As I stood there, teeth chattering, I couldn't help but think about how this morning was testing my patience. The conditioner, at least, smelled pleasant and familiar, a small comfort amidst the chilly ordeal. I took a deep breath, trying to stay positive despite the circumstances. Finally, after what felt like an eternity, I finished rinsing off and stepped out of the shower, relieved to be done with the ordeal.

Wrapping myself in a towel, I couldn't help but laugh a little at the absurdity of the morning. At least now my hair was clean, and I could move on with my day, hoping that the worst was behind me.

After taking my second shower, I brushed my hair once more, trying to smooth out the last few tangles. Aware of the low water pressure, I decided to brush my teeth next. I applied toothpaste to my toothbrush and held it under the weak stream of water. Suddenly, the water stopped flowing altogether, leaving me with a toothbrush in hand and a mouth full of unbrushed toothpaste. I then went into my parents' room to use their sink. Lifting the faucet handle, I was relieved to find that there was running water. Nearly gagging on the toothpaste that lingered in my mouth, I quickly leaned over the sink and rinsed it out. The cool water washed away the minty foam, and I felt an overwhelming sense of relief. I took a moment to catch my breath, grateful that their sink was still functional amidst the strange water issues plaguing the house.

Later, I considered going outside for a walk to get a bit of exercise. I felt somewhat out of shape and knew that stretching my legs would do me good. I didn't plan to wander too far, just a simple stroll around the neighborhood. The idea of getting some fresh air and moving my body sounded refreshing, especially after the unsettling incident with the water. As I laced up my sneakers, I imagined the cool breeze and the rhythmic sound of my footsteps on the pavement, hoping the walk would clear my mind and lift my spirits. The sky was clear, no cloud in sight. The air was warm and the breeze was calm, but cool.

I hadn't walked too far from home when I heard loud honks above me. I looked up and saw a large gaggle of geese flying over the mansion. Their wings flapped slowly as they soared freely along the breeze above. Then, splat, splat.

"Shit," I cursed, realizing what had happened.

I had no choice but to turn back and take yet another shower. Goose droppings were tangled in my hair, and the disgust and frustration welled up inside me. I wanted to cry. Scratch that, I wanted a shotgun to take them out. My leisurely walk had turned into a messy ordeal, and all I could think about was scrubbing my hair clean once more.

After drying myself off, I went to the mirror in my washroom. Taking a deep breath, I picked up my hairbrush and began to slowly and firmly brush my hair. Each stroke was deliberate, as I tried to work out the tangles and remove any lingering remnants of the goose droppings. The rhythmic motion of the brush was somewhat soothing, even as I felt a mix of frustration and exhaustion from having to deal with yet another unexpected mishap. I watched my reflection, seeing the weariness in my eyes, and resolved to take better care of myself despite the bizarre events of the day.

That moment of quiet calm was abruptly shattered by a loud, piercing scream. It was my mother. Her voice echoed through the house, filled with terror. The brush slipped from my hand as I rushed toward the source of the scream, my heart racing with worry and adrenaline. I dashed through the hallway, my mind racing with the possible reasons for her distress, hoping that whatever was causing her fear was something I could handle.

I rushed down to the entry hall and found Mother on the floor, her body curled into a tight ball as she sobbed uncontrollably. Her cries were jagged and desperate, each one cutting through the silence of the house like a knife. I felt a pang of fear and confusion—what could have happened to bring her to such a state? I knelt beside her, my heart racing, and gently placed a hand on her trembling shoulder. "Mother, please, try to calm down," I urged, my voice trembling as much as her body.

Father was nowhere to be seen, and the absence of his calming presence only heightened my sense of helplessness. I knew I had to take charge in this moment, to be the anchor she needed. I wrapped my arms around her, pulling her close.

"Mom!" I cried out. "What's wrong? What happened?"

Mother looked up at me, tears streaming down her cheeks. Her eyes were wide with terror, as if she had witnessed something horrific. She could barely speak through her sobs, her hand trembling as she pointed to the entry doors.

"Your father…" she managed to choke out, her voice trembling with dread.

"Dad?" I yelled, panic rising in my throat.

From outside, Father's voice echoed through the doorway, laced with urgency and fear. "Stay in the house!" he hollered.

Something terrible had happened.

I didn't listen to Father's commands and left Mother there to compose herself. Stepping outside, I was suddenly overwhelmed by the putrid scent of death. As my eyes adjusted to the harsh brightness, I was confronted with a dreadful sight. Father and I stood in the middle of the yard, surrounded by dozens of dead bodies. Dead geese littered the ground around us—dozens, if not a hundred. The sight was overwhelming, and the stench of decay filled the air.

The once vibrant yard was now a macabre scene, with feathers and blood creating a gruesome tapestry on the grass. Several geese hung limp in the trees, while many lay splattered across the lawn and on Father's truck. A few had even smashed through the windshield. I noticed a small pile of bodies in the back of the truck, their bodies contorted and lifeless. More were broken and twisted, bleeding on the front stairway and the roof of the mansion. The entire scene was a chaotic and grisly arrangement, with feathers drifting through the air like a morbid snowfall. The once serene landscape of our yard had been transformed into a nightmarish spectacle, and the air was thick with the metallic scent of blood.

"Dad?" I cried. "What happened?"

He quickly turned towards me and shouted, "I told you to stay back." He then paused and sighed. "I'm sorry. Is your mother okay?"

"She's crying. She'll live."

"Come, come look at this."

I carefully counted and stepped over seventeen dead geese as I followed my father. We came to a stop, and he pointed down at a couple of geese lying on the hood of his truck. He slowly examined one of their bodies, showing me there were no puncture wounds. Only blood seeped from its rostrum, its nose.

"Poison?" I asked.

"Not likely," he answered.

I shivered, feeling the chill of the eerie scene.

"Poison wouldn't have affected so many at once like this. Something must have spooked them. Must be a territorial thing. It's interesting how animals can act in unexplainable ways that lead to death. But this many? There has to be another reason. Worms, perhaps?" He quickly retracted his theory. "No, this is odd. I called animal control, and they're coming to investigate. Before they do, I want to collect one to examine it myself."

The tension in the air was tangible as we stood amidst the lifeless bodies of the geese, the mystery deepening with each passing moment. The warm early summer breeze rustled the lush green leaves of the surrounding trees, creating a stark contrast to the grim scene before us. The sky, a bright azure, seemed indifferent to the horror below. We exchanged uneasy glances, each of us silently questioning how these creatures had met such a sudden and unnatural end. The faint scent of decay mingled with the sweet fragrance of blooming wildflowers, adding to the surreal atmosphere. As the sunlight filtered through the canopy, casting dappled patterns on the ground, an unspoken fear gripped our hearts—if something had done this it was still out there, watching us.

Later, Sheriff Wittrock showed up with two other men. They couldn't drive up close to the house without running over the bodies that lay scattered around the driveway. He parked his vehicle at a safe distance and then walked across the yard to meet with my father. I noticed the two men unloading several black cases from the back of the vehicle. They were carrying some kind of equipment, but I couldn't make out what it was or what it was used for.

Sheriff Wittrock, or Luc as my father called him, asked my father a series of questions. I remember Luc well; he and my father have been close friends since childhood. I used to call him Uncle Luc when I was younger, though now that I'm older, I find that name less relevant. Despite the passage of time, he's still the only friend my father truly trusts.

Luc's presence seemed to bring a small measure of calm to the chaotic scene. His steady demeanor contrasted sharply with the grim spectacle around us. He listened intently as my father recounted the events leading up to the discovery of the geese. I could see the concern etched on both their faces.

The two men with Luc began setting up their equipment, positioning it carefully around the yard. Curious, I edged closer to get a better look. One of the men noticed me and gave a reassuring nod, though he said nothing. The black cases contained a variety of tools and devices—some I recognized from my father's stories about investigations, while others were completely foreign to me.

As the sun dipped lower in the sky, casting long shadows across the yard, Luc turned to me. His eyes, usually so kind, were now serious and probing. "What did you see?" he asked gently, yet firmly. I hesitated, glancing at my father for reassurance.

"Go ahead," my father urged. "Tell him everything."

I took a deep breath and began to recount the eerie stillness that had settled over the yard earlier that day, the unsettling sight of the geese lying lifeless, and the strange feeling that we were being watched. Luc listened carefully, occasionally jotting down notes in a small, worn notebook. Luc nodded thoughtfully as I finished my account. "Thank you," he said, his voice a mix of gratitude and concern. "We're going to figure out what happened here."

Whatever had caused this bizarre and tragic scene, we knew it was only the beginning. And as long as Luc was here, I felt a glimmer of hope that we might uncover the truth, no matter how terrifying it might be.

The two men continued their work, setting up what looked like cameras and other monitoring equipment around the perimeter of the yard. One of them held a device that beeped intermittently, adding to the tension in the air. The other man approached a tree with a long pole and a hook on the end. He started pulling geese bodies out from the branches and then laid them onto a wide blue tarp on the ground.

He stopped for a moment, wiped the sweat off his forehead, and then waved at me. "Nice weather we're having today, huh?" he said awkwardly. I wasn't sure if he intentionally made a pun or was simply making small talk. Either way, he had a pathetic way of trying to cheer someone up. His attempt at humor fell flat in the grim context of the scene, only emphasizing the unease we all felt. I forced a small smile in response, not wanting to be rude, but his words did little to lift any spirit.

As the two men continued their work outside, setting up equipment and collecting the geese bodies, Luc followed my father and me into our home to interview my mother. The house felt different, as if the tension outside had seeped into its very walls. My mother, clearly shaken, sat at the kitchen table, her hands wrapped tightly around a steaming cup of tea. Luc approached her with a gentle yet serious demeanor, pulling out his notebook and a pen.

"Amethyst, I know this is difficult, but I need to ask you a few questions about what happened today," Luc said softly. My mother nodded, her eyes wide with fear and uncertainty. She glanced at my father, who gave her a reassuring nod.

"I'll do my best to help, Luc," she replied, her voice trembling slightly.

We all took seats around the kitchen table, the familiar surroundings feeling oddly foreign in the midst of the unfolding mystery. Luc began his questions gently, asking about anything unusual she might have noticed leading up to the incident with the geese. My mother recounted a few odd noises and shadows she'd seen in the evenings, her voice trembling slightly.

It was at that moment I discovered I wasn't the only one seeing things in this mansion. As the interview went on, I couldn't help but glance out the window at the men working in the yard. Their equipment beeped and clicked, the sounds a constant reminder of the strange events that had brought us to this moment. Luc's steady presence provided some comfort, but the weight of the unknown loomed large over us all. The kitchen, once a place of comfort, now felt charged with an uneasy tension as we all awaited any revelation that might shed light on the mystery.

Mother went on to explain what she experienced. From what I could understand through her sobs, she had walked to Father's truck to drive into the city. She heard a gaggle of geese flying over the mansion. Thinking nothing of it at first, she proceeded to get into the truck and turned the key to start it. Suddenly, a goose fell through the windshield, its squawks filling the cabin with an eerie, panicked noise. It then choked and died, its lifeless eyes staring blankly at her.

Terrified, she bolted out of the truck and ran toward the front door of the mansion. As she ran, the sky seemed to darken, and geese bodies began to rain down like a bad storm. The thuds of their impacts echoed around her, each one a sickening reminder of the unnatural event unfolding. Despite her frantic attempts to dodge them, several geese struck her as they fell, their feathers brushing against her skin like cold, dead fingers. The horror of the scene left her trembling and breathless by the time she reached the door. That was when she came in screaming. My father immediately went outside to investigate. Shortly after, I followed him and joined him outside.

"Everything will be alright, Mrs. McWarlick," Luc said in a professional manner." Andrew and his brother Jason, the two men who arrived with me, are outside dealing with the problem as we speak. They'll have your yard clean and sterilized in no time."

Mother nodded, her face still pale, but the tension in her shoulders eased slightly at Luc's reassurance. She watched from the window as Andrew and Jason methodically worked in the yard, their movements efficient and practiced. She thanked him and then turned away from watching the process outside.

Two hours later, Father and I stepped outside, bracing ourselves to confront the gruesome task ahead. The yard was a gruesome sight, with blood-soaked patches marking where each goose had met its end. It looked like a macabre battlefield, the birds having plummeted to their deaths in some inexplicable disaster.

The stench of blood and feathers filled the air as we spent the next hour gathering the remaining bodies, adding them to the already enormous pile of carcasses. The silence of the aftermath was broken only by the sound of our shovels scraping the dirt and the occasional rustle of leaves. Although Sheriff Wittrock had been on the scene for some time, he approached us as we were finishing.

"We've collected four hundred and thirty geese," Sheriff Wittrock informed us. After a brief pause, he added, "So far." His eyes scanned the treeline, the implication clear—there could be more, hidden in the shadows of the trees, waiting to be discovered.

"Do you have any idea how this could have happened?" Father asked.

Luc clenches his fists, then quickly rests them on his hips and sighs.

"Actually, yes…" he begins. "As strange and bizarre as this might sound, Andrew, one of my investigators, examined one of the geese." He pauses, shaking his head slightly as if searching for the right words. "This may sound gross, but he cut open its skull to investigate further."

"AND?" I demanded, unflinching at the mention of the gruesome detail. "Continue!"

"Andrew informed me that when birds fly above a certain altitude, the pressure can cause their brains to…" Luc gulped, trying to force the words out. "Explode."

"AND?" Father asked.

"Well," Luc continued, "their brains were normal. There was nothing out of the ordinary that would explain this. Unless…" He hesitated.

"There's more?" I pressed.

Luc waved his hands in a dismissive gesture, as if trying to brush away his anxiety. "It's possible that the recent weather changes caused a significant stress on the geese, leading to their sudden deaths. The strange weather patterns, including the tornado that appeared out of nowhere the other night, might be a factor. However, a case like this has never been documented."

"And then there is fear," Andrew interrupted as he walked towards the vehicle he arrived in. "To be honest, there's a more plausible explanation for all of this." He continued, "The agitation caused by the anticipation or realization of imminent danger may have driven these animals to take their own lives. Not intentionally, I might add, but as a defense mechanism or due to confusion. Something must have spooked them."

Andrew continued to delve into various other possibilities, but most of what he rambled on about blurred into the background for me. I stepped away mentally, needing a break from the tedious scientific nerd talk. However, one detail stood out to me: the impact of weather changes on birds. Andrew explained that sudden shifts in weather can create immense stress for them, leading to alarming behaviors. Some birds might starve, others might turn aggressive, even attacking each other, or in extreme cases, resorting to cannibalism—either consuming their own young or even themselves. Although rare, these behaviors occur when the birds feel cornered or threatened by their environment.

I started to feel sick to my stomach. We guessed that something large had spooked them, but the possibility of multiple culprits stalking the birds couldn't be ruled out. Regardless, it remained one big mystery. But was it even worth solving? At that moment, all we cared about was that the carcasses were being removed and would soon be disposed of somewhere.

A few moments later, the rumble of a large dump truck broke the quiet of the early evening. The truck pulled into the clearing, its headlights casting long shadows as the sun dipped below the horizon. A rugged-looking man, dressed in work gear, jumped down from the cab. He greeted Luc and Andrew with a firm handshake, exchanging a few brief words that I couldn't quite catch. Without hesitation, he moved toward the grim task at hand, carefully loading the goose carcass into the back of the truck. The fading light added a sense of urgency to their movements, as if they were hurrying to finish before darkness fully set in.

Father thanked Sheriff Wittrock and his team for all their hard work and for doing everything they could to help with the situation. As they spoke, I slowly walked over to the remaining pile of geese, just before they were hurled into the truck. I felt a pang of sympathy for the poor creatures. Leaning down, I focused on one of them. Its lifeless eye seemed to stare up at me—glossy, empty, and frozen by rigor mortis. Suddenly, the eye twitched, and for a moment, it felt as though it was looking directly at me. Startled, I pulled back, stumbling and bumping into my father.

"It's okay, Dawn. It's over now," he said calmly.

I quickly turned and pointed at the bird, eager to show my father what I had just witnessed. But to my surprise, the goose's eye was now closed, as if it had been playing a cruel trick on me—or perhaps I was just seeing things. By then, Luc and his crew had left.

Father and I finally returned to the mansion. As we stepped inside, the comforting aroma of freshly baked pizza filled the air. Mother had prepared a homemade pizza for supper, something simple that didn't take much time. Without hesitation, we gathered in the dining room to eat. Thankfully, there was no goose on the menu. Mother, who didn't say much, kept muttering under her breath, "I hate birds," over and over.

After dinner, I decided to call it a day and headed off to get ready for bed. All I wanted was to slip into my comfortable nightgown and write in my diary, but first, I needed to shower again. The smell of the geese and the blood still clung to me, making my skin crawl. As I stepped into my washroom, my bad luck struck again—I stepped on a hairpin, and it drew blood from the bottom of my right foot. After tending to the small wound, I continued with my routine, taking care of my hygiene.

Once I was dried off and had brushed my hair, I slipped into my nightgown and settled onto my bed, ready to start writing. As I opened my diary, one thought lingered: *I hope tomorrow is a better day.*

MAY 26

Yesterday, the 25th, was uneventful. Aside from lounging around the mansion, I spent most of the day writing in my diary, recounting the strange events that had unfolded recently. It was a quiet day, and I didn't mind taking my time to reflect, even though I had no job to occupy my hours or earn money. Instead, my thoughts were consumed by the anticipation of our upcoming family camping trip. The idea of escaping the mansion, even for a little while, filled me with a sense of excitement. It wasn't just about the trip itself; it was about leaving behind the eerie happenings of the past few days and hoping for a return to normalcy, if only temporarily.

I didn't want to dwell on all the recent negativity, but the events of the other day kept replaying in my mind. The fear of what might happen next loomed over me. It felt like danger could strike at any moment, anywhere. A creeping suspicion began to form—maybe it was this house? Could it be a tomb of curses, trapping us within its walls? No, that can't be it. I could just be overreacting, the stress of everything clouding my judgment.

Mother's voice echoed in my memory, reminding me of her words of caution. She had told me how a woman's menstruation could wreak havoc on her body and mind—causing pain, confusion, frustration, hot and cold flashes, and in rare cases, even hallucinations. Was that what I was experiencing now? I shook my head, trying to dismiss the thought, but the unease remained.

"Anxiety," my mother said as she stepped into my room.

"What?" I replied, caught off guard.

"Anxiety," she repeated calmly. "It's an uneasy disturbance of the mind when faced with uncertain events. Also, you're narrating your thoughts out loud again."

"I am?" I asked, surprised.

"Yeah, you do that sometimes," she said, a smirk tugging at the corners of her mouth.

"Oh! I wasn't aware I did that. How long have I been—"

"Not long," Mother interrupted gently. "Don't worry, I wasn't eavesdropping for too long. I just happened to walk in as you were writing about feeling stressed." She placed a neatly folded towel on my dresser and turned to face me, her smile widening with a reassuring warmth. "Come," she added, her tone inviting. "Let's go for a walk. Some fresh air might do you good."

I hesitated for a moment, glancing at the half-filled page in my diary. The words I had scribbled down seemed almost foreign now, distant from the calm my mother was offering. But her presence was like a lifeline, pulling me back from the edge of my spiraling thoughts.

"Okay," I finally agreed, closing the journal and setting it aside. "A walk sounds nice."

Mother's smile softened as she opened the door wider, ushering me out into the hallway. The house was quiet, the kind of silence that felt heavy, like the walls themselves were holding their breath. As we walked, the faint creaks of the floorboards beneath our feet seemed to echo through the stillness.

Once outside, the air was cool and crisp. Not a cloud in the sky. It was nice. We walked side by side down the gravel path that led away from the house, neither of us speaking at first. It was as if the world around us knew we needed this quiet moment, just the sound of our footsteps and the occasional rustle of leaves in the morning breeze.

After a while, Mother broke the silence. "You've been under a lot of pressure lately," she said softly. "It's only natural to feel overwhelmed. But you don't have to carry it all on your own, you know."

"I know," I replied, though the words felt heavier than they should have. "It's just...everything feels so uncertain right now. And the things that happened—it's hard not to let it get to me."

She nodded, her eyes thoughtful as she looked ahead. "Uncertainty can be scary. But it's also a part of life, something we all have to face at one point or another. What matters is how we deal with it."

I glanced at her, searching her face for the reassurance I so desperately needed. "But what if I can't handle it? What if things get worse?"

Mother stopped walking and turned to face me, her expression serious yet filled with a deep, unwavering love. "You're stronger than you think," she said, her voice firm. "And you're not alone in this. Whatever happens, we'll face it together."

Her words settled over me like a comforting blanket, easing some of the tension that had been knotted in my chest. I nodded, feeling a small sense of relief. "Thank you, Mom."

Once we arrived at the spot where Mother wanted to walk, the lift in my spirits unfortunately faded. Before us stood the three arched entrances to the historic Electric Park, now a shadow of its former self. The playground where my cousin Dean used to play was in ruins, the once lively area now broken down and desolate. Trees were uprooted, their massive roots exposed like raw nerves, while debris was scattered across the meadow. The stream, which once flowed peacefully through the park, was blocked and flooded, its waters muddied and sluggish.

The only thing still standing was the park bench where I usually sat, a solitary reminder of what once was. It was a sad, haunting sight. The tornado had torn through everything in its path, leaving behind only remnants of the joy and laughter that used to fill this place.

"Come, sit with me," Mother insisted, her voice gentle yet firm. "I need to ask you something."

A knot of concern tightened in my chest, but I followed her to the bench and sat down beside her. She took a deep breath, her eyes scanning the wreckage before us, and then exhaled slowly. For a moment, she just sat there in complete silence, as if gathering her thoughts or perhaps mourning the loss of this once-beautiful park.

I waited, feeling a mix of unease and curiosity. Whatever she needed to say, it was clear it weighed heavily on her mind.

"I've noticed you've been writing a lot," Mother said, her tone curious.

"Yes, almost every night before I go to sleep," I replied.

"Is it anything good?" she asked, gently prying.

"I'm not sure," I admitted. "Probably not, if I'm honest."

"You could turn it into a book," Mother suggested, a hint of pride in her voice. "And I mean a pretty damn good one at that."

"What are you getting at, Mom?"

"Well," she continued, "to be honest, I want to ask you about something."

I looked around, my eyes scanning the dimly lit surroundings. The distant echoes of our footsteps had faded, leaving an eerie silence in their wake. The air felt thick, almost stifling, as if it were holding its breath. Shadows danced in the corners, and for a moment, I could have sworn I saw a figure move. But as my gaze settled, I realized we were truly alone. The once vibrant space now felt hollow, and a chill ran down my spine, amplifying the sense of isolation.

"How do you know Tanis Krieser?" Mother finally demanded, her voice sharp and eyes narrowing with suspicion. I felt a knot tighten in my stomach as I met her piercing gaze.

The truth was, I had no idea how to answer her question. The name Tanis Krieser was as foreign to me as the strange events that had begun to unravel around me. I had never heard of her before that day in the park when our paths inexplicably crossed. There was no logical explanation, no story I could weave to satisfy Mother's probing. The only escape from her relentless questioning was to tell her the truth—my truth—however unbelievable it might sound.

"I met her in person, right here, at this exact spot," I said truthfully, my voice barely steady as the weight of the admission settled between us.

Mother sighed, her question hanging in the air like an accusation. "How?" she asked, her voice tinged with a quiet urgency that made it clear she needed more than just a simple answer.

"It was the day Dean and I went to the park," I began, trying to steady my thoughts. "Some girl named Tanis sat next to me and just started talking. She was with the kid who Dean was playing with. I think it was her son? If I remember correctly, his name is—"

"Leon," Mother interrupted, her tone flat but loaded with an unspoken tension. It was as if she knew more than she was willing to say, and my stomach churned at the realization that this was more than just a casual encounter.

"Look," Mother said, her voice softening but still firm. "I know you were already told this the other day, but Tanis has been dead for seven years. There's no way you could have—"

"I know, Mom. I know," I interrupted, my voice dropping as I sulked, the weight of her words settling heavily on me. "I honestly don't understand it either." My mind raced, trying to piece together the impossible encounter. I had seen Tanis, heard her voice, felt her presence. None of it made sense, and the more I tried to rationalize it, the further the truth seemed to slip away.

Knowing it has been a rough week for all of us, I tried to divert her questioning. Nothing seems to make sense. Although, a tornado in May isn't very common in Nebraska. Tornado season typically starts from June through July. But, this one happened, and we were sitting in its rubble.

"Maybe you're clairvoyant?" Mother suggested, her tone wavering between skepticism and the faintest hint of hope. She studied my face, searching for a reaction, as if the idea could somehow explain the unexplainable. But all I could do was stare back, caught between disbelief and the unsettling possibility that maybe, just maybe, she was right.

"So," I said, eager to steer the conversation away from the unsettling topic. "What makes you think my writing would make a good book? What writing are you talking about?"

"I've been reading your diary," Mother admitted, her eyes meeting mine with a mix of guilt and determination. My heart sank, a wave of anger and betrayal washing over me. I hadn't expected this invasion of privacy, not from her, and the weight of her words hit me harder than any revelation about Tanis ever could.

"Uh, why?"

"You also read your fathers journal."

I imagined myself blindfolded, standing before a firing squad, ready to take me out. I felt guilty for reading Father's journal. As the weight of my actions sank in, I became increasingly nervous and fidgety, my discomfort growing with each passing moment. I wasn't physically caught red-handed, but my own words, written in ink, betrayed me.

"Hey," Mother said, wanting my attention. "It's okay."

I felt a wave of relief wash over me when I heard her say that. I was still a bit confused, uncertain about what she truly meant, but at least I knew she wasn't planning to punish me. For now, that was enough to ease the knot of anxiety tightening in my chest.

Mother's gaze was heavy with sorrow as she looked at me.

"I can't be a hypocrite," she confessed, her voice wavering. "I've noticed you haven't been yourself these past few weeks, and I wanted to understand what was going on with you. I tried to figure you out, but I failed. I saw you writing in your diary more often, and I hoped I might find some clarity there, some insight into what you were feeling… what you weren't telling me."

Mother and I looked at each other, a tense silence hanging in the air. Then, almost unexpectedly, we began to giggle. The giggles grew, bubbling up into deep, hearty laughter that seemed to release the tension between us. It felt good, almost like old times, to talk openly with her about my troubles. Now that I knew she had discovered my secrets, I thought I should bring it up myself—but she beat me to it.

"Now you know about the 'odd' thing your father and I were arguing about," she continued, her smile fading into a more serious expression. "To be honest, I think there may be some truth to what he's been saying… even if it sounds far-fetched."

"But how could you give in to his story so easily?" I asked, bewildered. "I mean, he was drunk and…"

"True," Mother interrupted, her tone growing more serious, "but I've been having these dreams lately." She paused, as if weighing her words. "One night, I woke up for no apparent reason and saw a dark figure floating above me, just floating in the air. At first, I was terrified—frozen with fear. Then, suddenly, a strange calm washed over me, like the comforting presence of someone you know and trust. I wanted to reach up and touch it, to see if it was real, but I couldn't move. My arms felt heavy, pinned down against the bed as if some unseen force was holding them there. I couldn't even lift a finger."

I sat there in silence, my heart racing as I watched her closely, hanging on every word. I could see a mix of fear and wonder in her eyes, a reflection of the same emotions stirring inside me. I listened, waiting for her to continue, trying to make sense of what she was saying.

"Then," she whispered, her voice barely audible, "a tiny gleam appeared above me, right in the center of the shadow's outline. It multiplied into two, like a pair of eyes—watchful. They twinkled like distant stars in the night sky, unblinking. I tried to scream, but no sound came out. It was as if the air had been stolen from my lungs. The harder I tried, the more the silence pressed in around me, suffocating me.

"The figure drifted down to the foot of my bed, hovering there as if it were studying me, deciding what to do next. Then, without a sound, it rose to its full height, looming over me. And just as suddenly, I felt something release me—like invisible chains falling away. I shot up, gasping for air.

"Your father didn't even stir. He was right there, fast asleep, completely oblivious to what had just happened. The figure slowly hovered out of our bedroom and into the hallway until it disappeared into the darkness, and I couldn't see it anymore.

"I realized then that I was breathing heavily, each breath ragged and sharp. I sat there, in the dark, cold night, with my heart pounding in my ears, dreading that something else was about to happen. The room felt colder, like the air itself had turned to ice. I kept expecting to hear the creak of the floorboards or see the shadow reappear in the doorway. But there was nothing—just a suffocating silence, as if the house was holding its breath along with me."

"What happened?" I insisted, eager to know more.

Mother sighed and looked away. As she did, I noticed a wisp of cold breath escaping her lips, as if the temperature in the room had suddenly dropped. I knew the weather outside wasn't cold enough for that to happen.

Mother continued.

"Not long after the shadowy apparition moved down the hallway and disappeared into the darkness, I heard whistling."

"Whistling?" I asked.

"Yes, whistling," she confirmed, her eyes wide with fear. "An unfamiliar tune, drifting through the dark. It was soft at first, almost like a lullaby, but there was something wrong about it—something… off. I felt a shiver creep down my neck. I shook your father, trying to wake him, but he wouldn't budge. I called his name, over and over, but it was like he was in a deep trance, lost to me. That's when I decided, against every instinct, to crawl out of bed and follow the sound."

I gasped, unable to hide my fear.

"I was relieved not to find the figure in the hallway," she continued, her voice barely more than a whisper. "But as I made my way toward your bedroom, the whistling grew louder and more sinister. The moonlight cast a ghostly pallor over the room, its cold glow spilling across your bed. There you were, asleep, while the terror seemed to hover just beyond the shadows. Then, the whistling stopped."

At that moment, I wasn't sure I wanted to hear any more.

"I slowly turned back into the darkness of the hallway. I glanced up and didn't see the shadow figure—just the twinkling eyes. They stared at me from within the darkness, watching. I stopped, unsure of what to do, but then I saw the eyes shift toward the stairwell. It wanted me to follow. The figure hovered away, drifting down the stairs. I moved cautiously, and when I reached the entry hall, I saw the dark shape slowly fade through the front door."

She paused, taking a breath, her face pale. "I ran to the door and threw it open. As soon as I did, a tall man stood there, his eyes burning like fire as he looked directly at me."

A sharp pinch twisted in my stomach, a sudden reminder of the figure I had seen in my closet.

"I screamed as loud as I could," Mother explained. "Then I sat bolt upright in bed. Your father grabbed me, trying to calm me down. He said I was about to leap off the bed."

"I didn't wake up?" I asked, struggling to recall the episode.

"Thankfully, no, you didn't," she replied, her voice breaking. "That was the night your father found you unconscious in the woods during the storm." Tears welled up in her eyes. "We thought you were dead."

"But I'm okay now, Mom." I fought to hold back my own tears.

I wrapped my arms around her, pulling her into a tight hug, trying to reassure her that I was still here. I understood her fear. I'm her only child, and the thought of losing me would be a nightmare for any parent to face.

As I hugged my mother, something caught my attention in the corner of my eye. I slowly pulled away from her and noticed movement where the playground once stood. Squinting to get a clearer view, I focused on a young woman wearing a blue negligee.

"Tanis?" my mother mumbled under her breath.

I gasped. Mother could see her too! I wasn't losing my mind. Relief flooded through me, mingled with confusion. My mother wrapped her arms around one of mine, squeezing tightly, a big smile spreading across her face. I knew she felt the same as I did, mesmerized.

Tanis showed no sign of acknowledging our presence. Her spirit moved with a graceful stillness, reaching an arm out. Suddenly, an elderly woman appeared from thin air and took her hand. I didn't recognize her.

Mother stood up from the bench and slowly, cautiously, stepped toward them. The elderly woman and Tanis glanced at each other, their smiles gentle and knowing, before turning and walking away from us, disappearing into the shadows of the woods. Their laughter was soft and melodic, drifting back to us as they faded into thin air.

"Mom?" I whispered, my voice barely audible.

Mother seemed not to hear me. She had a serene smile on her face, even as tears rolled down her cheeks.

"God bless you, Wanda! God bless…" she murmured, her voice breaking with emotion.

"Who was that?" I asked, still staring into the distance.

"Wanda Krieser," Mother replied with a sigh of relief and joy. "Tanis's mother."

A wave of realization washed over me—we had just witnessed Tanis and her mother crossing over into the afterlife. It was a deeply emotional and profoundly beautiful moment, one I knew I would never forget. As I gazed into the woods, I couldn't help but wonder if this was what Mother meant when she spoke of "seeing" Tanis one last time. If so, it was the most breathtaking and extraordinary moment I had ever experienced.

MAY 27

I jolted awake, my heart racing. Panic set in as I realized I had forgotten to pack my things yesterday for today's camping weekend with my parents. My mind raced, trying to remember everything I needed. I didn't care much about what to wear, so I grabbed a few light shirts, shorts, and a sun hat, tossing them into my bag along with an extra set of clothes, just in case.

I got the impression I wasn't the only one dragging my feet about leaving. I heard the frantic shuffle of feet racing down the hallway. Peeking around my bedroom door frame, I saw my mother darting into her room.

"Wake up, you lazy goof!" she yelled at my father. "We need to be on the road soon, so get up and load the truck!"

"I don't want to go to school today, Momma," my father mumbled, half-asleep.

"TODD!" Mother barked. "Get up NOW!"

My father sat up like a zombie emerging from the grave, groaning dramatically. "I'm all ready to go, you Hellspawn," he muttered.

I hoped he was joking. But with Dad, you could never be too sure.

"Showered?" she questioned him, eyeing him suspiciously.

"Two hours ago, while you slept like a precious little kitten, snuggled up like a bug in a rug on a Tuesday," he joked with a grin. "Unlike some people, we don't spend hours packing, primping, and putting on a new face every day, Miss Grouch. You might want to swap that mask of yours for something a bit more... pleasant."

Before he could smirk any further, there was a loud THUD! as Mother smacked him on the back of the head with a hardcover book, a copy of War and Peace—because if she was going to hit him, it might as well be with a classic.

Father rubbed the back of his head, wincing. "Ow! I was just kidding!" he whined, though a mischievous grin remained on his face.

Mother stood over him, brandishing the book like a sword. "You'll be eating more than your words if you don't get moving," she warned, her eyes narrowed but with the slightest hint of a smile breaking through.

Father's grin widened as he stood up, feigning a salute. "Aye aye, Captain! Just keep the literary artillery to a minimum, will ya?"

Mother rolled her eyes, but I could see a laugh trying to escape her lips. It was always like this—Dad pushing her buttons just enough to get swatted but never enough to get truly scolded. And, truth be told, she seemed to enjoy the game as much as he did.

I was packed and ready to go, sitting in the dining hall, waiting patiently for my parents. As I waited, I clutched my diary, grateful I had remembered to bring it. It was my lifeline, my escape, and I knew it would keep me entertained during the long hours ahead. Thank God I had it with me.

I had enough time to write in this diary as I waited. Nothing exciting happens when you're waiting on others, supposedly. But sometimes, waiting can get you into trouble.

So, I made sure I had everything ready to go.

After breakfast, my parents and I loaded the truck with our belongings. Father made sure to bring his tackle box and a couple of fishing poles, convinced that fishing in the mountains would be an adventure. He kept going on about how the fish up there are supposed to be much larger than the ones in the flat plains. I wasn't sure how much I cared about the size of the fish, but I had to admit, it sounded fun. Besides, our destination was somewhere I'd never explored before: South Dakota.

We drove halfway through Lincoln, weaving through the city's traffic, heading towards the interstate. That's when it hit me—I might have forgotten to pack the rune stone I found at the lake the other day. My stomach sank a little at the thought. That stone had felt important somehow, like it was meant to come with me. But then I remembered I had grabbed a book about runic stones from Father's library to read on the trip. At least I'd have that.

I glanced out the window, watching the city fade into the distance as we headed north. The thought of unraveling the mystery behind that rune stone filled my curiosity. Who knows what the symbol carved into it really means? Maybe it's ancient, maybe it's just some kid's art project from years ago, or maybe… it's something more.

Now that we were leaving home, escaping the oddities that seemed to have been thrown at us lately, I felt relief and anticipation. I decided then and there that I'd face whatever came my way on this trip. South Dakota, with all its unknowns, awaited us, and I was ready to explore every bit of it.

It was still early in the morning, and the roads were quiet, with only a few cars passing by. The sidewalks were empty, the city still waking up. As we drove, I noticed a construction site where a new hotel was slowly taking shape, its metal frame catching the soft morning light. Nearby, a movie theater was also under construction, its outline barely formed among the scaffolding. These new additions felt almost out of place, standing stark against the calm, quiet streets.

Unfortunately, we had to drive east towards Omaha. That city is a story all its own, with a sense of unease that hangs over most areas. Still, I'm hopeful that, in time, things will change for the better. Mother once described Omaha as a tiny slice of New York, bustling and vibrant in its own way. Lincoln, on the other hand, doesn't have nearly as much to offer in terms of entertainment, but there's even a rumor that the two cities might merge one day.

Although Lincoln is smaller than Omaha, I'm content in my quieter city. I love Nebraska—its vast, open fields, endless skies, and the sense of peace that comes from living in this farm-filled state. I plan to never move away from here. This will forever be my home.

Later…

Luckily, we didn't have to drive into Omaha. Father decided to head north instead. The landscape was a boring sight, but somehow memorable. Cornfields stretched endlessly, farmhouses dotted the horizon, and trees were scattered across the flat lands, with plenty of livestock grazing in the fields. During the drive, I saw pigs, sheep, cows, horses, and even chickens if I paid close attention. I often noticed a rafter of turkeys strolling along the side of the road as we passed by. And then, as we entered the Great Plains, I caught sight of buffalo roaming in the distance, their massive forms moving slowly across the open prairie a rare and awe-inspiring sight.

I had only ever seen buffalo in photos, whether in articles or books that provided general information. Seeing one in person, however, is an entirely different experience. The more you observe them, the more fascinating they become. Unlike the common cow or bull, buffalo are a rare sight, especially in and around Lancaster County. For those of us who live in or near the city, we have to travel quite far for even a chance to spot one. They remind me of miniature woolly mammoths, though without the tusks or elongated snouts. Despite their rough appearance, they possess a unique beauty. A kind of charm that is both awkward and oddly captivating at the same time.

I'm finished writing in the diary, at least for the time being. Since this stretch of road seems to go on endlessly, it feels like the perfect opportunity to do some sightseeing and enjoy the fresh air. Maybe I can clear my mind, soaking in the scenery. I'm even hoping to steal a short nap if the quiet hum of the journey lulls me to sleep. There's something calming about the gentle rhythm of the road, offering a brief escape from everything on my mind.

I could hear the wind blowing through the trees.

"Dawn," a voice whispered.

"Hmmm?"

"Dawn!"

"What?"

"Wake up."

"Why?"

I woke up to find myself lying in a field of green grass. A warm breeze brushed against my skin as the blades of grass swayed like waves on the ocean. My mind was still foggy, struggling to make sense of where I was or why someone had been calling my name. There were no trees, yet I could hear the wind rustling through them. No other plants were rooted in the ground. I stood alone in the tall grass—except for an unknown apparition that hovered before me.

Although it had no physical body, the white, mystic figure drifted slowly toward me, its presence almost hypnotic. Its almond-shaped eyes gleamed with a glossy sheen, their surface appearing almost liquid. Yet beneath that glossy facade, I could see a mesmerizing swirl of colors—blues, greens, and faint touches of gold—like the reflection of a distant galaxy hidden within them. Despite their otherworldly appearance, there was a haunting beauty in those eyes, a quiet depth that spoke of ancient wisdom and secrets untold. They held me captive, drawing me in with their silent allure, as if they were windows to a world beyond comprehension.

A soft, greenish-white glow clung to its ethereal form, pulsating gently, mimicking the rhythm of breathing. It floated without substance, moving not by steps but as though carried by the whims of the warm breeze that surrounded us. Despite the heat in the air, an unnatural coldness seeped into my bones, chilling me from the inside out. Strangely, there was no pain, no anxiety, no fear—just a profound stillness, a sense of peace that blanketed my mind. The apparition's head lifted slowly, guiding my gaze upward. Without hesitation, I followed its movement, my eyes drawn to the vivid blue sky above.

Meteors began to streak across the heavens, each one brighter than the last, a cascade of colors and sizes that defied reason. They shot by with dizzying speed, their trails leaving faint shimmers in their wake, as though the sky had come alive to perform an endless ballet of light and motion.

For a moment, time seemed to pause. The world beneath me faded into insignificance, leaving only the celestial display and the silent, otherworldly figure by my side. The cold in my chest deepened, but it wasn't unwelcome. It felt as though I had crossed a threshold, teetering between two realms, standing on the edge of something far greater than myself.

It turned toward me, gazing deeply into my eyes. Though it didn't speak, I felt its words resonate in my mind, like the mental connection Mother and I sometimes shared.

"What do you see?" the voice whispered, its presence both intimate and alien.

The connection was immediate, its thoughts flowing into my mind as though we shared a silent, unspoken language. There were no audible words, yet the weight of its message was clear and impossible to ignore.

"I see... you," I replied, my voice trembling with uncertainty.

The figure tilted its head, as though deep in thought, curiosity flickering in its gaze.

"Who am I?" it asked.

"I... I don't know," I admitted, though the question felt strangely familiar, like a forgotten memory just out of reach.

"Who do you wish me to be?"

"My friend," I said without hesitation, the honesty of my own words surprising me.

The figure seemed to consider this, its tone shifting to something both curious and unsettling.

"Yes," I replied, my throat tightening as an inexplicable lump formed. A sudden wave of emotion washed over me—raw, unnameable. I wasn't sure if I wanted to cry or scream. Something about this interaction struck a nerve deep within me, though I couldn't quite understand why.

"What... What is your name?" I managed to ask.

The entity stood motionless, its presence both captivating and unnerving. Slowly, it raised a misty arm and placed its translucent hand on my chest, just above my heart.

A strange warmth bloomed where it touched, spreading through my chest and glowing with a bluish-green hue. The light pulsated softly, in perfect rhythm with my heartbeat. For a moment, the sensation was comforting, like an unspoken bond forming between us.

Then, without warning, the glow turned fiery red, its heat escalating with every passing second. The warmth transformed into searing pain, and I gasped as it felt like my chest was igniting from the inside out.

I suddenly awoke, disoriented. My heart pounded wildly in my chest as if it hadn't yet caught up to the fact that I was no longer in that strange, haunting place.

"Are you okay, dear?" my mother asked, her voice gentle as she sat beside me in the truck. The engine idled softly, filling the silence between us, and she glanced over with that look of quiet concern. I could feel her eyes searching my face, waiting for a response, but the words felt stuck in my throat.

"Yeah... I'm fine," I lied, forcing a smile that didn't quite reach my eyes. My stomach twisted in knots as I avoided her gaze, knowing she could see right through me. The tension in the air was thick, and I needed a moment to breathe, to collect myself. "Could we pull over? I need to use the restroom."

I hoped the excuse would buy me time—time to gather my thoughts, to shake off the lingering unease that had been gnawing at me since I woke up. My mother hesitated for a second, her brow furrowing in concern, before she nodded and signaled to my father to pull over at the nearest rest area. The truck slowed as we approached, and I could feel her eyes on me, filled with the questions she wasn't asking out loud.

A few miles down the road, my father pulled the truck into the nearest rest area. From the outside, it looked surprisingly well-kept, surrounded by tall trees that gave the place a peaceful, almost inviting atmosphere. As I stepped inside, I was relieved to find it clean. Bright overhead lights illuminated the space, and the faint smell of disinfectant hung in the air. It was far better than the rundown, grimy stops I had imagined.

Near the entrance, I noticed an information booth brimming with travel pamphlets and brochures. Each one advertised scenic routes, local attractions, and roadside diners. The colorful displays felt strangely out of place in such an ordinary rest area, like they belonged to a more adventurous traveler's journey. Still, I found myself lingering for a moment, staring at the pamphlets as if they held answers I wasn't sure I wanted.

I walked into the women's restroom, only to be startled by a man walking out. He was an old, white-haired man with a hunched posture, his movements slow but deliberate. In his hands, he carried a dripping mop, leaving faint wet streaks across the tiled floor. His faded blue jumpsuit looked worn from years of use, the name "Jack" carefully etched on a patch sewn into the top left side.

"Excuse me, little miss," he apologized, his gravelly voice surprisingly gentle as he brushed past me. "I didn't see you there," he added. "It's all nice and clean just for you!"

There was a faint scent of cleaning supplies clinging to him, and as he shuffled by, I noticed the slight weariness in his eyes—eyes that spoke of long hours and countless shifts spent cleaning spaces like this one.

"Thank you!" I replied, giving him a respectful nod.

I stepped into the restroom and glanced around, noting three open stalls, each spotless and ready for use. The faint scent of disinfectant lingered in the air, and the polished tiles gleamed under the fluorescent lights. The quiet hum of the ventilation system was the only sound, adding to the sterile, almost too-perfect atmosphere.

After a short while, I made my way to the sink to wash up. As the cool water ran over my hands, a strange sense of calm began to settle over me, and I almost convinced myself that everything was okay. But just as I started to relax, flashes of my dream crept back into my mind—haunting, fragmented images that refused to disappear. My chest tightened as the unsettling feeling returned, gnawing at the edges of my thoughts.

Watching myself in the mirror, I hesitated before unbuttoning the top few buttons of my shirt, exposing the left side of my chest. My breath hitched as I stared at the faint red handprint pressed over my heart, as if someone, or something, had left its mark on me. Goosebumps crawled up my arms and down my neck, sending a shiver through me. I gulped.

I quickly buttoned myself back up as I heard the distinct sound of shoes clicking against the tiled floor, the echo amplified in the quiet, sterile atmosphere of the public restroom.

My mother walked in, her expression worried as she passed by. Without a word, she hurried into one of the stalls and closed the door. A few moments later, I heard her let out a relieved sigh.

"Oh my, I thought I was going to burst," she said with a chuckle of relief.

I couldn't help but laugh softly in response, the tension between us easing for just a moment.

"Are you about ready to hit the road again?" she asked from behind the stall door.

I told her I was ready, though my thoughts still lingered on the strange mark I had seen earlier. As we headed back to the truck, I couldn't shake the feeling of unease. Once inside, I discreetly unbuttoned my shirt again, stealing a glance at my chest. But this time, the handprint was gone. No trace of it remained, as if it had never been there at all. I buttoned back up, my heart racing, trying to make sense of what had just happened.

Before I knew it, we were back on the road. I hadn't realized that we were already in South Dakota. My mother mentioned that I'd been asleep for several hours, and my father had even stopped for gas once while I slept.

As the scenery blurred past the window, I became aware of a gnawing hunger settling in my stomach. I haven't eaten since... Well, I couldn't even remember the last meal.

I started eating my father's jerky.

"Don't eat so much of my jerky, you jerk," Father joked. "You'll fatten up."

I playfully slugged my father on the shoulder. "Haven't you heard? I want to be just like you when I grow up," I joked back. "Short, plump, and salty."

Mother laughed.

"Well then," he added, "just don't eat it all… please?"

Later, Mother asked to trade places with me so she could sit in the middle of the truck's cab, between Father and me. I didn't mind; in fact, I'd been hoping to sit by the window for a while. The cramped space inside the truck, stuffed with supplies, was starting to feel claustrophobic, and I was eager to stretch out a bit. The cool glass of the window offered some relief as I leaned against it, gazing out at the passing landscape. The fresh air was a welcome change after being squeezed in the middle, and I could finally relax, though the hum of the engine still vibrated through the floor.

We pulled over at a small roadside diner in the quiet town of Chamberlain. The restaurant sat on the edge of a vast, open landscape, where rolling fields stretched out endlessly beneath a sky painted in soft hues of dusk. The sun hung low, casting long shadows that made the peaceful scene feel both calming and a little eerie, as if the quiet carried secrets.

The truck's engine finally went silent as Father turned it off, leaving us in the stillness of the fading day. We stepped out of the cab, grateful to stretch our legs after the long drive. The smell of warm food and the sound of a distant train greeted us as we entered the diner.

Once inside, we grabbed a booth by the window, allowing us to watch the fading light while we studied the road map spread across the table, planning our next destination over plates of hearty food. It felt like a quiet pause in the journey, just the three of us, a map, and the road ahead to Rapid City.

The food at the restaurant wasn't bad at all. In fact, I'd definitely recommend it to anyone passing through. I was more than satisfied with my meal, a quarter-pound beef patty stacked with crisp green lettuce, fresh tomato, extra onions, slightly melted Swiss cheese, and a generous amount of jalapeño peppers. The whole thing was smothered in a perfect blend of honey and barbecue sauce, nestled between two thick slices of toasted sourdough bread. Just thinking about it makes my mouth water all over again. It was the kind of burger that lingers in your memory long after the meal is over, a perfect combination of flavors that felt both comforting and bold.

As I continue writing in this diary, I can feel fatigue slowly creeping in. We hit the road once more, and I sat by the window, resting my head against the cool glass as I gazed up at the vast night sky. The stars flickered like distant lanterns, and after spotting about six shooting stars, my eyelids grew heavy.

Glancing over, I noticed that Mother had already dozed off, her head resting gently on Father's shoulder as he drove, his eyes steady on the road, likely fueled by his third cup of coffee. The steady rhythm of the tires on the pavement, combined with the quiet hum of the engine, created a peaceful lull. I carefully cracked the window, letting a cool breeze drift in—refreshing and calming. Nestling a pillow beside me, I adjusted myself in the seat, hoping to drift into sleep as the world outside passed by in the shadows.

"Hello again," a familiar voice echoed.

"Hello? Who are you?" I asked.

"I am whoever you wish me to be."

"Do you have a name?" I pressed, glancing around. "I... I can't see you."

"Open your eyes."

Hesitantly, I blinked my eyes open. I was back in the same grassy field from my previous dream. A few feet ahead, a jagged cliff plunged into the churning ocean below. Perched at the edge was a figure dressed in a dark cloak, a wide-brimmed cowboy hat casting a shadow over his face. His cloak and long, dark hair swayed with the wind that whispered between us.

I took a step forward, but froze when his voice cut through the breeze.

"It's funny," the voice paused, lingering unnervingly in the silence before repeating, "It's funny how a person's life's work can manifest—an existence that separates itself from death, from lifelessness. It reproduces, it grows, all within the fleeting span between birth... and death." A heavy sigh followed, deep and full of unspoken weight. "The Earth thrives on life because of water—an element both sacred and sustaining, the reason you are even alive. Without it, the Earth withers... as it should. Without you, I become a wanderer. A traveler between dreams, drifting aimlessly, seeking meaning. I am a compromise, a temporary solution to life's difficulties, you might say. Perhaps even more significant than you realize."

The voice chuckled darkly, a sound that sent goosebumps on the back of my neck.

"And yet, I am not born of this lifestream of God. I am a defiance, a rebellious image against the order of good and evil. If you had never lived... I would never exist."

"Are you a guardian angel?" I asked.

The figure before me, still facing away, laughed—a deep, unsettling sound. "No, no, no. I was created, a living being, once human. Now, I am something more... an immortal being in the service of God."

Slowly, it stood and turned to face me. Its face shone like the sun, so bright that I squinted and raised a hand to shield my eyes, but the more I tried to look, the more they burned.

"I will not hurt you, child," it reassured me, extending an arm, an open hand reaching out toward me.

"What is your name?" I asked again, my voice trembling.

"My name," it paused before answering, "is Modus Vivendi."

I jolted awake, drenched in cold sweat. My heart raced as I glanced around, confirming I was still in the truck, safe with my parents. It was just a dream, or so I hoped.

But that name... Modus Vivendi. I'd known it for as long as I could remember. It was the name of my childhood imaginary friend.

* * * *

We drove further along that road, the silence thick and heavy, as if the world itself were holding its breath. In the distance, a light flickered like a lantern atop a hill, growing brighter with each passing moment as we approached. As I watched the light, it began to move, slowly pulsating and seemingly floating in the air, hovering a few feet above the ground.

Father remained focused on the road ahead while Mother stirred from her slumber, stretching after being crammed in the truck's middle seat for so long. They both kept their eyes on the road but didn't notice the object in the middle of the path. A red flickering light hovered close to the ground, almost as if it were calling out, a warning from the harbingers of death. I pointed at the direction of the light and asked Father what it was. I looked forward, focusing on the object ahead. He remained silent. Mother sat up and readjusted herself in the seat.

"Are we there yet?" She asked.

For a moment, no one spoke. Out of the corner of my eye, I saw Mother glance at me, following the path of my gaze. Her eyes locked onto the strange, pulsating red and white light in the middle of the road. It was closer now, its unearthly glow flickering like something from another world, casting eerie flashes across the ground. Father slowed the truck just as a bright light flashed, like the sudden burst of a camera's snapshot.

"It's coming this way!" Mother exclaimed in surprise as the light lowered to the ground. "What do we do, Todd?"

Father gripped the steering wheel tighter, his knuckles white. "Stay calm," he muttered, though his voice betrayed uncertainty.

The light, now just feet away, pulsed brighter, illuminating the truck's interior in a series of blinding flashes. The air grew thick with an oppressive weight, as if the very atmosphere around them was changing. Suddenly, the truck's engine sputtered and died. The headlights flickered once, then went dark, plunging them into eerie silence.

"Todd, what's happening?" Mother's voice was barely a whisper, her eyes wide with fear.

Before Father could answer, the light shifted, darting sideways, circling the truck as if inspecting them. It hovered, its pulsating rhythm growing slower, more deliberate, casting strange shadows that twisted and writhed along the road.

And then, as abruptly as it had appeared, the light stopped moving. It hung there in the air, silent and still, just outside the driver's side window. Without warning, a low hum reverberated through the truck, shaking the seats. The light flickered once more, then began to change shape—elongating, morphing into something vaguely humanoid, but still bathed in that unnatural glow. Father swallowed hard, his hand moving toward the door handle as if drawn to it.

"Don't open it!" I cried, but my voice sounded distant, drowned out by the growing hum.

Father hesitated, staring at the figure outside. The light from its form was now so bright it hurt to look at, but I couldn't tear my eyes away. Mother clutched my arm, trembling, her breath quick and shallow. The figure then slowly moved to my side of the truck, stopping just outside my window.

The figure slowly raised its arm, extending an open hand toward me, but I noticed it had only three long fingers and an elongated thumb. The truck's door lock clicked open with a sharp, metallic snap, echoing in the tense silence. The noise seemed to hang in the air, unnaturally loud against the surrounding quiet, making my heart skip a beat.

Then, all of a sudden, time froze. The pulsing light, the strange figure, even the wind that had been rustling through the trees—it all stopped. The world seemed to hold its breath, suspended in an eerie, unnatural silence. I blinked, my heart pounding in my ears. Everything was motionless, except for me. I glanced at Mother, her face locked in an expression of fear, her hand mid-reach toward Father. Father, too, sat frozen, his eyes wide, his grip still tight on the steering wheel, completely unmoving.

Even the light, once pulsating with life, had halted mid-flicker. The figure within it remained still, arm outstretched, its form distorted yet frozen in time. It was as if the entire world had been paused, and I was the only one untouched by the invisible force that had stopped everything.

Suddenly, I found myself outside the truck, with no memory of how I got there. I tried to speak, but no sound escaped my lips. My breath caught in my throat as the silence pressed down on me, thick and suffocating.

Then, without warning, the figure in the light turned its head—toward me. It moved, despite everything else being frozen in place. Its gaze locked onto mine, and I felt a cold chill run down my spine.

"You can still move," it said, though its mouth never opened. The words echoed in my mind. "That means you can see... what they cannot."

The air around me shifted, and the figure seemed to ripple, as if reality itself was bending around it. I wanted to run, to scream, but I was rooted to the spot, trapped in the stillness of this frozen moment.

"What are you?" I managed to whisper, though I wasn't sure if the sound left my mouth or if it was just a thought I projected.

The figure tilted its head, as though considering me. "I am the reason you are here," it said. "And the reason you cannot leave."

I squinted, trying to make out its face, though the pulsating light distorted its features. At first, it was just a blur—a shadow in the glow. But as I focused, the figure's face began to take shape, though nothing about it seemed human.

Its skin was pale, almost translucent, like thinly stretched wax. Hollow, black almond shaped eyes stared back at me, void of emotion or life. Its mouth, a thin, jagged line, didn't move as it continued to speak in my mind. There was no nose, only a smooth expanse of skin where it should have been. The more I looked, the more its face seemed to shift, as though it wasn't fully solid, constantly rippling in and out of focus.

"Stop looking," the voice warned, though now it sounded sharper, more insistent. "You are not meant to see."

But I couldn't stop. My eyes felt locked onto it, drawn deeper into its hollow gaze. Something about it was both terrifying and mesmerizing. The edges of its form seemed to blur, almost like it was unraveling, and for a moment, I thought I saw something even darker behind it—something vast, ancient, and cold.

Suddenly, a searing pain shot through my head. I gasped and clutched my temples, the pressure unbearable. The figure's face rippled again, shifting into something unrecognizable, twisted and warped beyond comprehension.

"Look away!" it hissed.

But it was too late. The pain intensified, and my vision blurred as I felt myself slipping away, the frozen world around me spinning into darkness. My ears began to ring, a high-pitched whine that drowned out everything else. The light around me looked as though it were melting, dripping away like liquid, distorting the world in strange, shimmering waves. The ringing in my ears grew louder, piercing through the silence, and the world around me seemed to warp, bending under the weight of something I couldn't understand. The melting light dripped away until everything around me was plunged into shadow.

My mother's words echoed in my mind, "Don't always trust your imagination." But this felt too real, too vivid to be a trick of the mind.

Suddenly, the figure that had been frozen in the light began to move again, its body jerking as if waking from a deep slumber. Its head turned sharply in my direction. Eyes, or what I assumed were its eyes, fixating on me. I felt a cold dread settle in my chest.

I took a step back, instinctively moving away from the truck, away from the figure. The air around me felt thick, like moving through water. My body felt sluggish, unresponsive, as if something was holding me back.

Then, in the darkness, I saw another flicker of light—this one far off, in the distance, barely more than a glow on the horizon. A small part of me wanted to run toward it, to escape whatever was unfolding around me, but my legs refused to move.

The figure took a slow step forward, the ground beneath it rippling unnaturally with each motion. I opened my mouth to scream, to call out for help, but no sound came out. The air itself seemed to choke my voice, keeping me silent.

This can't be real, I thought, panic setting in. But I could feel the coldness creeping closer, the figure looming larger with each passing second. I remembered my mother's warning again, but this was beyond imagination. This was something else entirely.

As the figure took another step forward, a voice—not in my head, but out loud, called my name. "Dawn, stop!" It was sharp, urgent, and strangely familiar.

I whipped my head toward the sound, and standing at the edge of the darkness, just beyond where the light had melted away, was... me.

It wasn't a reflection or a trick of the light. It was me, down to the same clothes, the same terrified expression. But this version of myself seemed more... solid, more real, while I suddenly felt ghostly, like I was the one who didn't belong here.

"Don't listen to them!" the other me yelled, their voice panicked. "You need to wake up! This isn't real!"

I froze, confusion crashing over me. "What—?" I tried to speak, but my words felt weak, fading as soon as they left my mouth.

The figure in the light turned to face the other me, its head tilting unnaturally, as if intrigued by the sudden shift in reality. Then, without warning, it rushed toward her—toward me—with inhuman speed, its form unraveling into a mass of shadow and light.

"No!" I screamed, finally finding my voice, but it was too late. The figure collided with the other me in an explosion of light and darkness, and everything around me shattered—literally.

The world fractured like broken glass, splintering into a thousand pieces, each shard reflecting back distorted images of the truck, the road, my parents, and the figure.

I stumbled backward, falling to the ground, gasping for breath. The shards hung in the air around me, floating in the void, each one showing fragments of the world that had just existed moments before.

And then I heard the voice again, this time much closer, almost whispering in my ear.

"You were never supposed to wake up."

I woke up, gasping for air, my heart racing as if I had just sprinted a mile. The world around me was suddenly bright and familiar, the interior of the truck bathed in soft, warm light. I blinked rapidly, disoriented, struggling to piece together the remnants of the nightmare.

"Are you okay?" Mother's voice pierced through my foggy mind, her face etched with concern. She reached out, her hand trembling as she brushed a lock of hair from my forehead. "You were screaming."

I looked around, taking in the sight of my parents sitting beside me, the road stretching out ahead, the moon casting a silvery glow over everything. Shadows stretched across the ground, and the stars twinkled overhead like distant eyes watching from the darkness. But the memory of the other me, the figure in the light, and the shattering world clung to my mind like a dark shadow.

"Yeah, I'm fine," I lied, my voice shaky. But deep down, I knew I wasn't fine. I could still feel the echoes of that other reality whispering at the edges of my consciousness.

"What happened?" Father asked, glancing over at me. "You looked like you were in a trance."

"I... I don't know." I swallowed hard, trying to shake off the lingering dread. "Just a bad dream."

Mother frowned, clearly not convinced. "It felt more than that. You were really scared."

I wanted to reassure her, to dismiss it as just a nightmare, but the memories surged back, my other self, the figure, the ominous warning.

"Maybe it's just stress from the trip," I said weakly, forcing a smile. "I think I need some air."

"Okay," Father replied, easing the truck to a stop on the side of the road. "Just take a few deep breaths."

I stepped out of the truck, the cool breeze hitting my face, grounding me. I leaned against the side, trying to calm my racing heart. As I gazed into the distance, I noticed something out of the ordinary, a flicker of red light pulsing faintly at the edge of the woods nearby.

Was it just my imagination, or was the darkness returning to claim me? At this point, I knew it was best not to trust my imagination. The memory of the figure loomed large in my mind, and as I stared at the light, I couldn't shake the feeling that this was far from over.

The flickering glow pulsed in rhythm with my heartbeat, beckoning me closer, taunting me with its familiarity. I took a deep breath, feeling the weight of what had happened settle heavily on my shoulders. I couldn't let my fear consume me; I had to face whatever this was.

I scribbled my final thoughts in a hurried scrawl. If I don't write this down, it might vanish like a dream upon waking. But I know this isn't a dream. I can feel it. The darkness is real, and it's coming for me. Whatever happens next, I need to be ready.

With a final glance at the ominous light, I'll close the diary, sealing my fears within its pages.

MAY 28

I woke up to the sound of someone knocking on the truck's window, but I ignored it. I was too tired to move or deal with anyone at that moment. Stretching out along the long single seat in the truck's cab, I felt a bit disappointed that I had to get up to help my parents unload our camping gear. But it had to be done. The sun was bright, shining down on my face until a shadow crept over me. I looked up to see a strange man peering at me through the windshield, knocking. His face was painted white, with black masking his eyes, giving him a haunting appearance. Feathers jutted out in several directions from around his head, adding to his wild, almost primal look. Around his neck hung a band of dried beads, and at its center dangled a small skull—perhaps of a bird or some other small creature.

"Little girl?" he called out, his voice raspy yet insistent. "Little girl?" he repeated, demanding an answer. "Wake up! Come join us. We have fun."

His skin was deeply tanned, like he'd been stranded on a desert island for way too long. I was a little caught off guard by his bizarre appearance, but before I could process it, two small children slowly popped into view, as if they'd been summoned from thin air. They also had paint on their faces—the boy with red slash markings, and the little girl with a colorful sunflower on one cheek and a butterfly on the other. Great, I thought. Now we've got an audience.

I had no clue what was going on. Was I dreaming again? That would explain a lot. With a heavy sigh, I rolled my eyes and sat up, muttering to myself, "Fantastic. Just what I needed, mystery man and his pint-sized sidekicks. What's next, a circus parade?"

"She looks silly, Papa," said the little girl, standing between the man and a boy who was probably her brother.

"That's not a very nice way to greet our guest, Hopper," the man replied, glancing down at her with mild disapproval. "She just arrived…'

"Can I scalp her, Papa?" the boy interrupted, his tone disturbingly casual for such a question.

"No, you cannot, young man," the man scolded, raising an eyebrow. "We've talked about this. No scalping without permission," he joked.

I shoved the truck door open, secretly hoping it might knock over the little brat for asking such a ridiculous question. As I stepped out of the cab, my irritation quickly gave way to confusion. All around me, people were dressed as Native Americans—men, women, and children alike. Some walked leisurely across the grounds, while others tended to fire pits, cooking over open flames. Children raced around, laughing as they chased each other with toy tomahawks and bows and arrows, completely absorbed in their play.

It felt like I had just stumbled into a time warp—or maybe a reenactment event—but something about the whole scene seemed a little too real. I couldn't help but wonder, Where am I, and what did I just step into?

"I'm so sorry, little miss," the man apologized. "Please forgive my daughter. She's not the best at first impressions."

"It's uh, alright." I replied. "Where am I?"

"Oh!" he bellowed, his voice booming as if the introduction had been long overdue. "Allow me to introduce myself. My name is Prowling Wolf." He gestured proudly to the little girl beside him. "This sweet young lady here is my oldest daughter, Hopper."

He sighed, a tired sound escaping him, before continuing, "And this... is my son. He calls himself Manpeebehindbush." His expression was completely serious, and something about his demeanor made it clear he wasn't joking. He paused for a moment, then added, with a hint of exasperation, "You can just call him Screaming Buffoon."

Almost on cue, his son let out an ear-piercing shriek and bolted after his older sister, arms flailing wildly as he chased her around. I watched in disbelief, trying to figure out if I had stepped into some kind of fever dream or if this was just a very strange day.

Prowling Wolf spread his arms wide and gave a slight bow. "Welcome to the Ecstatic Dance Festival," he said, completing the bow with a flourish in my direction.

"I don't understand," I said, feeling both confused and curious.

"No worries! I can fill you in," Prowling Wolf said, his tone light and reassuring. "For starters, we all have given names here. To receive one, you must meet with the camp elders. The eldest among them will 'speak'"—he raised and bent two fingers in air quotes—"to your soul, and it will reveal your true name, one that carries your essence and purpose."

He smiled as if this were the most natural thing in the world while I stood there, still trying to wrap my head around what he had just said. "Your mother, 'Fasting Broom,' and your father, 'Master Winchester,' have asked me to summon you to join us for this glorious day."

"Glorious day?" I asked, genuinely curious.

"Of course!" he cried, his eyes lighting up with enthusiasm. "This is the…"

"It's the day of paranormal visions and of the dead!" Screaming Buffoon interrupted, his voice echoing through the air like a trumpet.

Prowling Wolf shot a bemused glance at his son, then continued, "Yes, exactly that! Today, we celebrate the connections between our world and the spirit realm."

"Never heard of it," I admitted, feeling a little out of place amidst their excitement.

Just then, an odd-looking woman approached, draped in a mane of feathers around her neck, a blue and red handprint painted across her face. She wore a white silk tunic paired with a dark red skirt around her waist. There was something awkwardly familiar about her, but I couldn't quite place it.

"Hey, kiddo! How do I look?" she asked, grinning widely as she shifted uncomfortably, adjusting the southern region of her inner thighs.

I blinked, trying not to laugh. She looked like she had just wrestled a peacock—and won, I thought, but wisely kept it to myself. "You, uh, look great?" I said, though it sounded more like a question than a compliment.

"This skirt really lets the air in," she replied, fanning it a bit for emphasis.

I quickly looked away, hoping my awkwardness wasn't too obvious. Yeah, definitely not what I needed to know.

"Your mother's over there," she said, pointing between two trees and a couple of tents, right next to a hammock, not too far from the truck. "She's helping the ladies brew a pot of stew," she added with a proud smile. "My favorite."

That's when it hit me. "Dad?" I asked, my voice a mix of disbelief and horror.

He blushed, shifting uncomfortably.

I decided to take a stroll around the campground, eager to experience the vibrant culture that surrounded me. Everywhere I looked, there were bursts of color and activity. Children laughed and played, chasing each other with toy weapons, while the women busied themselves chopping a variety of fruits, vegetables, and meats. Others were painting faces or tattooing each other with a dark, yellowish-brown dye. I overheard someone mention "Henna art" and found myself wondering, "Whatever that is?"

By the lake, men were either fishing from canoes or skinning deer along the banks. I paused for a moment, watching a man near the dock patiently teach a little girl how to filet a fish, her face lighting up with concentration and pride as she followed his instructions.

Not far from there, several young adults, along with others who seemed close to my age, were sitting in a circle, making beaded jewelry. The rhythmic sound of beads clicking together and the soft murmur of conversation created a peaceful atmosphere. For a moment, I forgot where I was. It truly felt like I had stepped back in time, wandering through a serene Native American village, where life moved at a slower, more intentional pace.

I soon realized it wasn't all Native American-themed. People were dressed in Ancient Egyptian and Greek clothing as well. I even met a man who explained that he was crushing and grinding herbs to create a mixture that could induce clairvoyant episodes.

"Nope, I'm out," I told him, backing away slowly.

A man who introduced himself as Delphi proudly told me that his daughter, Tawny, was one of the leading goddesses in the Ecstatic Dance and Magical Rituals. His eyes lit up as he spoke about her, clearly impressed by her role.

"She embodies the spirit of the festival," he explained. "When she dances, it's like she's channeling the energy of the gods themselves."

I nodded politely, trying to picture it, though the idea of people dancing to summon magic sounded a bit... out there. Still, the way he spoke made it seem like some kind of mystical performance was about to unfold, and part of me was curious to see what this "goddess" could do.

To what I understand, the "ritual" is a sacred event where the goddesses perform the Ecstatic Dance, a powerful and mesmerizing ceremony that holds deep meaning. Their movements are not just a display of grace but a form of ancient communication, invoking divine energies and connecting the physical world with the spiritual realm.

Each step, spin, and gesture is imbued with symbolic significance, weaving together stories of creation, destruction, and rebirth.

The atmosphere during the ritual is charged, with flickering torchlight casting shadows that seem to dance along with the goddesses. The rhythm of the drums builds in intensity, creating a hypnotic pulse that syncs with the heartbeats of all present. As the goddesses dance, it's as if the very earth responds—trembling slightly underfoot, the air thickening with unseen power.

For those witnessing, it's not merely a performance but an invitation to transcend the ordinary and glimpse something beyond the veil of reality. The ritual signifies an ancient tradition, passed down through generations, where the divine meets the mortal in a fleeting moment of unity. The Ecstatic Dance is more than just movement; it's a channeling of forces far greater than anyone can fully comprehend, leaving those who watch in awe, forever changed.

But that story will have to wait until later.

I learned that clairvoyance can manifest in many different ways. For some, like fortune tellers, it comes through visions seen with the "inner eye"—a mystical sense that goes beyond ordinary sight, although what exactly that means can be elusive. These visions may feel as real as the physical world around us, momentarily replacing the present time and surroundings. In those moments, the boundaries between reality and the unseen blur, making the experience both eerie and profound.

In shamanism, however, clairvoyance takes on a different form. Shamans enter what they call a "non-ordinary" reality, a realm that exists parallel to our own. In this altered state of consciousness, they embark on spiritual journeys, searching for lost souls that wander aimlessly between our world and the spirit world. These souls, often separated from their bodies due to trauma or suffering, can cause illness or distress if not retrieved. The shaman acts as a healer, using their vision and guidance from spirit allies to restore balance by returning the lost soul and mending the sick.

Both fortune tellers and shamans tap into forces beyond the material world, yet their experiences differ in purpose and practice. While the fortune teller's visions may reveal glimpses of the future or hidden truths, the shaman's sight is a tool for navigating the spiritual landscape, often with life altering consequences for those they help. This deeper understanding of clairvoyance shows that it is not a single phenomenon but a complex gift, experienced and used in countless ways throughout various cultures and traditions.

While Tawny introduced me to different groups of individuals gifted with second sight, I found myself learning a great deal about the afterlife—both its comforting and unsettling aspects. Each group had their own unique insights, and there was so much to absorb. From the concept of second sight to the vision quests of Native Americans and shamans, to encounters with ghosts and spirits, the variety of experiences was staggering.

It became clear that every culture has its own interpretation of the veil separating life and death, and each has developed its own ways of glimpsing beyond it. Some saw visions through dreams, others through spiritual journeys, while many described encounters with entities from the spirit world. This exploration of the afterlife revealed a profound, interconnected understanding of what lies beyond, shaped by countless beliefs and traditions across history.

Those who possess the gift of clairvoyance have been revered, feared, and even misunderstood. These individuals, whether known as oracles, prophets, diviners, wizards, witches, or something else entirely—were often seen as bridges between the physical world and the spiritual realm. They could interpret messages from the beyond, foresee events yet to unfold, or reveal hidden truths. From ancient civilizations to modern times, clairvoyants have played pivotal roles, their abilities shaping beliefs about the afterlife and influencing decisions of great consequence.

The sheer variety of ways people have encountered the afterlife through visions, dreams, spirit communication, and mystical experiences made me realize how complex and layered our understanding of it truly is. Each story, each belief, paints a different picture of what might await us beyond this life.

I thanked Delphi and Tawny for sharing their insights, grateful for the knowledge they had passed on. With their words still lingering in my mind, I continued to explore the goings-on around the campgrounds. As I wandered through the tents and fires, I could feel the subtle shift in the atmosphere, as if the very air was charged with a sense of mystery and anticipation. The distant sounds of whispered conversations and the flicker of shadows dancing in the firelight added to the growing unease. Every corner seemed to hold its own secrets, waiting to be uncovered.

Later, I noticed another group of people gathered across the lake. From a distance, I could see that they too were engaged in some sort of festivities, but their appearance was markedly different. They wore dark, tattered clothing, as though it had been ravaged by time or the elements. Their hair was streaked with black and white, giving them a ghostly, almost otherworldly look. What stood out the most, though, were the symbols painted on their faces, each one distinct, intricate, and seemingly filled with meaning. The symbols, though unfamiliar to me, hinted at something ancient and perhaps ritualistic, as if these people were connected to a darker, more primal force.

Candles were set up on a worn picnic table, their flickering flames casting eerie shadows across the scene. The group moved in a rhythmic, trance-like dance around the table, chanting words that seemed to resonate with the very air. Their voices rose and fell in a haunting cadence, while they lifted thick sticks above their heads, as if calling down some unseen power. The glow of the candles and the sound of their chanting combined to create an atmosphere that felt both mesmerizing and unsettling, as though they were on the verge of summoning something ancient from the depths of the night. Centered on the picnic table was an unmistakable symbol—an upside-down cross, its presence commanding attention amid the flickering candlelight. The cross seemed crudely carved into the surface, yet its significance was clear. As the group danced and chanted around it, the dark symbol took on a more sinister quality, amplifying the unsettling nature of their ritual. It felt like more than just a mark; it was as though the cross was a focal point of their ceremony, a deliberate connection to something darker, fueling the eerie energy that pulsed through the air.

They appeared to be enjoying themselves, but in their own twisted way. There was something unsettling about the group—an air of malevolence that lingered in the shadows. They looked almost sinister, their dark clothing and strange symbols giving them an evil, ominous appearance. The trees surrounding them cast long, creeping shadows, and their small campfire struggled to provide enough light, flickering weakly as if starved for fuel. It seemed as though someone had neglected to tend the fire, leaving the group enveloped in a gloomy, suffocating darkness. The sun's rays barely penetrated the dense canopy above, blocked entirely by the thick branches and leaves. Something in my gut didn't feel right about this scenario.

As I observed more closely, my attention was drawn to an altar draped in a tattered red tapestry. Carved into the side of the altar was a pentagram, its sharp lines catching the light of the sun that managed to filter through the leaves. Resting on top was the carcass of a small animal, lifeless and cold—a possible sacrifice offered to whatever dark force they were invoking. The scene was deeply disturbing, with the altar radiating an unsettling energy, as if it were the very center of their ritual, the focal point of something dark and forbidden.

"Wiccans," a woman said from behind me.

I turned to face a strikingly beautiful woman with no facial paint. She wore a flowing silk red dress with elegant red fabric linings that shimmered in the dim light. Her blonde hair cascaded past her shoulders, slightly curving outward at the ends. As she watched the group across the lake, a grimace formed on her face, her expression a mix of disdain and concern.

"Pardon?" I asked, my curiosity piqued. She snapped out of her gaze and smiled down at me, though the warmth in her smile didn't quite reach her eyes.

"They're evil, alright," she replied, her voice low and steady. "But not in person," she added cryptically, as if there was something more to her warning that she wasn't willing to disclose. "A ritual, not a religion. A festival much like ours, friendly, but forgotten." she added.

What she said didn't make much sense at first, but I continued listening, intrigued by the seriousness in her tone. Her eyes narrowed as she glanced toward the gathering across the lake.

"The ones you should really worry about are them," she said, pointing toward a group of people standing in a circle around the altar, each dressed in black and red hooded cloaks. Their faces were obscured in shadow, adding to the unsettling air that surrounded them.

"Do you see?" she asked in a hushed voice. I followed her gaze and noticed the other group of individuals, the ones I had originally seen, quietly backing away from the hooded figures, almost as if they sensed something they couldn't bear to confront. "Those you met were pagan—they're the good ones," she explained. "The ones embracing nature, celebrating the light and the earth. But the ones in the dark cloaks... they're something else entirely." Her voice dropped, filled with a hint of dread. "They are the Wiccans, and their practices are steeped in something far darker. What you saw was no ordinary ritual. They deal in powers that corrupt and destroy."

A chill crawled down my spine as her words took hold. The hooded figures around the altar appeared more menacing with every passing second, their true purpose obscured by a disturbing mystery. I couldn't shake the feeling that something far more dangerous lurked beneath the surface of what I had initially assumed.

The woman went on to explain more about the two groups and the significance of the ceremony for Samhain. She described how the Wiccans, a religious group deeply rooted in ancient pagan traditions, observed Samhain as one of their most sacred and important days. It marked the end of the harvest season and the beginning of winter, the darker half of the year. Samhain was a time when the veil between the living and the dead was believed to be at its thinnest, allowing spirits to pass freely between worlds.

For the Wiccans, Samhain was not just about honoring the dead but also about embracing the cycle of death and rebirth. It was a time for fasting, merriment, and, in some darker sects, even sacrifice. They believed that through these rituals, they could gain power, insight, or favor from the spirits they communed with. The bonfires, the chants, and the offerings were all designed to draw the spirits near, to guide them or seek their wisdom. However, this group seemed to take those ancient practices to a much darker extreme, their rituals more sinister and foreboding than any simple celebration of nature or life.

As she spoke, the weight of her words settled in. This wasn't just a ceremony; it was a dangerous invocation of forces I wasn't sure anyone should be tampering with.

As I stood frozen in place, my breath hitched while the hooded figures closed in around the altar. Even in the bright daylight, the scene felt suffocating, as though the sun itself refused to touch the ritual. The flickering candles seemed out of place under the midday sky, their flames small but steady, casting warped shadows that danced across the ground. The rhythmic chants grew louder, reverberating through the open air, cutting through the serene environment like a blade.

I saw the goat now, tethered to the altar, its wide, terrified eyes gleaming in the sunlight. The bright day only made its trembling more vivid, its small body tense with the dread of what was about to happen.

Despite the clear sky, a strange heaviness hung in the atmosphere, thick with unspoken intent. One of the cloaked figures raised a gleaming, curved blade, and the sunlight glinted off its surface, blinding for a moment as the chant hit its peak. Time seemed to slow, and with a single, decisive motion, the blade sliced through the goat's flesh. The sound, a sickening, wet thud, was unnervingly sharp in the midday stillness. The goat's cry was brief and hollow, its body collapsing onto the altar, where its blood began to spill, a dark crimson against the glaring brightness of the day. The liquid pooled around the stone, streaming down its edges, glistening in the sunlight as if mocking the life it had just taken. The chanting surged, their voices rising in unison, ecstatic and powerful. The scent of blood, thick and metallic, wafted through the warm air, mixing with the scent of burning wood from the dying fires nearby. Though the sun beat down, the warmth felt wrong, too intense, as if the very world was recoiling from what was taking place.

I wanted to turn away, to run, but I couldn't move. I was rooted to the spot, horrified by what I was witnessing in the clear light of day. Their ritualistic movements were slow, deliberate, and primal, as if they were drawing on something ancient, something darker than the sunshine around them should allow.

The lead figure stepped forward, dipping their fingers into the goat's blood, raising their hand to the sky. The sunlight bathed the scene in an almost surreal glow, but even then, I could feel it, something was shifting. The air turned colder despite the daylight, and the atmosphere thickened with an oppressive weight.

As they continued their ritual, I realized this wasn't just an ordinary ceremony. This was a deliberate act of power, a blood offering to dark forces unseen, their influence creeping into the daylight, corrupting even the sun itself. And I, helpless, could do nothing but witness it all unfold.

"The dead are honored," the woman stated, her voice calm yet unsettling as a small goat was led along the line of dark-hooded figures. The goat, timid and unaware, seemed out of place among the foreboding presence of the cloaked individuals.

"Samhain is considered a sacred time," she continued, her gaze never leaving the ceremony. "It's a moment when the veil between the living and the dead is thinnest, making it ideal for communing with spirits. But it also marks the start of a new cycle, a new season of crops and growth."

As the goat neared the altar, the tension in the air thickened. The dark figures, shrouded in their robes, stood motionless, their faces hidden, as if waiting for a signal to begin something far more sinister. I could sense the weight of the ritual bearing down, a mix of reverence and fear that clung to the surroundings like a heavy fog.

A masked, naked woman approached the altar, her figure striking and commanding. Her long, fiery red hair cascaded down her shoulders, framing her full, curvaceous form. Her bust rose and fell with each deliberate breath as she moved with a slow, purposeful grace. Suddenly, her gaze shifted in my direction, locking onto me with an unsettling intensity from behind the mask.

She paused for a moment, standing tall behind the altar, then raised both arms slowly, her movements deliberate and ritualistic. In her hands, she gripped a curved blade, its edge gleaming in the fading daylight. The way she held it, poised and ready, suggested that the blade's purpose was far darker than I dared imagine.

Two hooded figures approached the altar, lifting the small, trembling goat in their arms. With careful precision, they laid it upon the cold stone, the animal's soft bleating fading into the unsettling silence that followed. The rest of the group moved methodically, forming a tight circle around the altar.

As they gathered, each figure bowed their head in unison, their hoods obscuring their faces, and a low, eerie chant began to rise from their midst. The words, strange and ancient, floated across the small lake, their meaning lost to me but carrying a weight that felt both dark and powerful. The cadence of their voices was hypnotic, growing louder with every passing moment, as if calling to something beyond the visible world. The sunlight, though still strong, seemed to dim slightly, as if the very air thickened with the gravity of the ritual. I could feel a growing sense of unease, as though whatever they were invoking was stirring, waiting just beyond the edge of perception.

The masked woman began panting heavily, her gaze still fixed on me with an unsettling intensity. She slowly raised the blade high over her head, the sharp edge glinting in the light, poised to strike. Instinctively, I covered my eyes.

"No, you must watch," the woman beside me insisted, but this time her voice wavered, betraying a hint of unease. Her grip tightened as she pulled my hands away from my face, but there was no longer calm assurance in her touch. "You need to see this... something isn't right."

The group's chanting swelled, their voices merging into a low, eerie drone that seemed to vibrate through the very air. Somewhere in the distance, drums began to pound rhythmically, a deep, primal beat that reverberated through the trees. A horn blared, its sharp, mournful sound cutting through the forest, but I couldn't see anyone playing the instruments. It was as if the sounds were conjured from the very surroundings.

Most of the words in the chant were indecipherable, lost in the chaotic noise, but one word rose above the rest. It echoed through the clearing, clearer and louder with each repetition, growing more haunting with every utterance. The word carried an unsettling weight, filling the air with a dark resonance that made my skin crawl.

"Rakshasi... Rakshasi... Rakshasi!"

That single word echoed in my mind, perfectly clear, each syllable vibrating through the air like a dark incantation. It carried an ominous weight, as though it was summoning something ancient and malevolent. The masked woman's panting grew heavier, more frantic, her chest rising and falling with labored breaths. Her trembling hands wobbled as they struggled to keep the blade steady.

"Oh, fuck, this isn't good," said the woman next to me.

Then, the masked woman drove the blade into the goat, swift and brutal. Blood splattered across her naked body, staining her pale skin with streaks of crimson. The chanting grew louder, almost feverish, as if the act had unleashed something uncontrollable.

She glanced nervously at the scene unfolding around her, her earlier confidence shattered. The ritual was spiraling out of control, and even she seemed uncertain about what she had just set in motion. A loud scream of horror escaped her lips, a visceral reaction to the shock of her actions, as if she had been hypnotized by the chanting. But then, that horrifying scream morphed into a loud, aggressive laughter.

She cocked her head at an unnaturally sharp angle, the motion slow and deliberate, as if her neck might snap under the strain. Her eyes, wide and glassy, locked onto mine with an intensity that sent another chill down my spine. There was something deeply wrong in the way she moved, as though her body was no longer her own, and the stare, unblinking, hollow, seemed to pierce straight through me, void of humanity, as if she were something far beyond human, studying me with cold detachment.

In one swift motion, she tore the mask from her face, wiping the blood from her skin with her fingers before bringing them to her lips. Slowly and deliberately, she ran her hands across her chest, smearing the blood with a twisted sense of intent. Her eyes, locked onto mine, held a cold, unsettling gaze that was as menacing as the ritual itself.

I closed my eyes and took a deep breath, desperately trying to steady my nerves. I knew I could simply turn and walk away, but something deep inside told me this was more than just a nightmare—it was real, no matter how much I wished it wasn't. When I opened my eyes, the scene before me twisted into something far worse. The deranged woman now wore the goat's intestines like a grotesque necklace, prancing around the altar like a court jester. Her maniacal laughter filled the air, her eyes wild with a madness that sent a cold wave of terror through me. I felt sick to my stomach. I couldn't tear my eyes away, no matter how much I wanted to. The chanting had become a deafening roar, filling the air with an almost unbearable pressure.

The ceremony came to a sudden, jarring halt as the woman froze mid-laugh, her unsettling cackle dying in her throat as though she had been yanked back to reality. The chanting cut off in unison, leaving an eerie silence hanging in the air. It was as if the entire ritual had unraveled in a blink. The hooded figures exchanged nervous, bewildered glances, their hands slowly dropping to their sides, unsure of what to do next.

The woman at the altar, still drenched in blood, wobbled backward, her wide eyes darting frantically as if she had no idea where she was or what had just happened. Panic flashed across her face. She took a few disoriented steps before collapsing to her knees, the blade slipping from her trembling hands, hitting the ground with a soft thud.

In an instant, chaos erupted. The figures scattered, their dark cloaks swirling as they fled into the forest, vanishing as quickly as they had appeared. It was as if they were running from something far worse than what they had been trying to summon.

"I'm so terribly sorry, dear," the woman beside me said softly, her tone unnervingly calm. "I didn't introduce myself."

"Wh... what just happened?" I stammered, my voice shaky.

"What do you mean?" she asked, her expression unreadable.

"All of that!" I shouted, gesturing frantically toward the lake, where the group of people had just been—but now there was nothing. Not a trace.

She smiled faintly, her eyes narrowing. "Trust me, girl. You do not want to meddle with those people." Her words hung in the air, carrying a weight that chilled me to the bone.

My heart raced as I looked back across the lake, hoping to catch a glimpse of anything, anyone, but it was as if the entire group had vanished into thin air.

"What do you mean?" I pressed. "Who were they?"

"Those people…" The woman sighed, her gaze distant, as though she was piecing together memories too dark to share. "They deal in things that twist the world. Powers far beyond what you or I can understand. You're lucky they didn't notice you."

"Notice me? They looked right at me!" I whispered, the fear clawing at my chest.

She turned toward me, her expression solemn, eyes reflecting something. "No," she said, her voice barely above a whisper. "If they truly saw you, you wouldn't be standing here."

"Who are you?" I finally asked.

As she smiled, the corners of her lips curled ever so slightly. "You may call me Prosperity, Granddaughter of Angelina," she said, her voice soft but commanding. With a graceful bow, a gesture that felt strangely formal in the eerie stillness, she continued, "It was an honor meeting you, Dawn, Daughter of Amethyst."

My heart skipped a beat at the mention of my mother's name.

"If you don't mind me asking, who is Rakshasi?" I asked eagerly, my curiosity getting the better of me.

Prosperity paused for a moment, her back still to me. She didn't turn around, but I saw her shoulders tense slightly. "A dangerous force," she said at last. "One you're better off not knowing." She glanced over her shoulder, her eyes dark and unreadable. "Curiosity like yours can lead to places you're not ready to go, Dawn."

"I can handle myself."

"That woman you saw was Rakshasi, but in her human form."

"You actually believe that?" I asked, raising an eyebrow.

"Not exactly," she replied, hesitating. "Sort of." She glanced around cautiously before continuing, "Come with me, please. There's someone I want you to meet."

As Prosperity walked forward, a sudden chill swept past me, carried by an unnerving breeze that seemed to whisper through the trees. The hairs on the back of my neck prickled, and I felt a cold, piercing stare burrowing into the back of my head. My heart quickened, dread pooling in my stomach. Slowly, I turned, my body stiff with unease.

Standing at the lake's edge was a man, his posture rigid and unnatural. His gaze, intense and suffocating, locked onto me like a predator stalking its prey. A dark hooded cloak draped over him, identical to the figures who had vanished moments earlier, yet there was something far more sinister about this one.

For a brief moment, the clouds parted, and a sliver of sunlight revealed what lay beneath the hood: a twisted, crooked smile, sharp and cruel, stretching across a face half-hidden in shadow. The air felt thick with menace, as if the very atmosphere shifted in his presence. He stood perfectly still, his eerie grin a silent, mocking challenge.

My blood ran cold. Something was very, very wrong.

I turned and grabbed Prosperity's shoulder, halting her to point out the mysterious man. But when I looked back, he was gone, as if he had vanished into thin air. There were no signs of anyone walking along the banks of the lake or disappearing into the trees.

After a brief walk with Prosperity to her campsite, she introduced me to her grandmother, Angelina, a lovely older woman with long white hair and striking blue eyes. As we sat by the fire, Angelina explained that she practices Angelic Alchemy, a spiritual art passed down through generations in her family. She described it as a sacred blend of ancient wisdom and divine energy, used to heal, protect, and connect with higher realms. Her calm yet powerful presence suggested that this practice was more than just ritual; it felt like a way of life, deeply intertwined with the unseen forces that surrounded us.

Angelina began explaining her beliefs, delving into the core of her practice with a sincerity that made her words linger. I couldn't remember all the details, but certain parts stood out. She described how her practice wasn't entirely unlike Christianity; at its heart, it centered on the eternal struggle between light and dark, good and evil, a balance she believed shaped all existence. It was a battle of forces: much like God versus Lucifer in Christian belief, her own spirituality focused on harmonizing these forces within oneself and recognizing their presence in the world. The dualism reminded me of stories from religious teachings—a persistent tension between life-giving virtues and the allure of darkness, each side vying for control over one's soul and purpose.

As our conversation unfolded, things started to get a bit muddled. Angelina mentioned that angels exist within a celestial realm, what many might call heaven. Her words implied that this wasn't merely a symbolic place but a realm distinct from our own, inhabited by beings of pure spirit who align with divine order. She spoke as if these celestial forces were engaged in an eternal purpose, echoing traditional beliefs that angels serve as messengers and protectors, bridging the distance between the divine and the earthly. Her insights painted a layered picture of the universe, where heaven wasn't just a place but a realm of harmony and purpose, ordered yet mysterious.

"Think of it like this," Angelina explained, leaning in with an intensity that caught my attention. "This realm I'm talking about isn't the heaven you might have learned about in church. Instead, it's a space that exists between worlds—a sort of void, or a gap between dimensions." She paused, letting the weight of her words settle, then continued, "It's a place where beings exist that aren't tied to our reality, nor any other. We refer to them as celestials, though some might even call them extraterrestrials, given their nature."

Her description blurred the lines between spiritual and otherworldly, and with each detail, I felt myself growing more confused. Was she suggesting that these entities were both divine and alien? Her words hinted at a realm that was neither entirely holy nor wholly cosmic, a liminal space where boundaries dissolved, and beings of uncertain origin moved freely, transcending the limits of earthly understanding.

After listening intently to Angelina's detailed account of fallen angels, she offered me a porcelain cup of tea, its surface intricately decorated with celestial symbols. Stars and planetary motifs, delicately painted in gold and cobalt, shimmered under the light, giving the cup an almost otherworldly aura. As I took the cup, I noticed how even this small object seemed to echo Angelina's words, a reminder of the cosmic forces and beings she believed were still at work, somewhere in the spaces between light and darkness.

I took a sip of the tea, its warmth seeping through the porcelain cup into my hands. The flavor was unexpectedly sweet, with subtle floral and honeyed notes that lingered on my tongue. It had an unusual, almost enchanting quality—both comforting and unfamiliar, as if it held some secret connection to the celestial themes Angelina spoke of. The drink seemed to reflect her world: rich with mystery, layered with hidden nuances, and just enough sweetness to keep me captivated.

"May I ask you a question?" I asked, taking another sip of the tea, savoring its floral sweetness.

"Of course you may," Angelina replied, her voice as calm and composed as ever.

From across the room, Prosperity raised her eyebrows, her gaze sharp and knowing, almost as if she already anticipated what I was about to ask. It felt as though she could sense the curiosity swirling in my mind, or perhaps she'd heard this line of questioning before. Her silent attention added a new weight to the moment, deepening the mystery that seemed to hang in the air.

"What do you know about Rakshasi?"

Angelina fell silent, her expression darkening as she processed my question. A flicker of irritation crossed her face, making it clear that something about my inquiry had struck a nerve—or maybe it was the fact that I had dared to ask at all. Her eyes, usually so serene, had taken on a sharper edge, and I felt a sudden chill in the air, as if I'd unknowingly trespassed into forbidden territory. Her response, or lack thereof, left me uneasy, and I wondered if I had crossed a line that couldn't easily be mended. Angelina lifted her cup, pausing briefly as if lost in thought, then took a long sip, finishing her tea in two swift gulps. She set the cup down with a soft but deliberate clink, her gaze unwavering as though daring me to continue or perhaps waiting for my reaction. Her quick, almost dismissive way of drinking seemed to hint at her impatience, a subtle but unmistakable cue that the conversation was edging into territory she would rather avoid.

"Now, dear, I'll ask you a question," she replied at last.

Angelina's expression shifted, her face becoming noticeably sharper, almost calculating. I hadn't intended to provoke her, but the intensity of her gaze told me I'd touched on something personal, perhaps even guarded. Her reaction left me feeling exposed, as if she were now seeing through my intentions, weighing them carefully before responding.

"And how is it that you know about her?" Angelina asked, her voice steady and composed, but with a hint of guarded curiosity. She looked at me carefully, her expression unreadable, as though weighing how much I really understood. The calmness in her voice was almost more unsettling than anger—it suggested that whatever I'd touched on was serious, something she was more than willing to discuss, but only if I had the right answers.

I took a deep breath, gathering my thoughts before explaining to Angelina what Prosperity and I had witnessed at the lake. I described the eerie stillness that had settled over the water, the way the moonlight danced on the surface like silver, and how we had seen a figure emerge from the shadows, flickering in and out of view. I struggled to find the right words to convey the sense of foreboding that had enveloped us, the mixture of fear and fascination that gripped my heart.

"It was as if time stood still," I said. "There was something there. I couldn't shake the feeling that something was watching us, waiting."

"And you heard them chanting Rakshasi's name?" Angelina asked, her eyes narrowing slightly as if weighing the significance of our encounter.

"Yes, Grandma, I heard it too," Prosperity chimed in.

Angelina explained that the name Rakshasi evoked tales of a formidable being from folklore, a demon known for its ability to shapeshift. Often depicted as a beautiful woman with striking red hair, she possessed an alluring charm that could easily manipulate men and young boys. Angelina's voice grew more serious as she continued, detailing how this demon could twist desires to her advantage. If a man rejected her advances, legend had it that she would wear his organs around her body as if they were jewelry, a gruesome reminder of the fate that awaited those who dared to defy her. This realization made my heart race; we were treading into territory that was far beyond our everyday reality.

Angelina reached into a worn-looking sack by her side and pulled out an old sketchbook. She flipped through the pages with purpose before suddenly stopping. With a swift motion, she slammed her finger down onto one particular page, her expression intense. Rotating the book to show me, she revealed a drawing of a dark figure with four elongated arms, each ending in three long fingers. Its legs were similarly long and ended in three toes, and the body was a dark gray, distinctly female in form.

What unsettled me the most, however, was the figure's face. It had a familiar teardrop-shaped head with two black, almond-shaped eyes that seemed to pierce through the page. The nostrils were merely slits, and the mouth was small and unsettling. A strange sense of déjà vu washed over me; something about this creature felt eerily familiar, as if I had seen it somewhere before but couldn't quite place where.

"Rakshasi is known to be nocturnal, as most demons are," Angelina explained. "Many believe she, like other demons, never sleeps and harbors grotesque habits. She is said to feast on human flesh, drink from the skulls of her victims, and manipulate children by disguising herself as a lost child. She lures them into wooded areas, where her true intentions reveal themselves, and she eventually consumes them."

Angelina paused, her gaze drifting to Prosperity before settling back on me, her expression unreadable. "If I'm being honest, I don't believe she's that kind of entity," she said quietly, her demeanor shifting, her usual confidence tinged with a wary apprehension.

"How so?" I pressed, sensing the weight of what she was about to reveal.

Angelina's eyes took on a distant, haunted sheen, as though she were staring into a darkness only she could see. "I feel she's something far worse than a demon," she murmured. "Rakshasi may very well be an entity from…a world between worlds. Neither purely good nor wholly evil; she is both and yet neither, an enigma that defies all definitions. This isn't just some vengeful spirit; she's older, far older, beyond our conceptions of morality." Her words sank in, and Angelina continued, her voice barely above a whisper. "Picture a curious child playing in the woods after dusk. They wander deeper and deeper, following a voice only they can hear. Days, months, even years later, the child is found, but they're... different—if they're found at all. Legends say that Rakshasi takes these children up into the stars, to the place she's from. And she's not alone," she added, her gaze hardening. "There's more than one of her kind."

Her words painted a haunting image of beings that existed beyond the earthly concepts of light and dark, a realm where morality blurred, and intentions were a mystery. I felt a rising dread as I realized that this wasn't merely a tale of possession or hauntings, it was about forces beyond human understanding, entities that could cross into our world at will, taking what they pleased, leaving behind a void of unanswered questions and shattered lives.

I noticed the time was merging late in the afternoon and I should be getting back to my parents. I thanked Angelina and Prosperity for their hospitality.

"I didn't mean to frighten you dear child," said Angelina. "I assure you that you have nothing to worry about as Rakshasi is just a myth."

"No, no," I assured her. "I promise you that I appreciate everything you have shared with me."

Angelina held out her old woven bag, her eyes narrowing thoughtfully. "Reach inside," she instructed, her voice low and deliberate. "Take the first thing your hand touches."

Curious, I reached in, feeling a variety of items brush against my fingers. Just as I began to explore further, Angelina pulled the bag back, her expression firm. "Only the first thing you touch," she insisted. I promised to respect her request and opened my hand to reveal what I'd pulled, a necklace with colorful beads, each bead intricately carved with unique designs. At the center hung a stone pendant, carved into the distinct shape of an eye, colorless but hauntingly detailed.

Angelina's eyes softened as she looked at the necklace. "Keep it," she said, her tone final. "The Evil Eye pendant will show you the truth." When I asked her what the Evil Eye meant, she responded with a weak grimace, narrowing one eye while the other fixed me in a piercing stare.

A chill ran through my body, cold and unyielding, and I felt an intense unease, as if I'd been judged and silently condemned. But then, just as swiftly, she smiled, and the sensation vanished, leaving me feeling oddly restored.

"Now, go with Prosperity before I tell you another story," Angelina said with a gentle but firm tone, ushering me on.

I thanked her deeply for her hospitality and all she'd shared. As I turned to leave, the sweet taste of the tea lingered faintly on my tongue, a reminder of our strange encounter.

Prosperity led me to several other campsites, where I was treated to a variety of foods. We sampled fruits and cheeses from around the world, and I painted my face with triangular tribal symbols before dancing around fire pits to the rhythmic beat of Celtic music. One woman roasted honey-covered almonds at her site, filling the air with a sweet, smoky aroma, while her husband demonstrated how to load and shoot a bow and arrow. The excitement of the evening surprised me, leaving me with a sense of wonder and the warm memory of a new friend made along the way.

Prosperity and I walked along a narrow trail leading to a grassy field beyond the main camp, the sounds of laughter and music growing faint behind us. We settled under the sweeping branches of an old willow tree, its leaves creating a quiet, secluded haven. There, we joked about boys, swapped stories about life and school, and talked about our families. I learned Prosperity was two years older than me, but age didn't seem to matter, our interests aligned, and a natural bond was forming between us.

As the conversation deepened, we shared more about our lives, piecing together little details of who we were and where we'd come from. While the Ecstatic Festival was new to me, Prosperity explained that this was her third year attending. This annual gathering, she said, was a world all its own, a place where people came to celebrate freely and express themselves.

Eventually, our stories drifted to where we grew up. Prosperity shared that she was from Arizona and had never been to Nebraska before. Then, leaning closer, she confided her real name: Angela Rothermond. I felt a quiet thrill at her trust and a sense of mutual understanding. Smiling, she offered to give me my own Ecstatic name, something unique for me to carry through the festival.

After a moment of thought, she christened me "Karma Petra Winchester," a name that felt both strange and powerful. With a grin, she explained that each part symbolized something unique, a bit of my spirit, my newfound place here, and the journey we were now part of together.

While still sitting under the willow tree, I suddenly felt something change—like someone was watching us. Memories of the strange occurrences back home flooded my mind. I felt comfortable with Prosperity, trusting her enough to share the odd and unusual events happening in my life. But just as I was gathering the courage to speak, she began telling me a story of her own.

UNDER THE WILLOW TREE

Once, there was a young Native American girl named Aiyana, whose heart overflowed with curiosity. She found magic in every pebble and river, but it was trees that held her spirit. She especially loved the graceful willow trees, with their long, sweeping branches that seemed to dance in the wind.

One late afternoon, while exploring near her village, Aiyana discovered the most beautiful willow tree she had ever seen. Its branches hung like green curtains, and sunlight filtered through its leaves in a gentle, golden glow. Aiyana's heart raced with excitement as she approached it, eager to climb. She wrapped her small hands around the knotted trunk and began her ascent, feeling each branch sway slightly beneath her, as if welcoming her to the top.

At last, she reached the highest point, where the leaves parted just enough for her to see the valley stretching far below. The world looked so peaceful from up there, cradled by the quiet strength of the willow tree. Enchanted by the view and lulled by the rustling leaves, Aiyana soon drifted off to sleep.

Time passed, and night descended over the valley. The soft, cool darkness enveloped Aiyana, who slept soundly, unaware of how late it had become. Eventually, she stirred awake, hearing a familiar voice, her mother's voice, calling out her name with gentle urgency. Aiyana blinked in surprise, realizing where she was and how dark the world had grown around her.

In her sleepy confusion, she shifted on the branch, trying to call back to her mother. But the branch beneath her shifted too, and before she knew it, Aiyana had lost her balance. She slipped and tumbled, her fall cushioned only slightly by the willow's sweeping branches.

That night, Aiyana's spirit joined the willow she had so dearly loved. Her people believed she became part of the tree, a guardian spirit watching over the valley. On moonlit nights, when the wind would pass through the branches, her mother would look up at the swaying willow, feeling Aiyana's presence in the gentle rustle, knowing her spirit lingered in the beauty and grace of the ancient tree.

But that's not the end of the story. Legend has it that Aiyana's mother, guided by her mother's intuition, found her daughter lying at the base of the willow tree. Aiyana's body lay broken—her neck twisted and her arms and legs bent at unnatural angles. Overwhelmed with grief, her mother gently dug a grave beside the ancient willow. With tears streaming down her face, she laid Aiyana's broken body to rest in the earth, believing that ending her suffering would bring her spirit peace.

They say that if you stand before this very willow tree just after dusk, you can still hear the mournful cries of the grieving mother calling out to her lost daughter. And if you linger long enough, waiting in the hushed darkness, you might hear Aiyana's scream as she tumbles down from the branches, ending with the sickening crack of her fall.

Over the years, people claim to have seen Aiyana's spirit wandering the hill where the old willow tree stands. Her ghostly figure is a chilling sight, twisted in a way that seems both unnatural and tragic. Her head lolls backward, her body arched unnervingly, as if still marked by the trauma of her fall. Mud clings to her pale skin, and nightcrawlers slip from her open mouth, writhing as they fall to the ground. If you're unlucky enough to be caught in her gaze, you'll be frozen in place, paralyzed by her empty, haunting eyes. In that moment, a cold, suffocating sensation will seize you. You'll gasp for breath, only to feel thick, wet mud filling your mouth, the taste earthy and foul. Worse still, you'll sense the squirming of worms slipping down your throat, writhing with each breath as though alive inside you. Those who've survived such encounters say the feeling lingers, a chilling reminder of Aiyana's curse, leaving them forever haunted by the taste of earth and decay.

MAY 28: BEFORE SUNSET

After relaxing under the willow tree with Prosperity, we were startled by the sound of two men arguing near the trail we had walked along earlier. Peering through the branches, we saw a stocky, bearded man leaning heavily on a lumber ax, its blade sunk deep into the earth at his feet. His expression was intense, his brows furrowed as he spoke in a low, gravelly voice.

Beside him stood another man, tall and wiry, dressed in worn overalls. He listened in silence, chewing thoughtfully on a piece of hay, his gaze steady and almost detached as he watched his companion. The tension between them hung thick in the air, and we could feel an unease radiating from their conversation.

"Ha!" the bearded man laughed, though there was no humor in his voice. "You seriously doubt what I saw?"

"Naw, now, don't go thinkin' that, friend. That ain't at all what I'm implyin'," the man in overalls replied calmly, his Southern accent stretching each word with a slow, deliberate drawl. "You got it wrong. Them lights—they got themselves a reason for showin' up to folks like you."

Their words piqued my curiosity, and I leaned closer, eager to hear more.

"It was a UFO," the bearded man whispered, as if sharing a forbidden secret. He paused, his eyes shifting as he glanced around, then added, "Or should I say UFOs?"

The man in overalls didn't flinch. He just tilted his head. "More than one, you say?" he drawled.

"Two, maybe three," the bearded man insisted, his hand tightening around the handle of the ax. "Lights in the sky, moving in ways no human machine could. They hovered right above that hill and then"—he snapped his fingers—"gone in an instant."

The wiry man chewed his hay thoughtfully, his expression unreadable. "Those lights got their reasons, I'd wager. Seen more'n my fair share of strange things myself,"

By now, my curiosity was burning. What exactly had these men seen, and why were they so convinced there was something otherworldly in those lights?

Were they talking about the three ghostly lights I had seen the night before? It dawned on me that it might not have been a trick of the mind or a figment of my imagination, these men had witnessed the same strange lights. Could it really be the same eerie glow I had seen hovering silently in the dark? The thought made my pulse quicken, and I leaned in closer, hoping to catch every word, eager to confirm if our experiences were truly connected.

I leaned in closer, barely breathing, as the man in overalls spoke again. "You say they just vanished? Without a sound?"

The bearded man nodded slowly, his eyes distant. "Just... blinked out. One second they were there, and the next, only darkness. Almost like they'd never been there at all. But I swear, I could feel them watching me."

A shiver rippled through me. Watching. The word echoed in my mind, tugging at a memory I'd tried to bury. When I'd seen the lights, I hadn't just been looking at them, I'd felt their gaze as if they were studying me, assessing me. The lights had felt foreign yet oddly comforting, as though they held a quiet reassurance. It was like reconnecting with a forgotten memory from childhood, one that had lingered in my mind, hazy but warm.

"Haw haw!" laughed the man in overalls, a sly grin spreading as he spoke. "UFOs or not, I done seen lights like that before. I'm tellin' ya, them were Corpse Lights, sure as I'm standin' here."

"Excuse me!?" I interrupted. "I couldn't help but overhear."

"HOLY SHIT, I PEED A LITTLE!" the man in overalls

yelped, his eyes wide with shock. "Good Lord, you scared the livin' daylights outta me, little girl!"

"Ha ha," the bearded man chuckled.

The man in overalls let out a long sigh. "Sorry 'bout that," he drawled, tipping his hat with a polite nod. "Can we help y'all with somethin', ladies? Name's Jacob, by the way," he added warmly as he greeted Prosperity and me. "And this husky fella here is Ned."

"Yes, nice to meet you both," I replied, a bit sheepish. "I don't mean to eavesdrop, but may I ask—what exactly is a Corpse Light?"

Before Jacob could answer my question, Prosperity gave my arm a gentle tug, her eyes shifting toward the darkening sky. "We should probably head back to camp," she murmured, a hint of urgency in her voice. The sun was sinking low, casting long shadows across the trail, and I could feel the evening chill beginning to settle.

"I think I've seen those lights too—whether they're UFOs or Corpse Lights, whatever you call them," I pressed, my curiosity getting the better of me. "What are they, really?"

Jacob paused, giving me a long, thoughtful look, as if weighing whether he should answer. The bearded man, Ned, shifted his stance, his expression turning serious. I sensed that whatever they were about to share wasn't a story to be taken lightly.

"Look," Ned replied, his tone polite. "I don't wanna get all technical on ya, figurin' you might not be too deep into the science of it."

"Go on," I urged, eager to hear more.

"A Corpse Light is also known as a phosphorescent ghost light seen floatin' around in the night air," Ned explained, his voice lowering as though sharing a forbidden secret. "They shimmer white, blue, even red, twinklin' like stars in the night sky. Some folks have seen 'em outdoors, others right inside their own homes. They look like distant candle lights or lanterns, just floatin' out there."

Here's where things started to get confusing, but I'll do my best to recall it as clearly as I can.

"Foolishly," Ned continued with a wry grin, "some folks like to explain 'em away as swamp gas. But the funny part? They show up in places where there ain't a swamp for miles."

Ned explained that the Corpse Lights had been seen late last night, flickering on and off between nine o'clock and midnight. Each time they vanished, they would reappear a few minutes later, hovering in different formations as though moving to an unseen rhythm. He said the lights were known to linger near those who would soon face doom.

"We saw three of 'em off to the east, just over the hills," he continued, his face darkening with a somber expression. "Don't know who was out there that might've drawn them lights. I only pray the good Lord will save the souls of whoever was unfortunate enough to face their fate—if that's truly what those lights came for."

I thanked them both for the creepy information. I then grabbed Prosperity by the hand. We walked back to the camp safely, yet creeped out about the conversation that took place. While Prosperity and I were alone, I told her everything about what I saw on our way here last night as we headed back to our campsite. She seemed uneasy about my encounter. We laughed that maybe it was a UFO, although I sort of doubt it.

When we got back to camp, I noticed two tents staked firmly into the ground on our plot, their fabric rustling lightly in the evening breeze. Just as we arrived, Mother and Father returned as well. I introduced them to Prosperity, and the greeting went smoothly. Mother mentioned they'd been planning to join the Ecstatic Dance that evening but decided to stop by camp to rest for a bit.

Prosperity then told me she should head back to her grandmother but agreed to meet up later for the Ecstatic Dance and festival. After she left, I unzipped and rolled out my blue flannel-printed sleeping bag, setting a couple of pillows aside, and settled down to record everything in my diary—the strange encounters, Ned and Jacob's eerie tales, and the flickering lights I'd seen. I decided to keep today's odd events to myself, at least for now.

MAY 28: SUNSET

8:30 PM

As the sun dipped lower, casting a warm, golden glow over the camp, we gathered around the small fire that Father had carefully tended to life. The sky faded from amber to deep purple, and a faint chill began to settle in the air. We huddled close, savoring the warmth of the flames and the comforting crackle of wood.

Mother laid out a spread of simple but hearty provisions: crusty bread, fresh fruit, and a stew that simmered over the fire, filling the air with a delicious, earthy aroma. Father sliced the bread, handing pieces to each of us, and we laughed, telling stories and sharing memories under the vast evening sky. The firelight danced in our eyes, and for a brief moment, it felt as though the world beyond our campsite faded away, leaving only the warmth of family and the quiet comfort of a meal shared in the open air.

The cool, crisp mountain air wandered restlessly, carrying the sharp scent of burning wood from the other campers scattered nearby. In the distance, the deep, resonant beat of drums began to echo through the trees, joined by the haunting sound of wind and string instruments. Together, they created a rhythmic, almost hypnotic melody that wove through the night air like an ancient song calling us closer.

It was as if the whole camp was alive with anticipation, pulling us deeper into the evening's energy. The music mingled with the crackling of our own campfire, wrapping around us in a warm, harmonic embrace. The rhythm was inviting us to leave our seats, to follow the sound through the trees to wherever it might lead. We exchanged glances, feeling the pull of the music in the depths of our bones. The sound was magnetic, tempting us to leave the comfort of our fire and join whatever gathering lay beyond the trees.

Father was the first to rise, a faint grin on his face as he gestured toward the source of the sound. "What do you say?" he asked, his eyes sparkling with the same curiosity I felt.

Mother chuckled softly, brushing a stray hair back as she stood up as well. "It's been a while since we let loose," she admitted with a wink. "Shall we?"Excitement built within me as we left our small campsite, guided only by the rhythm. The trees loomed tall around us, their silhouettes swaying against the starlit sky. The path wound deeper into the woods, each step bringing the music closer, louder, more enveloping. Shadows flickered in the distance, cast by the fires from the larger gathering just ahead.

As we rounded the final bend, the scene unfolded before us—a circle of campers, some seated, others already swaying to the music, hands clapping in time with the beat. Colorful lanterns hung from tree branches, casting a warm glow over the crowd, and the flames from a large bonfire danced wildly in the center.

I felt a thrill of exhilaration as we joined the crowd. People were laughing, singing, and dancing, their faces lit with pure joy and freedom. The night seemed endless, a world apart from the ordinary. In that moment, with my family beside me and the music weaving through the air, I felt part of something timeless, as though we were stepping into a ritual as old as the mountains themselves.

The ambient atmospheric music was delicate and ethereal, flowing like a soft breeze through the trees. Wind instruments, perhaps flutes or panpipes, drifted with a haunting, echoing melody that rose and fell, each note lingering in the air as if carried by the mountain mists. String instruments, likely a harp or a lute, gently plucked in soft, rolling arpeggios, adding a tender warmth to the melody that balanced the cool night.

A low, humming drone in the background gave the music an expansive feel, as though it were stretching out into the starlit sky. Occasionally, faint chimes or bells would shimmer in, their tones like glimmers of light dancing over water, adding a touch of mystery to the sound. Together, the instruments formed a mesmerizing, layered harmony, blending seamlessly with the rustling leaves and the quiet whispers of the night, as though the music was a natural part of the forest itself. The atmosphere was serene yet filled with an underlying magic, inviting listeners to lose themselves in its timeless melody. Every moment felt like heavenly bliss.

Occasionally, a soft, crystalline chime would ring out, bright and pure, like droplets of light falling from the heavens. The music held a warmth that wrapped around you, calming and uplifting, giving the feeling of being carried to a realm of peace and beauty. It was as if the mountain itself was breathing, and each sound was a prayer to the night, a serenade of gratitude and grace that reached the very soul.

We feasted on a variety of dishes from the other camp chefs, moving from one site to the next as we sampled everything on offer. Some foods were extraordinarily delicious, while others were simply pleasant, but each had a unique flavor that reflected the individuality of the cook behind it. Every person, every taste—it was all distinct. Tradition holds that to eat and drink is to show honor to the Ecstatic Chief, and I embraced this wholeheartedly, finding not one dish to my disliking. I was fully satisfied.

One of my favorites was Prosperity's grandmother's Grim-Grog, a wild, fruity concoction made from grapes, apples, and honey with a strong undertone of alcohol. The flavor was rich and sweet, with just the right amount of warmth, and it seemed to fill me with a sense of celebration. The drink felt as though it carried its own story, aged and mysterious, like Prosperity's grandmother herself.

After her second cup of Grim-Grog, Prosperity began to sway a bit, awkwardly trying to steady herself with little success. The drink was potent, and it was clear it had worked its magic on her. Around us, laughter and music filled the air as people sang, danced, and feasted on the array of dishes everyone had contributed. The warmth of the bonfire cast a golden glow on everyone's faces, illuminating a night that felt like pure celebration.

Just as I thought this was the peak of the evening, two sturdy men emerged from the crowd, carrying a large, ornately carved altar. They placed it carefully in the center of the circle, near the bonfire, drawing everyone's attention. The crowd's energy shifted from lively chatter to a hushed anticipation, as if some secret ritual was about to unfold.

From the shadows, a tall, thin man stepped forward, his movements deliberate and graceful. He wore a flowing lavender cloak that brushed the ground, and in one hand, he held a long, gnarled staff topped with a small crystal that glimmered in the firelight. He approached the altar with a quiet authority, his face partially hidden by the hood of his cloak. The crowd fell silent, their eyes fixed on him, waiting. The entire atmosphere changed, heavy with mystery, as if we were about to witness something powerful.

"Ladies and lads," the tall man called out, his voice deep and resonant. "I welcome you all to the ancient Celtic Ecstatic Ritual." Around the circle, people knelt in reverence, including Prosperity and my parents.

"NO!" he shouted abruptly, his tone firm but not unkind. "You have no need to worship me, for I am a man of no higher power."

The crowd slowly rose to their feet, and as a gesture of unity, each person bowed respectfully to one another. Prosperity, a bit unsteady, wobbled toward me with her arms open. I reached out to steady her as she hugged me, her laughter warm and carefree.

"That's Priest," Prosperity explained, her words slightly slurred. "He's actually a priest. 'Priest' is the name they gave him here. He's cool." She hiccuped, and the sharp scent of strong alcohol lingered on her breath.

At the altar, Priest raised his arms high, his hands stretched wide to the star-filled sky. "May the feast fill you all on this glorious night. God is with you, each and every one…" He clasped his hands in a gesture of prayer. "Dear Lord, who art in heaven, we thank you for this bountiful feast. We pray to you, God—"

Suddenly, his words were cut off by the powerful sound of drums pounding from across the lake. The rhythmic drumming grew louder, echoing across the water and filling the air with an intensity that seemed to pulse in time with the beat of our hearts. A murmur spread through the crowd as everyone looked toward the lake, wondering what this unexpected sound might mean, and the ritual moment hung in suspense, charged with mystery.

A dozen or more hooded figures moved silently across the bridge on the creek side of the lake, their footsteps in eerie unison as they approached. The flickering firelight cast shadows over their cloaked forms, giving them an almost spectral appearance. They moved with purpose, each step measured and deliberate, as if drawn by an invisible force to the heart of our gathering. Conversations around the bonfire hushed, and the crowd parted slightly, an unspoken tension filling the air as we watched the mysterious procession make its way toward us.

"This isn't good," Prosperity whispered, her voice in a panic.

I glanced at her, "It's who I think it is, isn't it?"

"Yeah," she nodded, her eyes wide with a mixture of sincerity and drunken enthusiasm.

Several campers quickly gathered their children, glancing anxiously at the hooded figures and whispering urgent instructions as they began to back away from the unfolding scene. The hooded figures moved with calm precision, forming a line near the edge of the firelight, each one holding a lit torch that cast a warm but unsettling glow over their shrouded faces. The flickering flames reflected in their eyes, intensifying the sense of foreboding that hung thick in the air.

The drumbeats came to an abrupt halt, leaving a silence so profound it felt as though time itself had paused. For just a heartbeat, the stillness weighed heavily, stretching into an eternity. Then, faint gasps and whispers began to ripple through the crowd as people strained to make sense of what they were seeing.

At the far end of the line of hooded figures stood a woman, familiar to some of us yet now strangely altered. She was completely naked, her skin clean and free of the blood that had previously stained her. Her expression was blank, almost trance-like, as if she were unaware of the crowd or her own vulnerability. The tension thickened as she stood there, silent and unblinking, her gaze fixed on something.

That something was me.

Her flaming red hair flickered unnaturally, seeming to catch the torchlight and transform her head into a living flame. The light twisted around her, casting eerie shadows that made her silhouette seem to writhe like a specter. Her hair seemed almost too vibrant, too alive, as though it were a fire burning from within, flickering and crackling with a sinister energy. The flames from the torches seemed drawn to her, casting an unsettling glow that painted her skin with an unnatural hue, as though the darkness around her was coming to life, and then it hit me, the figure before us wasn't just some ritualistic participant.

Rakshasi moved with a slow, deliberate grace toward Priest, her flaming red hair catching the light of the torches as if it were alive. Her demeanor wasn't threatening—at least, not in the usual sense. There was an unsettling sensuality to her movements, a sort of predatory allure that sent a shiver crawling up my spine. It felt less like a gesture of submission and more like a calculated act of dominance disguised as reverence.

She knelt before Priest, her eyes locked onto his with an intensity that seemed to freeze the air around them. Slowly, she raised her arms, her palms open as if offering something unseen, something intangible yet heavy with meaning. The murmurs from the gathered crowd grew louder, a mix of confusion and unease rippling through the circle.

One of the hooded figures stepped forward, their movements precise and measured, as though rehearsed. They draped a deep crimson velvet cloak over Rakshasi's bare shoulders, the rich fabric pooling around her like blood against the earth. The moment felt ritualistic, almost sacred, yet tinged with an ominous air that made it impossible to look away.

Priest remained motionless, his expression unreadable, yet the tension between them was undeniable—an electric charge crackling in the air, ready to ignite at any moment. Finally, Priest extended his hands, grasping Rakshasi's with deliberate care. He pulled her gently to her feet, their movements slow and deliberate, as if every gesture carried profound meaning.

"Let the Ecstatic Festivities BEGIN!" Priest bellowed, his voice carrying across the gathering like a thunderclap.

The crowd erupted in cheers as fireworks suddenly burst into life, painting the night sky with brilliant colors. Fiery blossoms of red, gold, and violet illuminated the trees and the lake below, their reflections dancing on the rippling water. The explosions echoed like distant drums, blending with the crackling of the campfires and the murmur of excited voices.

Laughter and applause filled the air, and the atmosphere shifted from tense anticipation to joyful celebration in an instant. The vibrant display seemed to ignite the spirits of everyone present, uniting them under the dazzling spectacle above.

Rakshasi smiled gracefully, offering a slight bow accompanied by a delicate curtsy, her velvet cloak swaying gently with the movement. I let out a deep sigh of relief, the tension in my chest easing as it became clear that these people meant no harm. It dawned on me that all the theatrics—the hooded figures, the eerie silence, and even Rakshasi's unsettling entrance—were merely part of an elaborate act. A performance meant to heighten the mystique of the festival.

Prosperity and I continued to celebrate, each of us clutching goblets filled with the sweet, fruity Grim-Grog. The night buzzed with laughter and music, the air thick with the scent of roasted foods and burning wood. Out of the corner of my eye, I noticed Prosperity's grandmother, Angelina, tiptoeing toward us, a mischievous smirk playing on her lips.

"Y'all look like you could use a top-off," she teased, her voice slightly slurred but warm. Carefully, though not without a hint of clumsiness, she tilted her pitcher and poured more of her potent, nectar-like liquor into our goblets.

"Thank you, Angelina!" I said, trying to stifle a laugh as she gave us a conspiratorial wink before giggling and wandering off into the lively crowd. Her colorful shawl fluttered behind her, blending into the sea of dancing figures. Prosperity raised her goblet with a grin.

"To Angelina—our enabler," she joked, and we both laughed, clinking our glasses as the festival carried on around us.

We danced in the night like there was no tomorrow. We danced wildly, our movements uninhibited and carefree, twirling beneath the flickering glow of firelight. We drank deeply, feasting on foods that seemed to taste better with each bite. The music throbbed through the air, louder and more intoxicating as the hours wore on. The crowd thickened, their energy feeding into the electric atmosphere.

I felt weightless, almost untethered, as though the earth itself was spinning beneath my feet. My head swam, but I didn't feel ill—just euphoric. Fires flared high, their golden tongues licking at the dark sky, while shadows cast by the dancers seemed to join in, swaying and leaping alongside us. Prosperity doubled over with laughter at my attempts to keep up, my swaying and bobbing more comical than graceful.

"Here, drink this," Prosperity said, grinning as she handed me another goblet. This one was filled with a clear liquid that smelled faintly sweet but nothing like her grandmother's Grim-Grog.

"What is it?" I asked suspiciously, taking the goblet.

"You're a bit out there," she teased, mimicking my unsteady movements. "This should help you."

Trusting her, I took a big gulp, only to instantly spit it out, coughing and sputtering as the taste hit me.

"What is that?" I asked, my voice hoarse.

"Coconut water!" Prosperity said with a mischievous grin, shoving the goblet back toward me. "Come on, finish it—it's good for you!"

Reluctantly, I accepted the goblet again. Her insistence and the sparkle of humor in her eyes were hard to resist. I took another cautious sip, grimacing as the taste lingered on my tongue.

"Well," I muttered, "it's no Grim-Grog."

She laughed, linking her arm through mine. "Yeah, but at least you'll be able to walk straight in the morning."

We both giggled, and despite my protests, I drank the rest as the vibrant festival carried on around us. The night was alive with freedom, laughter, and the timeless rhythm of celebration. We eventually returned to my camp to collect ourselves and take a much-needed break.

MAY 29: MIDNIGHT-FIFTEEN

I didn't want to overexert myself and risk passing out, missing whatever else the night had in store. The festivities were far from over, and the air buzzed with anticipation. Back at camp, I settled into a quiet moment of reflection, pulling out my diary to jot down hurried notes about the evening's events. The swirling memories of dancing, laughter, and mysterious encounters demanded to be preserved, even if I could barely keep my thoughts straight. I promised myself I'd revisit these pages later to fully capture the surreal, enchanting chaos of the night.

Prosperity was still wide awake, her eyes sparkling with an energy that hadn't dimmed all night. She was fiddling with the hem of her sleeve, but it wasn't the nervous kind of fidgeting—it was the kind that came with bubbling excitement.

"You okay?" I asked, curious about the sudden shift in her demeanor.

She turned to me, her grin wide and almost mischievous. "I've got an idea," she said, practically bouncing in place.

"Oh no," I teased, narrowing my eyes. "What now?"

"You're gonna love it," she replied, her tone practically singing. She leaned in closer, her voice dropping to a conspiratorial whisper. "Let's go find Rakshasi and have her do a fortune reading for you."

I blinked, caught off guard. "Rakshasi? The naked fire lady?"

"She's not naked anymore!" Prosperity said, laughing. "And yeah! Think about it—she's mysterious, powerful, and clearly knows stuff. I bet she could tell you something incredible about your future. Wouldn't that be amazing?"

I hesitated, glancing toward the direction where Rakshasi had last been. "I don't know. What if she's just putting on a show for the festival?"

"Even if she is, so what? It's all part of the fun! Come on, Dawn," Prosperity urged, grabbing my hand and giving it a playful tug. "When else are you gonna get a chance like this?"

Her enthusiasm was infectious, and I couldn't help but smile despite my initial doubts. "Fine, but if she says something creepy, you're the one who has to explain to my parents why I'm up all night thinking about it."

"Deal!" she chirped, already pulling me toward the glowing firelight ahead.

We wandered through the camp, the warm glow of firelight and lanterns guiding our way as we searched for Rakshasi's tent. The lively sounds of laughter, music, and distant chatter filled the air, but each step seemed to stretch time, making our journey feel like it took forever.

Prosperity clutched my arm, her excitement palpable. "It's gotta be around here somewhere," she said, scanning the tents around us.

I wasn't exactly sure what we were looking for, perhaps something mysterious, marked with symbols or glowing with an eerie light, but every tent we passed looked completely ordinary. The anticipation, mixed with the lingering effects of the night's festivities, made my heart race with each wrong turn.

Prosperity stopped, pointing ahead. "There! That's gotta be it."

In the distance, a tent stood apart from the others, its fabric a deep, rich purple, almost black, with flickering candles casting strange, elongated shadows on its surface. The closer we got, the more an unusual aroma filled the air—something floral, but sharp, mingled with a faint trace of incense.

"Are you sure about this?" I asked, hesitating.

Prosperity grinned and tugged me forward. "Absolutely. Let's go meet your destiny."

Above the entrance to the tent was an etched runic symbol that immediately caught my eye, its sharp lines eerily familiar and brimming with an unsettling energy. It was the same marking I had seen carved into the weathered stone I stumbled upon while fishing with my father weeks ago. The sight of it here, glowing faintly in the firelight, filled me with an unsettling sense of déjà vu.

The tent itself seemed darker than its surroundings, as though it absorbed the light instead of reflecting it. The fabric appeared aged, with strange, almost organic patterns etched into its surface. A low hum seemed to emanate from within, barely audible but deeply disconcerting, like a whispered warning only I could hear.

I froze, my hand instinctively gripping Prosperity's arm. "Prosperity," I whispered, my voice trembling. "That symbol... I've seen it before."

She glanced at me, her excitement fading into unease. "You have? Where?"

I hesitated, swallowing hard. "On a stone I found while fishing with my dad. I thought it was just... nothing. But seeing it here..." My voice trailed off as a chill crept over me, making the hairs on the back of my neck stand on end.

"What do you think it means?" Prosperity asked, scratching her head in a slightly drunken daze.

"I haven't figured that out yet," I admitted, my eyes still fixed on the strange symbol above the tent.

The hum grew louder as we stood there. The tent felt almost alive, pulsating faintly, as though it were breathing and watching us, waiting for our next move.

"Do you think that's her humming inside?" Prosperity asked, her voice tinged with both curiosity and unease.

"I don't know," I replied, my gaze fixed on the mysterious tent.

"But it's rhythmic... almost hypnotic. There's something alluring about it, and yet..." My voice trailed off, the words caught in my throat as a shiver ran through me.

"Instead of standing out there, trying to unravel a mystery you know nothing about," a woman's voice called from beyond the tent's threshold, smooth and inviting, "why not come inside and join me?"

The words sent a shiver down my spine, not from fear but from the strange allure in her tone. Prosperity and I exchanged a quick glance, her wide eyes mirroring my own unease and curiosity.

A sudden gust of wind swept through from behind, forceful yet oddly deliberate, nudging us closer to the tent's entrance. Prosperity stumbled slightly, catching herself against my arm. As we stood frozen, torches lining the path extinguished one by one in a chilling, synchronized sequence.

Fwoosh... Fwoosh... Fwoosh. Each flame vanished, leaving only darkness in its wake until a single torch remained lit. Its flickering glow cast long, ominous shadows that seemed to stretch toward us like beckoning fingers.

The remaining light bathed the tent's entrance in a warm yet eerie glow, a stark contrast to the cold wind now biting at our backs. It felt less like an invitation and more like a summons—impossible to ignore. Prosperity clung to my sleeve, her earlier excitement now tempered with hesitation.

"This... this is it," she whispered, her voice trembling.

I nodded, swallowing hard. Rakshasi's domain.

"What time is it?" I asked, glancing nervously at Prosperity.

"Um..." She fumbled with a small pocket watch she retrieved from her jacket. "It's Midnight-fifteen."

"Uh, it's twelve fifteen?" I echoed in disbelief, my heart

skipping a beat. "We should get back to camp. I really need to write in my—"

"Don't even think about it, little one!" a low, sultry voice cut through the night from within the tent.

The words dripped with menace. They weren't shouted, yet they carried an unearthly weight, each syllable curling in the air like smoke and wrapping around my chest. Prosperity jumped, nearly dropping the watch, her eyes darting to the tent's entrance.

The torchlight flickered violently, casting Rakshasi's symbol above the tent in shadows that seemed to twist and writhe as if alive. The hum that had greeted us earlier grew louder, a haunting, pulsating vibration that felt as if it were coming from beneath the earth itself.

"Dawn..." Prosperity whispered, clutching my arm tightly. "Maybe this wasn't such a good idea."

We agreed to leave the tent behind and head back to camp. I took a few deep breaths to steady myself before turning away. But as we started walking, my steps faltered, and my breath caught in my throat. My lungs seemed to forget how to function as my eyes locked onto something ahead.

A figure lingered in the shadows, its pale, almost translucent skin glowing faintly in the dim light. At first glance, it resembled a deer, but something about it was disturbingly wrong. Its head was a bare skull, hollow-eyed and crowned with grotesquely twisted antlers, each curving in unnatural, chaotic angles. It stood upright, like a person, its bony hind legs supporting its skeletal frame. Its elongated arms hung low, swaying slightly, as if weighed down by an invisible burden.

It didn't move. It just watched.

The longer I stared at the creature, the tighter my chest felt, my breath trapped as though I had forgotten how to exhale. My entire body locked in place, frozen by an overwhelming sense of dread. It wasn't just fear—it was something deeper, something primal. The creature's empty eye sockets seemed to bore into my very soul, and though it made no sound, I felt its presence pressing down on me like a weight. It was as if the thing were speaking directly into my mind, its silent message chillingly clear: Don't move. Don't come closer. Or else.

The air around us grew heavier, oppressive, and the distant sounds of the campfire laughter and music faded into a muffled hum. Its pale, skeletal frame was barely concealed by what looked like shredded remnants of clothing—tattered fabric that seemed to belong to traditional Native American garb. Beads dangled from what was left of a torn sash across its chest, swaying with every subtle shift of its inhuman form. Feathers, filthy and bent, clung desperately to the rotting material as if they too had been corrupted by the creature's presence.

I could feel Prosperity trembling beside me, her hand gripping my arm tightly, but neither of us dared to speak or move. It was as if the slightest twitch would shatter the fragile thread of safety that kept the creature from advancing. Its jagged antlers, twisted and gnarled like the branches of a cursed tree, seemed to pulse faintly with an unnatural energy, amplifying the oppressive aura surrounding it.

The creature let out a guttural snarl, the sound reverberating through the stillness of the night, primal and menacing. Its jagged, skeletal jaw stretched unnaturally wide, exposing sharp, yellowed teeth that gleamed faintly in the moonlight. Its hollow eyes burned with an otherworldly intensity, locking onto us as if savoring our terror.

Suddenly, it raised one emaciated leg, the pale, taut skin clinging to the bone like paper stretched over a skeleton. With deliberate force, it stomped the ground, the impact sending a jarring vibration through the earth. Dust and pebbles scattered from the blow, the noise like a warning shot meant to rattle us further.

Its long, bony fingers, unnaturally sharp and grotesquely stretched, flexed and curled in a chilling rhythm. The claws at their tips gleamed as they scraped together, emitting a faint, nerve-wracking sound like nails on a chalkboard. The creature's gnarled hands hung low, swaying slightly, but their unnatural length made them seem almost predatory, as though they could snatch us from where we stood in a single lunge.

The creature leaned forward, its tattered Native American clothing swaying with the motion. Beads and feathers on its torn sash clattered faintly, a ghostly counterpoint to its otherwise ominous stillness. The sinewy arms extended toward the ground, the grotesque hands brushing the dirt as if testing its next move.

Then, it strutted a leg back, digging its claws deep into the soil with an ear-piercing scrape. The movement was deliberate and calculated, the stance of a predator preparing to strike. Its antlers, twisting at impossible angles, seemed to shimmer with life, casting distorted shadows that danced and leered like a hallucinatory nightmare.cIts snarl deepened, resonating with an almost telepathic menace, freezing me in place. Every muscle in my body screamed to move, but its hollow gaze and long, bony fingers seemed to grip my very soul, paralyzing me with the silent promise of unspeakable violence.

"Are you fucking stupid or something? Get over here!" a sharp voice cut through the air, snapping me out of my trance. I spun around to see Rakshasi standing at the entrance of her tent, her silhouette outlined by the eerie glow from within. She was waving at us urgently, her expression somewhere between fury and fear. "Get in here, now!" she barked.

Neither Prosperity nor I hesitated for a second. Panic had taken over, and her command was the only thing that made sense. Without a word, we bolted toward the tent, our footsteps pounding against the earth as if the sheer sound would somehow keep the monstrous being at bay.

I didn't stop to think about the absurdity of it all—why I believed that a simple tent, with its flimsy fabric walls, could possibly shield us from something that horrifying, that massive. My heart raced as we dove through the threshold, the strange humming within the tent abruptly silenced the second we crossed inside. The air inside was thick, suffused with an oppressive, almost otherworldly stillness. It felt as though we'd entered another dimension entirely.

Rakshasi quickly pulled the flap shut behind us, her hands moving with a precision that belied her apparent calm. "What the hell were you thinking, standing out there?" she hissed, her voice low but charged with urgency.

I looked at Prosperity, who was panting heavily, her face pale with terror. "What is that thing?" I managed to choke out, my voice trembling.

Rakshasi didn't answer right away. She peered through a slit in the tent's fabric, her face set in grim determination. "If it wanted you, you'd already be dead," she said finally, her tone cold. "But you've pissed it off, and that makes it dangerous. You're lucky it hasn't charged yet."

The tent felt suffocating, every shadow seemingly alive with menace. The distant sound of the creature's low growl reached us even here, a deep vibration that seemed to rattle the very air. I clutched Prosperity's arm, unable to shake the horrifying image of that monstrous form etched into my mind—its skeletal antlers, those impossibly long claws, the torn remnants of its clothing fluttering in the night.

"What do we do now?" I whispered, half-afraid of what her answer might be.

Rakshasi turned to me, her eyes gleaming with a mixture of intensity and something I couldn't quite place. "Now," she said, "we pray it loses interest—or we hope you're ready to fight for your lives."

"What?" I asked, my voice barely above a whisper.

Rakshasi's expression darkened as she met my gaze. "It would be a grave mistake to let yourself be killed by that... thing," she said, her tone grim, the weight of her words sinking into my chest like a stone.

Suddenly, the rhythmic pounding of Indian drums echoed from the other side of the tent, accompanied by haunting vocal chants. The sounds seemed deliberate, a powerful ritual in motion, as though the camp were collectively summoning courage to calm the beast—or ward it away from their fragile sanctuary. The air inside the tent vibrated with the primal energy of the chant, and for a moment, I dared to hope it might work.

"What is that… thing?" Prosperity asked, her voice trembling as she clung to my arm.

Rakshasi turned her piercing gaze toward Prosperity, her expression unreadable. "A shadow from ancient stories," she began, her voice low and steady. "A predator born of hunger, madness, and the cold emptiness of the wild. Some call it a guardian, others a curse. But most simply call it death."

The drums intensified, and the chants outside reached a haunting crescendo. Then, as if responding to the ritual, the heavy, oppressive presence began to fade. Rakshasi closed her eyes, tilting her head slightly as if listening to something only she could hear. After a moment, she opened them and said with a faint smirk.

"It's leaving." she said.

Prosperity exhaled sharply, her grip on my arm loosening as relief washed over her face. "Thank God," she whispered.

Outside, the sounds of the forest began to return—the rustling leaves, the chirping crickets. It was as though the world had been holding its breath and was now exhaling in unison.

Rakshasi stepped toward the entrance, pulling back the flap slightly to peek out. "The warding drums did their job tonight," she said, her voice calm but laced with an eerie certainty. "You're lucky they were prepared." She turned to us, her gaze sharp. "But luck only stretches so far. Next time, immediately run when you come face to face with a Wendigo."

"That was no Winnebago," Prosperity snarked, her words slurring slightly as she hiccuped.

"Is she... stupid?" Rakshasi whispered sharply, her eyebrows arching high in a mix of disbelief and seriousness. Her piercing gaze flicked to me, as if questioning my association with Prosperity.

I shrugged awkwardly, trying to defuse the moment. "She's... uh... had a lot to drink."

Rakshasi sighed, shaking her head. "Drunk or not, ignorance can get you killed." Her tone was cold, a stark reminder of the danger lurking beyond the thin walls of the tent.

"Everything is clear. We're safe. The drums warded it away," said Rakshasi, her voice steady but distant, as if her mind was already preparing for the next threat.

I tried to take comfort in her words, but unease clung to me like a shadow. My chest tightened as my thoughts spiraled—memories of the creature's skeletal form, its haunting stare, and the sheer malice radiating from its presence. My mind fluttered chaotically, juggling fear, confusion, and disbelief all at once.

"How can you be sure?" I finally asked, my voice trembling. "That thing... it looked like it wanted to tear us apart."

Rakshasi turned her gaze to me, her expression unreadable. "Because it follows rules. Rituals. These things are old, bound by customs even darker than themselves. The drums hold power, but the safety they bring is temporary. It will wander elsewhere—for now."

Her words didn't soothe me. The idea that the creature wasn't gone, just redirected, only made my unease grow. I glanced at Prosperity, who still seemed dazed, the weight of what we'd just escaped not fully registering on her drunken face. I couldn't shake the feeling that the night wasn't over—not truly.

"So, little one," Rakshasi said, her voice curling like smoke around her words. She stepped closer, her dark eyes piercing through me. "You're familiar with the rune just outside my tent, aren't you?"

I froze, the weight of her question pressing down on me like a heavy stone. My mind raced back to the fishing trip with my father, to the smooth, cold stone etched with the same cryptic markings.

"How... how do you know that?" I asked, my voice unsteady.

Rakshasi's lips curved into a knowing smirk, but her eyes remained serious. "Because it's not a coincidence you found it. That rune is ancient—older than this land, older than your fears. And yet, it found its way to you."

Prosperity blinked and looked at me, her drunken haze fading slightly. "Wait... you didn't tell me about this," she muttered.

"I didn't think it mattered," I admitted, my stomach twisting with regret. "It was just a rock."

Rakshasi let out a low, humorless chuckle. "A rock?" she repeated, her tone mocking but not unkind. "That 'rock' carries more power than you can imagine. It marks you now. Whether you meant it to or not, you've become part of its story."

Her words sent a chill through me. I swallowed hard, suddenly feeling exposed, like the air itself had turned against me. "What does it mean?"

Rakshasi tilted her head, the firelight casting eerie shadows across her face. "That," she said, her voice dropping to a whisper, "is for you to discover. But I'll warn you—such knowledge comes at a price."

"Oh, here we go!" Prosperity shouted, her voice loud enough to make me cringe.

I glanced over at her, a mix of annoyance and embarrassment bubbling up inside me. She was sitting beside an exotic plant with thick waxy leaves that glistened strangely under the flickering light.

"Prosperity," I hissed, my cheeks flushing. I had a sinking feeling she was about to say something wildly inappropriate, again.

"We pay this demon money just so she can tell us some random bullshit!" Prosperity declared, her words slurred and punctuated with another hiccup.

Before I could respond, Prosperity suddenly swayed, her eyes fluttering shut. Without warning, she toppled over onto the floor, landing with a dull thud. Her snores followed almost immediately, deep and unbothered, like she had just slipped into the most peaceful slumber of her life.

Rakshasi raised an eyebrow, her expression unreadable. "She's drunk," I mumbled awkwardly.

Rakshasi smirked but pointed a long, bony finger at the plant Prosperity had been leaning against. "Drunk, yes," she said. "But the plant helped. It's a rare specimen. Its spores are known to calm the most restless of minds and shut the loudest of mouths."

My stomach twisted as I stared at the plant. Its leaves shimmered faintly, and tiny, golden particles seemed to drift lazily from its blooms, hanging in the air like fireflies.

"Is she going to be okay?" I asked, nudging Prosperity with my foot. She let out another snore in response.

"She'll wake," Rakshasi replied nonchalantly. "Eventually." Her smirk widened. "Now, shall we focus on you, little one?"

Rakshasi sat gracefully in a high-backed chair on one side of a round table draped in deep purple velvet, its edges embroidered with intricate golden runes. She extended an open palm, her fingers long and elegant, gesturing for me to take the seat directly across from her. Her eyes, sharp and penetrating, seemed to assess every part of my being, leaving no room for hesitation.

The table was adorned with an array of mysterious items. Three unlit candles, arranged in a perfect triangle, surrounded a crystal ball that shimmered faintly, casting subtle rainbows across the dark fabric. Surrounding the setup were scattered tarot cards, a few small vials filled with liquids that glinted in the candlelight, and a delicate silver dish holding dried herbs, releasing a faint, earthy aroma. As I settled into the chair, Rakshasi raised her hand, her movements fluid and deliberate. Hovering her palm just above the wicks, she made a slow, sweeping gesture. Without warning, the candles flared to life, their flames dancing as though summoned by an unseen force. Warmth from the sudden ignition brushed against my skin, and the faint scent of beeswax mingled with the herbal aroma.

The crystal ball now glowed with a soft inner light, its swirling depths reflecting the flickering flames. Shadows danced across Rakshasi's face, accentuating her otherworldly features. She leaned forward slightly, her voice low but filled with an unsettling authority.

"Now," she said, her voice low and smooth, "we can truly begin."

As I glanced around the tent, I realized just how much I had overlooked when I first entered, caught up in the adrenaline and tension of the moment. Now that things had settled, the interior struck me as unexpectedly expansive, far larger than it appeared from the outside.

The space was meticulously organized, giving it a sense of purpose and mystery. A sturdy wooden dresser stood against one side of the tent, its surface adorned with small trinkets and a polished brass mirror. Nearby, a small wood-burning stove emitted a faint warmth, its black pipe curving upward and vanishing through the tent's ceiling. Next to it, a cabinet with intricately carved designs housed neatly stacked dishes and jars, its top serving as a makeshift counter with a well-used cutting board resting on it. A bed, large enough to comfortably fit two, was tucked into one corner, covered with layers of rich fabrics and furs that seemed to shimmer in the candlelight. At its foot, a heavy trunk with iron clasps hinted at secrets or treasures hidden within. The round table where we sat was surprisingly spacious, capable of seating four or more comfortably, yet it bore the intimate, charged atmosphere of a place meant for deeper connections and revelations.

I couldn't shake the feeling of unease mingled with awe as I took it all in. There was something unsettling about the space itself as though it shouldn't exist within the modest confines of the tent I had seen from the outside. The air felt thicker here, charged with an invisible energy that made every object seem significant, every shadow alive with possibilities.

Who is this woman? I wondered, my mind racing. And why does this tent seem impossibly large inside, as though it exists outside the boundaries of normal space? My gaze flickered back to Rakshasi, and a shiver ran through me. There was much more to her, and this place, than met the eye.

"Here, drink this," Rakshasi said, extending a steaming cup of tea toward me. Her voice was calm, yet her eyes sparkled with an unreadable glint. "Don't worry, it's not poison—or anything that will harm you."

"Thank you," I replied, hesitating for a moment before accepting the cup. The aroma was earthy and slightly sweet, calming in a way that felt almost unnatural.

The conversation that followed was as intriguing as it was bewildering. Rakshasi delved into the connections between the rune I found and the symbols adorning her tent. She spoke of ancient energies, forgotten traditions, and the thin veil separating our world from others. Her words hinted at a deeper, more mysterious truth that danced just beyond my comprehension.

Although I struggled to grasp the full meaning of what she shared, I tried to absorb as much as I could. The way she spoke, measured and deliberate, made it feel like every word held significance, as if the very air around her vibrated with the weight of her knowledge.

It was late, too late. My body grew heavy with exhaustion, and the pull of sleep was becoming impossible to ignore. "Thank you for sharing all of this," I said, suppressing a yawn. "I think I need to head back to camp and rest now."

Rakshasi nodded, her gaze intense yet serene. "Rest while you can, little one," she said softly. "You'll need your strength for what lies ahead. The rune you found signifies the dawn of a new beginning, one that will test you in ways you cannot yet fathom. There will be great deeds for you to conjure. But remember, all things in this world are bound by the flow of time, and nothing can halt its course. However," she paused, her eyes narrowing as if peering into a distant reality, "in another time, the flow can be bent, even altered."

I tried to piece together her cryptic words and their meaning, but it felt like grasping at smoke. Nothing she said made sense to me, yet the weight of her tone made it impossible to dismiss.

"Thank you again for your hospitality," I said, attempting to shake off the growing unease. I gently nudged Prosperity awake. She groaned and leaned heavily against me as we began to make our way out of the tent.

The cool night air hit us as we stepped outside, but before we could fully depart, Rakshasi's voice called out one final warning, each word carrying a chilling weight.

"See yourself from the other side, and know it may not be by your own bidding," she said, in an ominous voice. "But remember this, death can be a guide, one that helps you save those who need it the most."

I turned back, but there was nothing. The tent had vanished, leaving no trace it had ever been there. The clearing was empty, save for the faint outline of trampled grass where we had stood moments ago. A chill ran down my spine once more as the realization sank in. The only sound breaking the heavy silence was the chirping of crickets, their rhythmic song almost mocking the strange encounter. I glanced at Prosperity, who was too groggy to notice the tent's disappearance, and instinctively tightened my grip on her arm.

Had we really been there? Or was it all some strange illusion? The night suddenly felt darker, heavier, as we trudged back toward camp in eerie silence.

What the hell was in that tea?

MAY 29

A loud crackling roar of thunder jolted me awake, echoing through the stillness of the early morning. My heart pounded in my chest, and beads of sweat clung to my forehead—a lingering effect of the strange nightmare I had just endured. I lay still for a moment, listening. Despite the ominous thunder, the rain hadn't started yet, and the air outside the tent felt eerily still.

Shaking off the remnants of sleep, I quickly dressed and reached for the eye pendant Angelina had given me, its smooth surface oddly comforting in my palm. The memory of her words flashed in my mind: "This will protect you when you need it most."

Stepping out of the tent, I stretched, feeling the cool air prickle my skin. The campsite was silent except for the faint rustling of leaves. I rummaged through my supplies and prepared a simple breakfast, though the unease from the dream dulled my appetite.

As I gazed upward, the sky seemed clear, an expanse of pale blue unmarred by storm clouds. Yet, the thunder came again, splitting the air with a deafening crash. The sound was so intense it felt as if the earth itself trembled in response.

Suddenly, a cacophony erupted as hundreds of birds burst from the surrounding trees, their wings flapping frantically. They formed a dark, chaotic swarm against the sky, fleeing toward the lake as if escaping an unseen predator. Something felt wrong, though I couldn't place what.

The pendant in my hand seemed warmer now, almost alive. My fingers tightened around it as I scanned the horizon, trying to push aside the growing sense of dread that settled in my chest. Something was coming. I could feel it.

"There's no time to eat right now, Dawn," Mother said, her tone brisk but carrying a flicker of unease. She and Father had already dismantled their tent, rolling it up in hurried silence.

I grabbed a granola bar for the time being.

Next, they turned their attention to my tent, their movements quick and urgent. Mother yanked the stakes from the ground, her hands working faster than I'd ever seen. Father swiftly unfastened the poles, collapsing the frame with a practiced ease that barely masked his growing anxiety. Within moments, they had torn it down, rolled it tightly, and tossed it into the back of the truck with the rest of our belongings.

The metallic clatter of poles and the shuffle of canvas rang out unnaturally loud in the thick, expectant silence. It wasn't just the sound that felt off, it was the air itself. Heavy, charged, almost alive. Each breath I took seemed to carry the weight of something unseen pressing down around us.

From somewhere beyond the trees came that rumble again, deep and resonant. It wasn't thunder. It didn't fade like a storm rolling away; instead, it seemed to vibrate through the earth, growing closer, stronger, as if the source of the sound was alive and moving.

Mother's eyes darted toward the horizon, her lips pressed into a thin line. She secured the tailgate, her fingers trembling as she latched it shut. "Everything's packed. Let's go, now," she said, her voice firm but tinged with an unmistakable edge of fear.

Father climbed into the truck, glancing at me over his shoulder. "We don't have time to figure out what this is. Whatever it is, we don't want to be here when it shows itself," he said, his tone low and clipped.

Prosperity and her grandmother pulled up to our campsite in her grandmother's green Chrysler, the ash wood trim catching the faint light of the overcast sky. The car's low rumble blended briefly with the strange, distant sound that seemed to pulse from the mountain.

Prosperity stepped out, her face pale but determined. "I had to stop by before you left," she said, holding out a folded piece of paper. " This is my address. Write to me, okay?"

I nodded, taking the note with trembling fingers. "Of course. Thanks for coming, but… why do you look so worried?"

Her grandmother stayed by the car, her eyes fixed on the horizon. Prosperity stepped closer, her voice dropped to a hushed tone.

"Have you heard what people are saying? About the mountain?"

"What about it?" I asked, though the heavy air and the strange sounds made her question hit harder than I wanted to admit.

"A psychic named Harland, he's well-known around here. He told some campers last week that the mountain is sick, like it's dying or something. Nobody really believed him, of course. He said there'd be signs." Prosperity explained.

"Signs? Like what?" I asked.

Prosperity glanced back at her grandmother, then lowered her voice even more. "The first crackling sound came from the mountain. Harland said that would happen, saying it would mean something's wrong deep in the earth. Now people are starting to think he might've been right."

I swallowed hard, the weight of her words settling in my chest. "But what does it even mean for a mountain to be sick?"

Prosperity shook her head, her expression grim. "I don't know. But whatever it is, it's not good apparently. You need to be careful, Dawn. Promise me you'll be careful."

Before I could respond, her grandmother called out. "Prosperity, we need to go." Her voice was firm but carried a nervous edge, her gaze never leaving the distant peaks.

Prosperity gave me a quick, tight hug. "Don't forget to write," she whispered, then hurried back to the car.

I stood frozen as the green Chrysler pulled away. The rumble from the mountain seemed louder now, its unnatural tone echoing through the still air. Prosperity's words lingered, filling me with an unease I couldn't shake.

I felt a twinge of sadness about our sudden departure, a bittersweet ache that lingered as I watched the camp fade into the distance. Something about Prosperity's goodbye felt unfinished, though I couldn't quite place why.

Sitting in the cab of the truck, I unfolded the small, creased note she had pressed into my hand. The neat handwriting made me pause for a moment before reading: My real name is Angela Rothermund.

I stared at the words, letting them sink in, as if they held some secret significance. Beneath her name was her mailing address, carefully written in the same deliberate script.

A faint smile tugged at my lips. Even though the air around me was heavy with the strange tension of the mountain, this simple gesture reminded me that some connections, no matter how brief, had a way of lingering.

As we drove past a familiar campsite, I noticed Rakshasi standing outside her tent. The sight of her jolted me; I vividly remembered her tent vanishing into the night—one moment it was there, the next, it was gone without a trace. Yet here she was, standing still, her figure framed by the dim light of morning. She held a steaming cup in her hands, as if nothing was out of the ordinary.

Her gaze met mine as we drove by, unblinking, the same eerie calmness in her eyes that I had seen the night before. She took a long, deliberate sip from her green cup, never breaking eye contact.

My mind raced, trying to piece together the inexplicable events. How could she be standing there? How was it possible for her tent to simply disappear without a sign of disturbance? The chill in the air seemed to grow heavier, as if the very atmosphere was waiting for me to make sense of it all.

The truck rumbled forward, but I couldn't shake the feeling that Rakshasi knew something I didn't. That she was watching me, perhaps even waiting for me to ask the right questions. Her silence was more unsettling than any answer could have been.

The campsite was mostly empty now, with only a few others choosing to stay behind. Some of them, I guessed, either didn't believe Harland's warning or hadn't heard it at all. Despite the eerie stillness in the air, the remaining campers carried on as if it were any other day.

Children ran and played, their laughter cutting through the otherwise quiet atmosphere. Families tended to their routines—grilling over smoky barbecues, hanging clothes on lines that swayed gently in the faint breeze. It almost looked normal, but there was an undercurrent of tension I couldn't ignore.

I wondered if they felt it too, the heaviness that seemed to come from the mountain itself. Or maybe they simply chose to pretend nothing was wrong.

As we drove past the campsite, I couldn't stop watching the families who had stayed behind. One little girl caught my eye—she stood perfectly still, clutching a worn teddy bear tightly to her chest, her gaze fixed on the mountain. For a brief moment, she reminded me of myself when I was younger, holding my own teddy bear just as protectively. She wasn't laughing or playing like the others. She just stared, unblinking, as if listening to something no one else could hear.

"Dawn?" Mother's voice broke my focus. "You're quiet."

I shook my head. "It's nothing."

But it wasn't nothing. Something about that girl's expression sent a chill through me. I turned to look out the back window, but by then, she was gone.

We had driven a couple of miles from the camp when the

deafening sound hit; a thunderclap so sharp and explosive that it felt as though the very air had fractured.

The truck jolted, and Father cursed, his hands gripping the wheel tighter. "What the hell was that?"

"I thought it was thunder," Mother murmured, her voice trembling, "but the sky is clear."

The sound wasn't coming from above; it was coming from the mountain.

The truck vibrated beneath us, as if the shockwave from the sound had rolled through the ground. Father slowed the vehicle, his eyes darting to the rearview mirror.

"Damn it," he muttered, "what now?"

He pulled the truck to the side of the road and killed the engine. The sudden silence was almost worse than the sound.

"That wasn't normal," Mother whispered, her hand hovering near the door handle.

"No kidding," Father replied, stepping out to check the truck.

I stayed inside, my ears still ringing. That's when I noticed it. My gaze shifted toward the mountain's peak in the distance, then froze. I knew something was wrong.

I couldn't make sense of what I was seeing at first, but the longer I stared, the more the truth settled over me like a weight. The sharp, jagged peak I remembered from our arrival was… different. Blunted.

No, not blunted. Gone.

It was as if someone had taken a great hand and scooped away a massive portion of the mountain, leaving behind jagged edges and an emptiness that defied logic. Dust lingered in the air, caught in the golden light of morning, and the space where the peak should have been felt like a wound on the landscape.

Mother gasped, her hand clutching my arm. "Dawn… do you see that?"

"I see it," I whispered, my voice barely audible over the lingering ring in my ears.

But I didn't understand it. Not yet.

*** * * ***

We drove further toward the nearest town, the truck's tires humming along the empty highway. I fiddled with the radio dial, trying to get any kind of signal, desperate for answers, but all I could hear was static. The silence inside the truck was deafening, each of us lost in our own thoughts, unwilling to break the uneasy quiet. We kept driving and didn't look back.

A half hour later, we reached a small, weathered restaurant. Father turned onto the off-ramp without a word, his face set in a hard, unreadable expression.

We parked in front of the diner, which, despite the hour, had several other vehicles scattered across the lot. The flickering neon sign above the door buzzed intermittently, casting an eerie glow over the scene. It wasn't much, but at that moment, it felt like a small island of normalcy in an ocean of confusion.

"We'll get something to eat, figure out what's going on," Father said, his voice gruff. But I could tell he wasn't sure himself, like he was trying to convince us as much as he was convincing himself.

The place was busier than I expected. Several people stood near the entrance, waiting to be seated, their voices low but filled with frustration. The air was thick with the smell of sizzling bacon and freshly brewed coffee, a welcome contrast to the unease still lingering from our drive. Mother approached the host and gave our name, and we were soon led to a table that could seat four, positioned near the window.

As I settled into the chair, I noticed the soft hum of a radio playing in the background, the faint sound of a local news report mixed with a lively jingle. It was 9:35 a.m., but it felt like much later. The morning's events still clung to me, leaving my mind restless and my stomach uneasy, though hunger began to push through.

I remembered the granola bar I had grabbed before leaving the camp. I unwrapped it, the sound of the crinkling packaging filling the quiet around us. Just as I was about to take a bite, I noticed a little boy sitting across from us at a neighboring table, his eyes locked on me.

Without thinking, I held out the granola bar to him. "Do you want a bite?" The boy paused, then shook his head.

"Smart kid," I said with a light smile, almost automatically. "Never take anything from a stranger."

The boy gave me a small nod of agreement, but he didn't smile back. Instead, he focused on his plate, eating slowly.

I was about to take my first bite when I noticed his mother, sitting across from him. She was watching us with an odd, calculating look, her eyes sharp but distant, as if weighing something in her mind. A chill ran through me, though I couldn't say why. The moment lingered uncomfortably, but I shook it off, returning my attention to the granola bar. There were more pressing things to think about.

"This just in..." a voice crackled from the radio. "And what appears is..." The broadcast fizzled, the signal weak, only managing to get a few fragmented words out. "Lights filled the skies late last night while most people slept... One witness said... he and..."

The radio cut out again, the static swallowing the rest of the sentence. It was frustrating, but the noise in the restaurant made it even harder to make out what was being said. Dishes clattered, conversations blended into a dull hum, and the sporadic bursts of the reporter's voice only added to the confusion. I leaned in closer, straining to catch something more, but all I could hear was the low buzz of static between the words.

"There were three strange lights," a man reported, his voice crackling through the radio. "They were just flying over the trees."

"More like hovering, if you ask me," a woman's voice interrupted, sounding somewhat agitated. "My husband, Harold, here saw them up close. He said they were hovering right above the treetops, not moving, just... staring down at us."

"What do you think the lights were, exactly?" asked the news anchorman, his voice steady but edged with curiosity.

"Well, Harold here says they weren't anything natural," the woman interjected firmly, her tone carrying both certainty and unease. "He swears they moved like nothing he's ever seen before—silent, smooth, and... deliberate. Almost like they were watching us."

"Watching?" the anchorman echoed, his interest clearly piqued. "You mean observing people?"

"That's right," she replied, her voice dropping slightly as though afraid to say more. "And when they were gone, it was like the whole forest went quiet. No animals, no wind... just an awful stillness. Harold says it didn't feel right."

"Do you have anything you'd like to add, Harold?" the anchorman asked, his tone steady but probing.

Harold cleared his throat before speaking, his voice crackling faintly through the radio. "This wasn't the first time those lights have been seen in these mountains," he said, pausing as though choosing his words carefully. "It's the second time in just a few nights."

He hesitated for a moment before continuing. "UFOs. That's what they were—no doubt about it. They didn't fly off like you'd expect, though. They went into the mountains." His voice lowered slightly, filled with unease. "At least, I think they did. And you know what else? The mountain—"

The radio crackled loudly, cutting out part of Harold's response.

His voice came back in fragments, tinged with static. "...was dying. That's why it…" The rest of his words dissolved into unintelligible static.

The anchorman's voice broke through the silence, strained and uncertain. "Harold, what do you mean, the mountain was dying?" But no response came, only the hollow buzz of the static-filled broadcast.

Our waitress approached the table, a weary smile on her face. "I just wanted to let you know," she began, addressing my parents, "it may take a little longer for your food to arrive. We've had a sudden rush, but I promise it'll be hot and fresh when it comes out."

My father nodded, his expression calm. "Take your time," he said, reaching into his coat pocket to pull out his tobacco pipe. "As long as I can enjoy this while we wait, I've got no complaints."

Mother rolled her eyes but didn't comment, and for the moment, we were satisfied to wait.

A sudden commotion near the entrance drew my attention. The low murmur of the restaurant was interrupted by a small tussle. People shifted and stumbled as a young woman pushed her way through the crowd near the door. She wasn't just moving—she was weaving, almost dancing, her movements sharp yet fluid, like she was caught between trying to escape and trying not to draw attention to herself.

Her arms flailed slightly, and she spun to avoid bumping into a man holding a coffee cup, nearly knocking it out of his hand. She muttered a hurried apology but didn't stop. The look on her face was a mix of urgency and discomfort, her eyes darting toward the door as if she couldn't bear to stay a second longer. She hustled and darted towards me in excitement.

"Oh, thank GOD you're alive!" cried Prosperity—Angela Rothermund—her voice trembling with a mix of relief.

Her eyes shimmered with unshed tears as she reached out, her hands gripping my arms like she needed to confirm I was real. Whatever she had been through, it was clear it had shaken her deeply. Her breath hitched as if she had more to say but couldn't find the words.

"Of course I'm fine!" I chuckled nervously, trying to lighten the mood. "I'm happy to see you too. But... What's going on? I recognize several of these people—they were at the camp and the festival."

"We heard what happened, and I was so worried about you and your family—especially the other families who stayed behind," cried Prosperity, tears streaming down her cheeks.

"Heard what happened?" Father asked, puffing heavily on his pipe, his brow furrowing in concern.

"How could you not have heard?" a woman's voice called from behind Prosperity, sharp with disbelief.

I turned to see Angelina stepping into view. She gestured toward a television mounted in the corner of the restaurant, where a news broadcast flickered faintly above the noise of the room.

"It's all over the news," she said, her voice lowering slightly as if the weight of her words needed no embellishment. "Everyone's talking about it."

Mother stood up from her seat and wrapped Angelina in a tight hug. For a moment, they both stood there, holding on as if the world outside had stopped spinning. The warm embrace spoke volumes, no words needed to express the relief and concern they both shared.

The table was large enough to fit all five of us, with an extra chair pulled in to complete the circle. We sat down, the weight of the situation settling in as we all took our places. Once we were seated, the conversation began. As we started piecing together what had happened. Each of us had witnessed different fragments, but none of it made sense. Still, we tried to make sense of it together.

"So, what exactly happened?" Father asked calmly, his voice steady despite the tension in the air. He smudged out the burning tobacco from his pipe, using the back of a butter knife as a makeshift tool, his movements slow and deliberate. The action was strangely methodical, as though the routine brought him a sense of control in an otherwise chaotic moment.

"We left the campgrounds after saying our farewells to you all," Angelina began, her voice trembling as she spoke. "We drove eastward toward the Badlands, thinking we'd made it out safely." She paused, glancing toward Prosperity, who sat silently, her hands twisting nervously in her lap.

"We decided to take an alternate route to Keystone," she continued, her voice thick with emotion, "hoping for a better view of the mountain. Prosperity wanted to snap a photo of the peak, the one where someone claimed to have seen those mysterious lights."

"I think I heard something about that on the radio earlier," I interjected, my own voice uncertain. I wasn't entirely sure if what I'd heard matched what Angelina was describing, but the pieces felt like they were starting to connect.

Angelina drew a shaky breath and pressed on. "She had just climbed back into the car, and then it happened. There was this thunderclap—so loud it made my heart stop. It echoed across the sky, and then..." Her voice cracked, and she hesitated, gathering herself.

"That's when the mountain collapsed," she said, her words dropping like stones into the growing silence at the table.

Her hands clenched together as she continued, the horror of the memory written all over her face. "The peak, God help us, it just shattered. Before we even understood what was happening, the entire side of the mountain came down in a massive landslide. It wiped out everything. The campgrounds, the trees, the road, everything we'd just left behind was buried under tons of rock and debris."

A heavy silence fell over the table as the gravity of her words sank in. I could feel the tension in the air, a shared understanding of how narrowly we had escaped disaster. Angelina's voice wavered as she added, "We were so close. If we hadn't left when we did…" She didn't finish the thought, but the unspoken reality hung heavily over us all.

"What do we do now?" Father asked, his voice low and heavy, as if the weight of the question was too much to bear.

"Sadly, there's nothing we can do," Mother said, her voice breaking as tears welled up in her eyes. She clasped her hands together, trembling. "All we can do is pray… pray for those who stayed behind."

Her words hung in the air, each one a stark reminder of the helplessness we all felt. Father's gaze dropped to the table, and the only sound that followed was the faint hum of the restaurant's conversations and the occasional crackle of the distant radio.

Prosperity assured us that she had been listening to the radio. "Firefighters, police, and paramedics have been dispatched to the site," she said, her voice steady but carrying a hint of unease.

"They're doing everything they can," she added, glancing between us. "But it sounds like the area is so unstable that they're being cautious with their approach. The debris is making it hard to reach the campground quickly."

Her words painted a grim picture, and I could see the worry etched on her face. The thought of those left behind weighed heavily on all of us, an unspoken fear lingering in the air.

As the conversation at the table settled, Prosperity turned to me, her brows knitted in concern. "Dawn," she began hesitantly, "you said something earlier about Rakshasi… when did you see her?"

I swallowed, the memory of that strange moment flashing vividly in my mind. "It was right before we left the campground," I said, my voice quiet but steady. "We were driving past the other campsites, and I saw her standing outside her tent."

"Outside her tent?" Prosperity echoed, her tone shifting to disbelief. "Dawn, are you sure?"

I nodded firmly. "Yes. She was holding a steaming cup, just standing there... watching us as we drove by." My voice faltered, and I added, "It was strange, though. Her tent was gone the night before, vanished into thin air. I was half-convinced it was some kind of trick of the light or something, but then, there she was. Clear as day."

Prosperity leaned in, her expression intense. "But... you said the tent was gone? And then you saw her again after that?"

"Yes." I hesitated, unsure how to explain it. "It felt... off. Like she shouldn't have been there. The way she was just standing there, staring—it was almost like she knew something was about to happen."

Prosperity sat back, her hand over her mouth. "Dawn, that's... unsettling." She glanced at Angela, who was listening intently. "Do you think it could mean something? Maybe Rakshasi knew about the lights—or the mountain?"

I shook my head slowly, feeling a chill creep over me. "I don't know. But now, thinking about it, I can't shake the feeling that there was something more to her presence. Something we missed."

Angelina interjected softly, her voice thoughtful. "Rakshasi has always been... different. People at the festival spoke about her, said she had a connection to the land, some even called her a seer. Maybe she sensed the mountain's instability or... something beyond that."

Prosperity's eyes widened. "A seer?" she whispered. "Do you think she tried to warn us?"

The question hung in the air, unanswered, as we each became

lost in our own thoughts, the mystery surrounding Rakshasi deepening.

I felt a knot tighten in the pit of my stomach.

"What about the others who stayed behind? Or... those who were just preparing to leave?" I asked hesitantly, though the moment the words left my mouth, I wished I could take them back. Deep down, I already knew the answer, and the weight of it was unbearable.

Angelina's expression grew somber, her shoulders sinking as if the burden of the truth was too much to carry. "Some made it out just in time," she said, her voice laced with quiet sorrow. "But according to the news, everyone was caught in the direct path of the landslide..." She paused, swallowing hard before continuing. "They're gone."

Angelina took a deep breath, exhaling slowly as though bracing herself to say more. "It's estimated that two hundred seventeen campers hadn't checked out of the grounds before the collapse. Rescue teams are out there now, searching through the debris, but it doesn't look hopeful."

Her words hung in the air, heavy and suffocating. My mind raced, conjuring images of the bustling campground from just hours before—families laughing, children running, the smell of food cooking over open flames. Now, all of that was buried under tons of earth and rock.

I clenched my hands together tightly, trying to steady myself. "Are they... are they sure?" I whispered, not wanting to believe it. "That no one else could have survived?"

"They're doing everything they can," Angelina replied, her voice wavering. "But from what they've said on the news, the landslide's force was... catastrophic. If anyone is still alive under there, it'll be a miracle."

Prosperity reached out and placed a hand on my arm, her touch grounding me as my thoughts spiraled. "We just have to hope," she said softly. "Hope that some of them found a way out... somehow."

"Those stupid, ignorant sons-of-bitches thought their God would protect them," Angelina snapped, slamming her palm against the table with a sharp thud.

Realizing her outburst, she took a shaky breath and softened her tone. "Sorry," she muttered, glancing down at her hands. "It's just... it really pisses me off that someone could be so naïve, so blindly stubborn. They had warnings, and they still stayed."

Her hands trembled slightly as she folded them together, her emotions teetering between anger and sorrow. It wasn't just about being upset; it was the gut-wrenching grief of knowing that avoidable tragedies had claimed innocent lives.

"Oh good, our food's here!" Prosperity exclaimed, her face lighting up with a mix of relief and excitement. She leaned back slightly in her chair as the server approached, balancing a tray laden with steaming plates.

The aroma of freshly cooked meals wafted over the table—eggs scrambled to perfection, golden hash browns crisp on the edges, and buttery toast glistening under the restaurant's fluorescent lights. The clinking of plates and silverware filled the brief lull in conversation as the server carefully placed each dish before us.

Prosperity immediately reached for her fork, her earlier tension momentarily replaced by the promise of a warm meal. "This looks amazing," she said, taking a deep breath to savor the smell. "It's been a long morning."

Her words, though casual, carried an undertone that reminded us of everything we'd just discussed. Still, for a moment, the food provided a welcome distraction—a brief reprieve from the weight of the day.

THE JEWEL

After finishing breakfast at the bustling diner, my parents and I stood to say our goodbyes to Prosperity and her grandmother. Hugs were exchanged, and with promises to stay in touch, my mother added a heartfelt "Safe travels" to them before we parted ways. The weight of everything we had just discussed lingered as we stepped back into the truck.

Prosperity and I promised to write and stay in contact. She gripped my hands tightly as she spoke, her voice soft but steady. "You're the first real friend I've made in a long time," she admitted, her gaze dropping for a moment. "Since my father died, I haven't really… been very sociable."

The vulnerability in her tone made my chest ache. I wanted to say something to comfort her, but words didn't come easily. "I'm sorry," I finally managed, feeling the weight of her loss.

She smiled faintly, brushing a loose strand of hair from her face. "It's okay. He would've liked you, I think. He was always telling me to find friends who actually understood me."

I nodded, understanding more than I could say. "Well, you've got me now," I replied, giving her hand a reassuring squeeze.

As we hugged goodbye, I promised to write to her often, to share everything I could about my strange little world. She laughed softly, but there was hope in her eyes now—a spark of something that had been missing before.

"I'll write you back, too," she said. "Even if my letters aren't much more than doodles or bad poetry, you'll still get them."

"I'll treasure every one," I replied, grinning.

As she walked back to her grandmother's car, I felt a strange sense of calm. Despite everything we'd been through in the last few hours, it was comforting to know I wasn't alone. We waved goodbye as they drove away. I missed them already.

Father packed his pipe with a fresh pinch of tobacco, tamping it down with his thumb before striking a match. He lit the bowl, puffed a few times until the tobacco caught, and exhaled a thick plume of smoke. With a nod in our direction, he said, "You ladies behave now, and don't take too long."

Mother and I stepped into the small convenience store nearby, the bell above the door jingling faintly as we entered. The place was cozy, with worn wooden shelves stocked with an assortment of snacks, toiletries, and travel goods. A faint scent of coffee and newspaper lingered in the air.

We wandered the aisles, gathering what we needed for the long drive ahead—water, crackers, and a few indulgences like chocolate bars. Father wasn't one for unnecessary stops along the way; he prided himself on efficient travel, moving from point A to point B with minimal interruptions.

Mother added a folded paper map of the region to the basket, just in case we found ourselves on an unfamiliar road. "Anything else?" she asked, glancing toward me.

I held up a small bag of gummy bears. "Just this," I said with a smile.

She chuckled and added it into the basket. "You and your sweet tooth."

At the counter, Mother handed the items to the clerk, who packed them carefully into a brown paper bag. The clerk, a gray-haired man with kind eyes, mentioned something about an unusual number of travelers passing through lately. He wished us safe travels as we left, his voice tinged with curiosity.

When we returned to the truck, Father was tapping out the ash from his pipe, ready to get back on the road. The truck rumbled to life, and we pulled out of the parking lot, the morning sun glinting off the windshield. The horizon stretched out before us, a road full of uncertainty but also the hope of leaving the past miles behind.

As the truck hummed along, the wheels crunching over the occasional patch of gravel, I let my mind wander back to the camp and everything that had transpired. I tried to focus, to put everything into words, but the enormity of it all made my hand tremble slightly as I wrote.

I glanced out the window, watching the trees blur into streaks of green, their branches swaying gently in the wind as if waving us goodbye. The landscape shifted, giving way to rolling hills that seemed to rise and fall with the rhythm of the road. Somewhere in the distance, a hawk circled lazily, oblivious to the chaos that had unfolded just hours ago.

"Writing down everything?" Mother asked softly.

I nodded, the pen hovering over the page. "I don't want to forget anything. It all feels so surreal—like it didn't really happen."

Mother turned to face me, her expression somber but tender. "Some things, maybe it's better to forget," she said, her voice low, almost as if she were talking to herself.

I didn't reply, unsure if I agreed. This wasn't something I could just let fade into the background of my memory.

After a few more miles, the words started flowing easier. I wrote about the landslide, the deafening roar of the earth collapsing and the sheer terror that had gripped us all. I described the lights Prosperity's grandmother had spoken of and Harold's frantic recounting of what he'd seen. I even detailed the peculiar look Rakshasi had given me as we drove past her that morning, standing outside her vanishing tent with that steaming cup in her hand.

"That woman," I said aloud, breaking the silence.

Mother turned her head toward me. "What woman?"

"Rakshasi," I replied. "She was there at the camp, just standing outside her tent before… everything. I still can't figure out how her tent disappeared overnight or why she was looking at me like that."

Father, his eyes fixed on the road, let out a low hum. "Some folks are strange, Dawn. Could've been a coincidence. Or maybe she knew something we didn't."

"That's the thing," I said, leaning forward slightly. "It didn't feel like a coincidence. It was like she knew something was about to happen."

Mother shifted uncomfortably in her seat. "Let's not dwell on it too much. Whatever her intentions, she's not our concern anymore."

But the knot in my stomach refused to ease. I couldn't shake the image of her piercing gaze, nor the sinking feeling that Rakshasi and the strange lights were somehow connected to everything that had happened.

As we crested a hill, the horizon opened up, revealing the faint outline of a town in the distance. I closed my diary, pressing my pen between the pages to hold my place. Whatever answers I was searching for would have to wait—at least for now.

I was determined to capture as much detail as I could before the memories blurred. My pen scratched across the paper, describing the landslide, the strange lights, and Prosperity's tearful relief at seeing us alive.

As the miles stretched on, the landscape began to change subtly, with rolling hills giving way to wider, open spaces. Along the roadside, a series of billboards started appearing, each competing for attention with bold designs and vibrant colors. They painted a picture of what lay ahead, promising all manner of adventures.

One sign boasted an opportunity to pan for gold, its glossy lettering glittering in the sunlight like the treasure it promised. Another urged travelers to "Discover the Adventure of a Lifetime!" with an image of a family smiling as they descended into a shadowy cave.

Further along, a billboard invited us to "Explore the Legendary Badlands," its rugged cliffs and unique formations depicted in sharp contrast to the clear blue sky behind them. Not far from it, a sign advertised the historic town of Deadwood, where visitors could "Step Back into the Old West," complete with gunfight reenactments and saloons.

But the largest and most colorful of them all was for Wall Drug, declaring itself "The Most Popular Place on the Planet." It featured everything from a giant jackalope to promises of free ice water and five-cent coffee. The sheer audacity of it made me chuckle, even as I marveled at its iconic status.

The billboards were more than just advertisements; they were like glimpses into a different world, one brimming with excitement and nostalgia, beckoning travelers to make a stop and explore. Yet, despite their charm, I couldn't fully shake the lingering unease in the pit of my stomach. The events of the morning still weighed heavily on my mind, casting a shadow over the bright promises of the road ahead.

I hadn't experienced any of those adventures before, and my curiosity was burning like a wildfire. Boldly, I turned to Father and asked, "Can we wander deep into a cave?"

He paused for a moment, a glint of excitement sparking in his eyes, then smiled and nodded. "Why not?" he said. "Let's make it an adventure to remember. It's been years—since I was a child, actually—since I last ventured into a cave."

To be honest, Mother and I just wanted some free time to clear our minds, to take in the sights of South Dakota without the pressure of rushing back home. The open road felt like a much-needed escape, a chance to breathe after everything that had happened.

As we planned the cave visit, Mother turned to me with a gentle smile. "Make sure you bring your diary," she said. "You might find something worth sketching or jotting down. Caves hold some of nature's most fascinating secrets."

I nodded, already imagining the jagged stalactites, winding tunnels, and glimmers of minerals I might capture in words and drawings. It felt good to focus on something as simple and grounding as exploring the unknown. Although, the unknown always seems to find its way into my life, weaving itself into the most ordinary of moments and transforming them into something strange and unsettling.

* * * *

We drove south, looping back through Keystone to steer clear of the chaos that had unfolded earlier. There was an unspoken understanding among us that nothing more could be done to help those at the campgrounds. The weight of that reality hung heavy in the air as the miles stretched on.

Eventually, we arrived at the historic Jewel Cave. The entrance stood like a gateway to another world, its rocky facade promising secrets buried deep within the earth. I reached for the brochure I had picked up at a small gift shop several miles back, flipping through its pages as we prepared to explore.

Jewel Cave, as I read aloud to my parents, was discovered in 1900 by Frank and Albert Michaud, two adventurous brothers who stumbled upon a small opening while searching for mining claims. Using dynamite to widen the entrance, they revealed a cavern lined with sparkling calcite crystals, which gave the cave its name. It quickly became known as one of the largest and most intricate cave systems in the world, with over 200 miles of mapped passages.

As I read, I couldn't help but marvel at how this subterranean wonder had remained hidden for so long, its beauty concealed beneath the rolling hills of South Dakota. "It's like an underground palace," I said, glancing out the window at the modest visitor center that now stood at the site.

Mother leaned in to look at the brochure, her face lighting up with interest. "It says here that early explorers thought they had only scratched the surface," she added. "There are still parts of the cave that have never been explored."

The thought sent a shiver of excitement through me. What might be waiting in those uncharted depths? And, as always, a whisper of unease lingered—because the unknown seemed to follow me everywhere. Jewel Cave's legacy loomed before us like a beacon, a labyrinth waiting to be uncovered.

"Can you imagine being the first to step inside something like that?" I mused, my fingers tracing the edges of the brochure.

Father parked the truck, stepping out to stretch. "I imagine it's dark, damp, and full of bats," he said, smirking. "Let's hope we don't get lost."

Inside the visitor center, the air was cool and filled with the faint hum of voices from other tourists. Displays along the walls showed old photographs and tools from the early explorers. I couldn't help but stare at the black-and-white image of the Michaud brothers standing triumphantly at the cave's entrance. Their discovery had been accidental, yet it unearthed a world that seemed more alien than earthly.

"Look at this," I said, pointing to a plaque. "The cave got its name because the crystals sparkle like jewels when the light hits them."

Father chuckled, rubbing his chin. "Let's see if it lives up to the name."

We booked a guided tour and followed the group down a steep, winding staircase into the depths of the earth. The air grew colder with each step, and soon the walls around us sparkled faintly under the low light. I clutched my diary tightly, the urge to document every detail growing stronger.

Our guide spoke as we descended. "Jewel Cave is home to countless chambers and passages, many still unexplored. Some areas are as narrow as a crawlspace, while others open into massive rooms, one even large enough to hold the Statue of Liberty."

"Statue of Liberty?" I whispered to Mother, incredulous.

She smiled. "Hard to believe, isn't it?"

As we moved deeper into the cave, I felt a strange sensation, like the air itself was alive. I wasn't sure if it was the sheer magnitude of the space or something else entirely. The shadows seemed to shift oddly, playing tricks on my eyes. I couldn't shake the feeling that we weren't entirely alone.

I scribbled in my diary while the guide pointed out stalactites and flowstone formations. My pen faltered, though, as I recalled Prosperity's trembling voice and the way the mountain had collapsed. Jewel Cave had stood for centuries, its chambers untouched by time. What if it, too, held secrets waiting to be unearthed?

Mother leaned closer to me as the guide continued speaking. "You're quiet," she said softly. "Are you all right?"

I hesitated. "It's just... I keep thinking about the campground, about Rakshasi and the others."

She gave my hand a gentle squeeze. "Write it down, Dawn. Sometimes it helps to let it out."

I nodded, returning to my diary. As I wrote, the lights flickered briefly. The group paused, a nervous murmur rippling through the crowd. The guide reassured us it was just an electrical hiccup. For a moment, the unknown didn't feel so distant.

It felt like it was watching.

Ahead of me, clinging to the rough, shadowy wall of the cave, I noticed a flicker of movement. Narrowing my eyes, I realized it was an insect of some kind, its elongated legs and antennae giving it an alien appearance against the sparkling mineral backdrop.

Our tour guide, a tall, thin woman with neatly tied brown hair, noticed my interest and paused to address the group. She wore light green pants and a tan button-up shirt, the emblem on her chest clearly identifying her as a park ranger. Her badge read Jessica, and her calm demeanor suited her role.

"Ah, you've spotted one of our cave crickets," Jessica said, gesturing toward the insect with a faint smile. "These fascinating creatures are rarely seen outside the cave system—they're completely adapted to life in the dark. Unlike most crickets, they rely on their incredibly long antennae to navigate these tight, shadowy spaces."

I leaned in slightly, my curiosity piqued as the creature adjusted its stance, blending seamlessly with the jagged surface. "Do they ever leave the cave?" I asked, my voice echoing faintly in the cavern's stillness.

Jessica shook her head. "Not often. They're highly specialized for this environment, and stepping into the outside world wouldn't suit them. They're one of many examples of how life finds extraordinary ways to thrive in even the most unique conditions."

I pulled out my diary, the pages already filled with hurried notes and half-finished sketches from earlier in the tour. Balancing it awkwardly in one hand, I began jotting down what Jessica had said about the cave cricket, determined to capture every detail.

As I wrote, I glanced back at the creature, its spindly legs gripping the cave wall like it belonged to an entirely different world. Carefully, I attempted to sketch its peculiar shape, from the oversized antennae to the sharp angles of its limbs. My lines were shaky, but the act of drawing helped cement the memory. The cricket remained motionless, as if it were a part of the stone itself, oblivious to my clumsy attempt at art. I smiled faintly, thinking how strange and wonderful it was to discover something so unique in the hidden depths of the earth.

As we ventured deeper into the cave, Ranger Jessica's voice

droned on, her steady stream of information echoing faintly against the stone walls. The air grew colder and damper, wrapping around us like a living thing. The steady drip of water and the faint rustle of unseen creatures added a subtle unease to the atmosphere.

We turned a sharp corner and came face to face with a vast, dark archway carved naturally into the cave wall. It loomed before us, wide and gaping, its shadowy interior stretching into the unknown. The air around it felt heavier, almost as if the cave itself was breathing, ready to swallow us whole. The faint glisten of moisture on the stone walls gave the illusion of movement, heightening the eerie stillness.

Jessica, always prepared, reached into a nearby wooden crate and pulled out a sturdy lantern. Despite the flashlights clipped to her belt, she chose to strike a match, lighting the lantern with practiced ease. The flame flickered briefly before settling into a steady glow.

"This," she began, holding the lantern high, "offers a broader and softer illumination than the focused beam of a flashlight. Let's see what it can show us."

As she stepped closer to the archway, the light from the lantern spilled into the cavernous space beyond. What had been a shadowy void transformed into a dazzling display. The walls shimmered with crystals, their facets catching the warm light and reflecting it back like a million tiny mirrors. The effect was breathtaking, as though we had stumbled into the heart of a massive jewel. The room seemed to pulse with an otherworldly energy, and for a moment, the group fell silent, captivated by the sheer beauty of it.

I clutched my diary tighter, unable to tear my eyes away from the scene. This was no ordinary cave; it felt alive, holding secrets buried deep within its glittering expanse.

As the tour pressed forward, a subtle unease began to creep over me. The steady rhythm of footsteps and Ranger Jessica's voice faded into the background as a faint whisper reached my ears. At first, I dismissed it as a trick of my imagination, a sound carried on the still, damp air. But with everything that had been happening lately, doubt gnawed at me. Then, I heard it again—a soft, unmistakable whisper.

"Dawn," it said, clear enough to make my breath catch.

I froze, my heart hammering in my chest. There was no way anyone would know my name down here, deep within the earth, surrounded by strangers in this tour group. My pulse quickened as I scanned the dimly lit cavern, but the others seemed oblivious, their attention fixed on the glittering crystals and Ranger Jessica's lecture.

Could it have been a coincidence? The weight of the unknown settled heavily on my shoulders.

I hesitated, rooted to the spot, straining to hear more. The whisper didn't come again, but the air felt different now, charged, like the static before a storm. It was a familiar feeling. I glanced at Mother, who was listening attentively to Ranger Jessica's explanation about the cave's history, her face serene. She hadn't heard it. No one had. I took a slow breath and forced myself to move, though my legs felt like lead. The group was moving ahead, their lanterns casting shifting shadows on the walls. Every step forward felt heavier, as if the cave itself was resisting our presence.

Then, I noticed something in the corner of my eye. A flicker of movement just beyond the reach of the lantern's glow. My stomach churned, and I turned sharply, staring into the darkness. The shadows seemed to twist and ripple against the jagged rock walls, and for a fleeting moment, I could have sworn I saw a figure—vague and indistinct, lurking at the edge of the lantern's glow. Then, from the shadows, two fiery, burning red eyes appeared, glowing with an intensity that cut through the darkness. They held me in their gaze, unblinking, as if they could see straight into my soul. It reminded me of the red, burning eye shadow I'd seen lingering in my closet back home, a memory I had tried to dismiss but could never quite shake. The resemblance was uncanny, as if the two were somehow connected, their fiery gaze burning into my mind like a brand.

"Dawn, are you okay?" Mother's voice broke through my thoughts, her hand touching my arm gently.

I nodded quickly, swallowing hard. "Yeah, just... something caught my eye."

Mother gave me a curious look, but didn't press. "Stay close," she said, motioning for me to follow the group.

As we moved deeper into the cave, the walls began to close in slightly, the passage narrowing. The sound of dripping water echoed around us, and the cool air seemed to wrap itself tighter, clinging to my skin. The lantern's glow bounced off the walls, making the crystalline formations glimmer like a thousand tiny stars.

But I couldn't shake the feeling that something was following us—something unseen, yet undeniable. The whisper played over and over in my mind, that one word: Dawn.

I opened my diary and scribbled hastily, my pen scratching across the page as I tried to capture the moment. Writing had always been my way of making sense of the chaos, and right now, my mind was a storm.

Then the lights flickered.

The group stopped, a murmur of concern rippling through the tourists. Ranger Jessica raised the lantern higher, her brow furrowed. "It's nothing to worry about," she assured us. "The electrical system in the cave can be finicky, but we have backup generators in case of an outage."

Her voice was calm, but I caught the faintest edge of tension.

I closed my diary and clutched it to my chest, my eyes darting to the dark recesses of the cave. Whatever was down here, it didn't feel like it was part of the tour.

After a long hike through the cave and an equally lengthy

history lesson, Ranger Jessica guided us into an enormous cavern. The space was breathtaking, with walls that shimmered in brilliant, bright colors, reflecting the lantern light like a kaleidoscope of jewels. Another guide joined us, introducing us to the fascinating underground wildlife. They pointed out albino crickets, blind salamanders, and tiny fungi glowing faintly like stars in the dark. I took the opportunity to sketch some of the insects and plant life in my diary, capturing the strange beauty of the cave's ecosystem.

Curiosity got the better of me, and I wandered a short distance from the group, making sure not to stray too far. I found a smooth stone bench near a small stream that trickled gently through the cavern. The water was crystal clear, winding its way toward a deep hole in the rock. Leaning closer, I peered into the depths. The walls of the hole were smooth and polished, and I noticed three small tunnels branching off, likely channels for the water to flow to other parts of the cave.

Suddenly, a large air bubble emerged from the hole, rising slowly before bursting on the surface with a soft pop. The ripples spread outward, distorting my reflection in the water. Startled, I jumped back, my heart racing.

Then, just as the ripples stilled, I heard a soft giggle behind me. Turning quickly, I froze. A little girl stood there, wearing a faded blue gown and a bonnet. Her dress looked out of place, its style belonging to another century. She didn't speak but stared at me with wide, curious eyes, her presence as eerie as it was surreal.

In her arms, she cradled a worn teddy bear, its faded fur a patchwork of gray and light brown.

The little girl stepped toward me bashfully, a shy smile gracing her face. Then, just as slowly, she retreated into the shadows behind her. I hesitated before cautiously stepping after her, moving carefully into the darkness. With each step, I made sure not to lose sight of the tour group's light in the distance.

"Hello?" I whispered, my voice barely audible as I strained to keep it from echoing through the vast expanse of the cave. "Where did you go?"

The soft glow of the tour group's lanterns and flashlights began to fade, swallowed by the shadows around me as I ventured further into the darkness. Anxiety prickled at the back of my neck, but I pressed on, unwilling to leave the little girl behind.

"Wait!" I called out, my voice louder this time, bouncing faintly off the walls. "Where are you going?"

I quickened my pace, convinced she might wander too far and find herself lost—or worse, in danger. My footsteps echoed softly as I entered an open space, the air cooler and damp against my skin.

Before me, the cavern opened up into a breathtaking chamber. A waterfall cascaded from a jagged opening high above, its silver threads catching what little light seeped into the space. The water pooled into a shimmering basin at my feet, the sound of its endless rush muffling the pounding of my heart.

I scanned the chamber for any sign of the girl, but she was nowhere in sight. The stillness around me was unsettling, broken only by the steady rhythm of the falling water. My grip tightened on my diary as I took a cautious step forward, the weight of the unknown pressing down on me.

Where could she have gone? And why did this place feel so eerily alive?

I called out again, my voice louder this time, desperation creeping in. "Hello? Can anybody hear me?"

The cave seemed to swallow my words, the echoes fading into the vastness of the chamber. My heart pounded as I took another cautious step forward, eyes darting around the dimly lit space.

Suddenly, a sharp, commanding voice cut through the steady hum of the waterfall. "I SEE YOU!"

It was a female voice, distant yet clear, and it sent a jolt through me. I froze, my pulse racing as the words echoed ominously off the cavern walls. The tone was urgent, almost panicked, and it felt like it was directed at me, or someone nearby.

"Who's there?" I called back, my voice echoed.

I scanned the chamber frantically, looking for any sign of movement. Was she warning me? The weight of the unknown pressed heavily on my chest, and a creeping sense of dread began to take hold. The little girl's giggle echoed faintly again, somewhere beyond the shadows. What was going on in this place?

Someone grabbed my arm from behind, their grip firm and unyielding. A sharp jolt of panic surged through me, and I let out a scream, instinctively trying to wrench myself free.

Feeling trapped, I balled my fist, adrenaline taking over as I swung my free arm with all my might. My knuckles connected with something solid—a wall of muscle and flesh. The impact sent a dull ache through my hand, but it was enough to momentarily jar my captor.

"Dawn!" a familiar startled voice boomed.

As more light spilled into the cavern, illuminating the space, I froze in disbelief. Standing before me, rubbing his chest where my fist had landed, was my father, his face a mixture of concern and surprise.

"Dad?" I gasped, my heart pounding.

"What on earth are you doing out here?" he asked, his voice stern yet tinged with worry.

I opened my mouth to explain, but the words caught in my throat. The echoes of the mysterious woman's warning still lingered, and the sight of my father here only added to the confusion. Why had he followed me? And how much had he heard—or seen?

"I... I thought I saw someone," I stammered, glancing toward the shadows near the waterfall. My father's presence was comforting, but the unease in my chest refused to subside.

Thankfully my Father shrugged it off.

As the last leg of the tour wound down, the group found themselves in the grandest chamber yet—a massive, cathedral-like space where countless crystals shimmered in the warm glow of lanterns. The ceiling arched impossibly high, adorned with formations that sparkled like stars in a night sky.

Even after the strange events earlier, a sense of awe overtook me. Whatever whispers I thought I'd heard, whatever shadows had played tricks on my mind, seemed to melt away in the sheer wonder of this natural marvel.

Ranger Jessica stopped at the center of the chamber, her lantern casting soft light across the group. "Take a moment," she said with a smile. "Let this place sink in. This is what makes Jewel Cave one of the most remarkable wonders of the world."

I reached for my diary and sketched the chamber. My father, standing nearby, gazed at the formations with a rare expression of boyish wonder. Mother leaned into his side, her eyes reflecting the light like the crystals above.

"This," Father said quietly, "is worth the journey."

I smiled, my earlier fears finally subsiding. The echoes of giggles and mysterious whispers seemed so far away now, dwarfed by the beauty surrounding us. Jewel Cave felt alive, but not in a menacing way—it was vibrant, filled with a history that demanded reverence and respect. As we climbed back to the surface, the sunlight filtering through the visitor center felt almost foreign, a reminder of how far we'd traveled into the earth's depths. Yet, despite the strangeness, I carried something more than just sketches in my diary.

I carried a newfound appreciation for the unknown—both its beauty and its mystery.

THE VAULT

Past the gift shop, we stumbled upon a quaint little café, its exterior adorned with flower boxes brimming with vibrant blooms. The aroma of freshly brewed coffee and warm pastries drifted through the open doorway, beckoning us inside.

We settled into a corner booth, its wooden benches polished smooth by years of visitors. The café was cozy, with walls decorated in vintage photographs of Jewel Cave explorers and artifacts encased in glass displays. A ceiling fan spun lazily overhead, stirring the comforting scent of home-cooked meals. I glanced at the menu, my stomach growling in anticipation.

"What do you think, Dad? Sandwiches or burgers?"

He grinned, folding the menu. "Burgers. Always burgers."

Mother laughed softly, shaking her head. "I'll get a salad, and we'll split some fries."

When our meals arrived, the plates were generous and inviting. The burger was stacked high with fresh lettuce, ripe tomatoes, and a thick patty cooked to perfection. The salad, garnished with colorful vegetables, was crisp and vibrant. As we ate, the conversation drifted back to the tour.

"That last chamber was incredible," Mother said, dabbing at her mouth with a napkin. "I'll never forget how the light hit those crystals."

Father nodded. "Makes you wonder how much of the cave is still unexplored. Imagine the treasures still waiting to be found down there."

I hesitated, recalling the strange events earlier—the whispers, the little girl, and the mysterious figure. Part of me wanted to share it, but another part wasn't sure they'd believe me. Instead, I jotted a quick note in my diary, promising myself to document it fully later.

As the sunlight streamed through the café's windows, warming the wooden floors, I felt a sense of calm. The eerie sensations from the cave were now a distant memory, replaced by the comfort of being with my family, sharing a meal and laughter.

After lunch, we wandered over to a nearby souvenir stand, where I picked out a small crystal pendant. The delicate gem glinted in the light, a tiny fragment of Jewel Cave's beauty and a keepsake to remind me of our adventure.

Father excused himself to step outside for a cigar, respecting the café and gift shop's smoke-free policy. The faint aroma of his cigar lingered just beyond the door as Mother and I explored the shop.

Mother's eyes lit up as she browsed a display of Black Hills gold jewelry, trying on a dainty ring adorned with intricate leaf designs. "Isn't this lovely?" she asked, holding her hand up for me to admire.

"It suits you," I said with a smile before turning my attention to a corner of the shop filled with whimsical Bigfoot-themed collectibles. Plush dolls, mugs, and even a pair of fuzzy socks covered in Sasquatch footprints brought a playful charm to the shelves.

Mother chuckled as she picked up a Bigfoot figurine holding a sign that read *"Believe."*

A familiar face approached me. Her name tag read Ranger Cody. She was one of the staff members who had guided us through Jewel Cave earlier in the day.

"Enjoying your visit?" she asked with a friendly smile, her green ranger uniform neatly pressed, the badge on her chest catching the afternoon sunlight.

"Yes," I replied, holding up my small crystal pendant. "I just picked this up as a souvenir. It's beautiful here."

Ranger Cody nodded, her eyes twinkling. "That's a great choice. Every piece tells a story, just like the cave itself." She paused, glancing around at the bustling gift shop and café. "I hope the tour was memorable."

"It was," I said, recalling the dazzling formations, the vast chambers, and the strange unease I had felt. "Jewel Cave is unlike anything I've ever seen."

She leaned in slightly, lowering her voice. "It has a way of leaving an impression on everyone. Sometimes in ways we don't fully understand." Her words hung in the air for a moment, almost cryptic, yet delivered with a kindness that eased any lingering tension.

"It does," I replied, my voice soft but certain.

"Can…" she began, then paused, as though weighing her words carefully. Finally, she continued, her tone gentle but curious. "Can I ask you a question?"

"Uh, sure!?" I replied hesitantly.

"I don't mean to bother you like this," Ranger Cody said, her tone careful, "but I noticed you went in to explore The Vault."

"Oh my goodness, I'm so sorry!" I exclaimed, panic rushing through me. "I swear I didn't steal anything."

Ranger Cody raised her eyebrows and quickly reassured me, "You haven't done anything wrong." She hesitated briefly, then continued, "The Vault is the name of the cavern you explored—the one with the waterfall. It's been closed off for years due to…" Her voice trailed off as she glanced around, as if ensuring no one else was listening. After a moment, she added, "It's always been off-limits to tourists because of…" She paused again, this time nervously.

"I'm listening." I said.

Ranger Cody glanced around the room once more, her expression unreadable, then leaned in closer. "The Vault has a history," she began carefully, her words deliberate. "There are stories—things people have experienced there that can't be explained. I'm not supposed to discuss it with guests, but... you were in there, and I can tell something's weighing on you."

Her eyes locked onto mine, her curiosity mingling with something deeper, almost like concern. "I just need to know," she said softly. "What did you see?"

I paused, lost in thought. I wasn't sure what to say. The concerned look on Ranger Cody's face was unsettling, her eyes filled with a quiet urgency that seemed to press for an answer. I felt a pang of guilt if I didn't tell her the truth, it might feel like I'd let her down, like I'd dashed her hopes.

With a deep breath, I made up my mind. "All right," I said. "I'll tell you everything."

Ranger Cody's eyes lit up with delight as I recounted the strange, haunting experience I had in The Vault. She listened intently, nodding as I spoke, and explained that the museum values eyewitness accounts because of the role they play in preserving the cave's rich and mysterious history.

When I finished, curiosity got the better of me, and I asked her outright why The Vault was considered such a significant and haunted cavern. Cody hesitated for a moment, then excused herself. She returned shortly with a few sheets of paper in hand and offered it to me.

"This is a copy of a passage from a book I'm working on," she said, her tone almost conspiratorial. The title at the top read Historical Stories of Jewel Cave. "It's not published yet," she continued, "but I've been writing this book for a while. I thought you might find it interesting."

I accepted the sheet, running my fingers over the crisp paper.

"Thank you," I said.

"Please read it when you have a chance," Cody urged. "I'd really appreciate it."

"I will," I promised, touched by her thoughtfulness. "Thank you for sharing this with me."

Ranger Cody beamed, clearly pleased with my response. She expressed how much she enjoyed meeting new people and hearing their stories. Her enthusiasm was contagious, and I found myself smiling despite the lingering sense of unease that clung to me from my time in The Vault.

As our conversation came to an end, my father walked back into the restaurant, his cigar now extinguished, the lingering scent of smoke clinging to his jacket. We regrouped with my mother, who had already finished browsing the gift shop, her hands empty except for a small paper bag. Without a word, we stepped out into the cool evening air and headed toward the truck.

The ride back to Lincoln, Nebraska, stretched ahead of us, long and quiet. But my thoughts remain fixed on the eerie beauty of Jewel Cave and the secrets it seemed determined to keep.

HISTORICAL STORIES OF JEWEL CAVE

The Vault in Jewel Cave, South Dakota, is said to be haunted by the spirit of a six-year-old girl named Emily. Her story, steeped in cruel hatred and overwhelming sorrow, is one that lingers in the shadows of the cave, whispered by those who dare to explore its depths.

Emily's life was tragically short and marked by hardship. Born in the late 1800s to a family of settlers seeking fortune in the Black Hills, Emily was an afterthought in her family's pursuit of wealth. Her parents, hardened by misfortune and financial ruin, were indifferent to her gentle spirit, often treating her as a burden rather than a child.

Local lore says Emily was often left alone for hours, sometimes days, while her family worked tirelessly in the harsh wilderness. It was during one of these long absences that Emily wandered into the dark expanse of Jewel Cave. Entranced by the sparkling crystals, she ventured deeper and deeper until she reached what is now known as The Vault.

When Emily's parents returned and discovered her missing, a frantic search ensued, but the girl was nowhere to be found. Days turned into weeks, and hope dwindled. Her disappearance was written off as a tragic accident, though whispers in the town hinted at neglect and foul play.

Decades later, stories of Emily's spirit began to surface. Visitors to The Vault have reported hearing the soft giggle of a child echoing through the chamber, only to turn and find no one there. Others speak of a faint silhouette of a little girl in a bonnet and blue dress, clutching a tattered teddy bear, who appears near the waterfall within the cavern. Her presence is often accompanied by a chilling drop in temperature and the feeling of being watched.

Some accounts describe a darker side to Emily's haunting. It is said that her sorrow twisted into something vengeful. Those who enter The Vault with ill intentions or disrespect for the cave's history have reported unsettling encounters—disembodied whispers, the sensation of unseen hands brushing against them, and, in some cases, sudden accidents that force them to leave the cavern abruptly.

Despite these tales, many believe Emily's spirit is not purely malevolent. Some who claim to have seen her describe a deep sadness in her fiery red eyes, as if she is eternally searching for the love and attention she was denied in life. Rangers at Jewel Cave often leave small tokens, like flowers or toys, near The Vault as a gesture of kindness toward the restless spirit.

To this day, The Vault remains one of Jewel Cave's most enigmatic locations. Whether Emily's ghost is a manifestation of anger, sorrow, or a plea for connection, her story continues to captivate and haunt those who visit the cavern.

The true story behind Emily's tragic fate has been pieced together from fragments of historical records, eyewitness accounts, and chilling discoveries made in Jewel Cave over time. What really happened to Emily is far darker than the ghost stories suggest—and far more unsettling.

Emily wasn't just a neglected child; she was the scapegoat for her family's misfortunes. Her father, a struggling prospector, and her mother, worn down by years of hardship, saw Emily as a constant reminder of their dashed hopes. By the time they reached the Black Hills, their bitterness had boiled over into cruelty.

The truth began to unravel when a small, weathered journal was discovered, hidden beneath the floorboards of what was once the family's cabin near the cave's entrance. The journal belonged to Emily's older brother, Samuel, who recorded the events surrounding her disappearance. Samuel's writings described a family teetering on the edge of ruin. The parents fought constantly, and Emily often bore the brunt of their frustration. But there was something else—an unsettling influence that Samuel could only describe as "odd."

On the day Emily vanished, Samuel recounted how his father seemed distant, as if lost in a trance. His father muttered strange things under his breath, but deeply unsettling. At one point, his father told the family, "It's odd… but it says she's the one. It's Emily."

Samuel tried to ask what he meant, but his father dismissed him, his demeanor shifting between anger and something almost fearful. Later that evening, Samuel watched as his father led Emily toward the cave, saying they needed to "set things right." Samuel followed, begging him to stop, but his father ignored him, his expression blank and his eyes fixed ahead.

They disappeared into the cave, and Samuel, frightened by the overwhelming darkness and an eerie sound he couldn't explain, ran back to the cabin. He never saw Emily again.

The journal ended abruptly, but its final words were chilling:

"I begged him to stop, but he said the devil needed a sacrifice. The last thing I saw was her disappearing into the cave's mouth, clutching her teddy bear tightly in her arms."

Years later, spelunkers exploring a hidden chamber in The Vault made a haunting discovery. Deep within the cave, accessible only through a narrow passage, they found the remains of a small child clutching a decayed teddy bear.

Though no one knows exactly what happened in the cave that night, Samuel's account suggested a malevolent force may have been at play. The eerie laughter reported by visitors, the strange whispers, and the shadowy figure with burning red eyes seen in The Vault all hint at something far beyond human understanding.

Emily's story has since become a symbol of the unexplained mysteries of Jewel Cave. Visitors often leave small trinkets and toys near the cave's entrance, hoping to bring peace to her restless spirit. But whether these offerings soothe her—or the darker force that may have claimed her—is something no one truly knows.

THE WAY HOME

The truck hummed steadily as it navigated the winding road, the towering pines blurring into a distant green haze as we left the Black Hills behind. I was crammed between my mother and the passenger door, my legs stiff from the cramped space. My father gripped the steering wheel, eyes fixed intently on the curves of the road ahead. Beside him, my mother leafed through a stack of glossy brochures she'd picked up earlier at the Jewel Cave gift shop, occasionally murmuring about nearby attractions.

The air in the truck carried a mix of crisp pine from the open window and the faint chemical tang of the brochures in her hands. Every so often, the tires crunched over loose gravel, and the truck swayed gently with the winding terrain. I stared out at the passing trees, their dark silhouettes stretching toward the afternoon sky, my thoughts drifting as the forest closed in behind us like a forgotten secret.

It was going to be a long ride home to Lincoln, the kind that gives you too much time to think. Strange things have been happening to me and I've been grateful to have this diary to capture the memories while they're still fresh. Writing them down feels like clinging to fragments of a puzzle, hoping one day the pieces will fit together and make sense.

* * * *

The sun had long dipped below the horizon, and night had fully enveloped us, casting the winding road into shadows broken only by the truck's headlights. Several miles had passed in an eerie silence when my breath caught. On the side of the road, illuminated by the pale beams of light, stood a creature I had seen before—a creature I could never forget.

Its body was draped in tattered Native American garments that fluttered lightly, though there was no breeze. A deer skull, its surface cracked and ancient, served as its head, and from it sprouted massive, gnarled antlers that twisted impossibly, almost like they defied natural order. The creature didn't move, but its hollow eye sockets seemed to follow us as we passed.

Was it the Wendigo that Prosperity and I had encountered before, the same monstrous entity we had narrowly escaped with the help of Rakshasi? The memory of that night still haunted me, and now, as I faced this creature again, I couldn't shake the feeling that it was somehow connected—perhaps the same force, or something even darker, now following us. The terror of that past encounter gripped me again, the fear of being pursued by something so mysterious and hungry.

As we drove past, the creature let out a bone-chilling screech, the kind that rattled your bones and seemed to scrape at the very air around us. It was a high-pitched, unnerving cry, like the desperate wail of something caught between life and death, its twisted antlers scraping against the night. The sound lingered in the air for a moment, echoing in my ears, before it faded into the thickening darkness, swallowed by the silence of the night as if it had never been there at all.

The truck's engine hummed louder as we sped away, but the air inside felt colder, heavier. My heart was racing, a constant thrum in my chest that refused to slow. I tried to focus on the road, on the dimly lit stretch ahead, but every shadow seemed to flicker with memories of that screech, every rustling of the trees felt like it was the creature moving just out of sight. My eyes kept darting to the rearview mirror, half-expecting to see its twisted form following us, its eyes locked onto mine.

But the road was empty—silent.

Yet, the feeling of being watched didn't fade. It lingered, like a presence that had crossed into our world and was now trailing behind us in the dark, waiting for the right moment to strike.

The rest of the drive felt like a blur, time slipping by in a haze of tension and unease. The road stretched on forever, the blackness pressing in from all sides. My father kept his hands steady on the wheel, but I could see the tightness in his jaw, the way his eyes flicked nervously to the rearview mirror, too. He wasn't saying anything, but we both knew something was wrong.

Mother had long since stopped flipping through the brochures, her fingers still, her gaze fixed out the window as if she, too, was searching for something in the darkness. The silence in the truck was suffocating, broken only by the occasional rattle of the tires against the uneven road. Even the usual banter between my parents was absent, replaced by an unspoken tension we all seemed to feel. Honestly, I actually liked the silence now that I think about it.

*** * * ***

Several hours later we reached the outskirts of Lincoln, I could barely remember the last few miles. The creature's screech still echoed in my mind, like a haunting refrain that refused to fade. I barely noticed when we pulled into the driveway, the sound of gravel crunching beneath the tires pulling me back to reality.

Once inside, I couldn't shake the feeling that the night was far from over. There was an uneasiness in the house, a subtle shift in the air, as if it, too, had been touched by whatever we had encountered out on the road. I found myself retreating to my room, closing the door behind me, and sitting down on my bed. The stillness of the house only made the memory of that screech more vivid, and I knew I needed to write it down, to capture it before it slipped away into the fog of my mind.

As I put pen to paper, the weight of the evening settled in. The Wendigo, the Rakshasi, the strange creature by the road—were they all connected? Had we narrowly escaped something far worse than we realized? I didn't know, but I had to record it all. There was something about the events of the night that felt like a warning, and I couldn't let it be forgotten. Not now. Not ever.

I grabbed my teddy bear, Sorrows, and hugged him tight, the soft fabric offering a small measure of comfort against the heaviness in the air. His worn seams and faded fur were familiar, grounding me in a way that nothing else could at that moment. But even as I clutched him close, my mind couldn't escape the memory of what I'd read about Emily's demise in Jewel Cave. My grip on Sorrows tightened, as if holding him could somehow keep the fear at bay.

* * * *

Later, something woke me up, though I couldn't say what. The air in the room felt heavier, like it was thick with something unseen. I groggily turned my head toward the clock on my nightstand. The red digits glowed eerily in the darkness: 3:33 AM. I thought it was an odd coincidence. The time felt significant, as if it held some kind of hidden meaning, something sinister I couldn't quite grasp. As I lay there in the silence, I thought I heard a faint whisper, like a soft murmur coming from the corner of the room, just out of reach. I told myself it was just my imagination, but the unease gnawed at me.

I heard the floor creak near the foot of my bed. Slowly, I looked up, my breath hitching in silent fear. Standing just beyond the edge of my vision was a figure.

It was short, with pale, light blue-grayish skin, its features unnervingly still. Large, black, almond-shaped eyes locked onto mine, sending a surge of icy dread through my body. Its teardrop-shaped head was unnaturally smooth, as though it didn't quite belong to the rest of its fragile, sinewy frame.

As I stared, frozen in place, the figure's arm began to rise—slowly, deliberately—its spindly fingers extending as it pointed toward my bedroom door, beckoning me silently toward the hallway.

The instant it made this motion, a familiar, almost mocking hum began to drift through the air—a tune I could never forget. Greensleeves.

Suddenly, rapid and erratic footsteps echoed in the hallway outside my room, pounding toward the staircase that led down to the mansion's entrance. I snapped my gaze back to the figure, but it was gone—vanished as if it had never been there at all.

My heart hammered against my ribcage, each beat thundering in my ears. Cold sweat clung to my skin as I struggled to steady my breathing, desperate to comprehend what I had just seen.

Then, with an agonizingly slow, unnerving creak, my closet door began to inch open, its hinges groaning under the weight of some unseen force. Darkness spilled from within, deeper and more oppressive than the shadows around it, and I found myself unable to look away.

Without thinking, I leapt from my bed, heart hammering in my chest, and bolted for the door. I had to know who—or what—was behind the humming, who had just run toward the stairs. Whoever it was, they wouldn't get away.

I peeked out from my bedroom door, my fingers gripping the edge as I tried to steady myself. The hallway stretched ahead, draped in shadow, but the stillness was broken by the faint glow of a figure near the staircase.

It was Shelton. The little boy's spirit moved soundlessly, his translucent form shimmering with a faint blue light. His small frame seemed fragile, almost weightless, as though he might dissolve into the darkness at any moment. Shelton's head was slightly bowed, his steps deliberate as he made his way toward the stairs leading to the main hall.

I watched in silence. He didn't look back, didn't acknowledge my presence, but the air around him felt charged with an energy that made my skin prickle. It wasn't just his appearance—it was the way he moved, as if driven by some unseen purpose. The glow from his form cast faint shadows along the walls, dancing like the memory of a long-forgotten flame.

I wanted to call out his name, to ask him why he was here, but something about the scene kept me rooted in place, as though speaking would shatter the fragile moment. Shelton descended the stairs, his faint glow fading as he moved deeper into the house, leaving only questions—and an unsettling silence—in his wake.

I reached the bottom of the stairs, but Shelton was nowhere to be found. The house felt unnervingly quiet. Then, suddenly, I heard a commotion coming from the kitchen—a hurried shuffle of feet, followed by Shelton's frantic cry.

"Theodosia!" he yelled, his voice cracking with urgency. "Hurry, get out!"

I froze for a moment, the weight of his words sinking in.

"Help me, Shelton!" His sister screamed in terror. "He won't let go of me!"

A sudden movement caught my attention. From the far corner of the main hall, creeping slowly from the darkness, the figure with the almond-shaped eyes emerged, its silhouette barely visible against the shadows. It stood there for a moment, unnervingly still, before raising a hand and pointing toward the kitchen, its finger extended in a silent, deliberate motion.

The gesture was unmistakable—again, it was guiding me, leading me down the path of the commotion. The tension in the air thickened, and I hesitated for a heartbeat, unsure whether to follow or flee. But something in the figure's presence compelled me forward, as if it knew more than I did, as if it was pushing me toward something I couldn't yet understand.

I rushed toward the kitchen, my footsteps echoing sharply on the wooden floor. What was happening? Everything about this moment felt unsettlingly familiar, like a memory I couldn't quite place. The house seemed alive, pulsing with a strange, oppressive energy. Fragments of what I'd written in this diary flooded my mind, each word pulling me deeper into the unfolding scene. This time, there was no closed door barring me from stepping in to help.

As I entered the kitchen, my footsteps faltered. The room was colder than it should have been, a biting chill that seemed to seep into my bones. The dim light overhead flickered weakly, casting long, jittering shadows across the walls.

And then I saw him.

Standing above the open door to the basement cellar was a tall man, motionless. His frame dominated the space, casting jagged shadows that stretched unnaturally across the kitchen.

He didn't move or speak—he just stood there, looming above the cellar floor door as if guarding something unspeakable, something that shouldn't exist.

My breath quickened as I took in his form. There was something horribly familiar about him, though my mind refused to make the connection. His face hovered just out of focus, like a name on the tip of your tongue or a half-forgotten dream that slips away the harder you try to grasp it.

I stared harder, desperate to piece together the fragmented memory clawing at the edges of my thoughts. My mind spun, refusing to align, the pieces of recognition scattered and elusive. The longer I looked, the more a terrible realization began to gnaw at the back of my mind. His face lingered there, haunting and incomplete, like a puzzle I didn't want to solve—but couldn't avoid. The silence in the room was oppressive, swallowing every sound. The faint hum of the refrigerator and the creaks of the old house seemed to fade into nothing, leaving only the oppressive stillness of his presence.

Suddenly, a faint movement caught my eye—behind him. It was Theodosia, struggling weakly, her face streaked with blood. Her terrified eyes locked onto mine, pleading silently. In his grip, she struggled, dangling helplessly as he held her high in the air. Blood trickled down her face, staining her dress, and her small hands clawed weakly at his arm. His face was a mask of rage, twisted and unrecognizable, his eyes burning red.

"Let her go!" Shelton cried, his voice breaking as he appeared beside me. "Dad, please stop."

The man's head snapped toward the sound, his gaze towards Shelton. A cruel, twisted smile spread across his face, but he didn't release the girl. Theodosia was in trouble.

It was at that moment I got a better look at his face, and the realization hit me like a blow to the chest. It was him. I knew that face, etched deeply in the shadowy corners of my childhood memories.

It was Modus. My childhood imaginary friend. The one I had confided in, played with, trusted. But Modus wasn't real—he couldn't be. Could he? My mind reeled as fragments of forgotten whispers and laughter from years past clawed their way to the surface. The warmth of his presence I'd once cherished now twisted into something dark and unrecognizable. His expression was a grotesque mockery of the Modus I remembered, his features sharper, stretched unnaturally across his face. His lips curled into a sinister grin. His eyes—once comforting and kind—were now pits of blackness, void of any humanity.

"How?" I whispered, my voice trembling as I took a step back. My knees felt weak, threatening to buckle beneath me. "You're not real... you were never real."

Modus let out a guttural chuckle that reverberated through the kitchen, low and cruel. He tilted his head slowly, almost twitchingly, as he tightened his grip on Theodosia, her pained cries slicing through the air.

"This," Modus hissed, "is my house."

Before I could fully process what was happening, a sharp, guttural growl pierced the air, low and menacing. My heart leapt as Theodosia's small body was hurled through the air, as if she had been tossed like a rag doll. She hit the kitchen door with a sickening thud, her body crumpling to the floor. Her weak, pained cry snapped me out of my frozen state. My instincts screamed for me to run to her, but

Modus's overwhelming presence held me rooted in place.

Modus turned slightly, his movements unnervingly unnatural, his attention suddenly fixed on something hidden within the shadows. He tilted his head back slightly, as if curious about who or what had managed to draw his attention.

"No!" Modus bellowed, his voice reverberating with fury. "You will not take them from me!"

Then, without warning, there was a blinding flash of light. It filled the room, flooding every corner and obliterating all the shadows. I shielded my eyes, the coldness in the air replaced by an overwhelming sense of emptiness.

I stood frozen, staring at the empty bulkhead to the cellar. My mind screamed for answers, but there was nothing—no sound, no movement, no trace of what had just happened.

What had I just witnessed? Was it the lingering presence of Modus—a previous tenant who had murdered his own children in a fit of madness? But why? What could drive someone to commit such a horrifying act? I then realized that I witnessed the residual haunting of their death.

A wave of relief rushed over me, but it was fleeting. I turned quickly, my heart pounding, to check on Theodosia. "Theodosia!" I called out, my voice echoing off the empty walls. But she was gone.

Panic surged as I searched the room frantically, my eyes darting to every corner, but there was nothing—no sign of her. And then it struck me: Sheldon was gone too.

Then, I saw it.

The almond-eyed figure was there again, peeking from the black void within the cellar entrance. Half of its pale, teardrop-shaped head was visible, and its large, inky black eyes locked onto mine with a chilling intensity—unblinking. It didn't make a sound. It didn't move closer. It simply watched, its gaze unrelenting.

It wasn't going to do anything until I made the next move.

Okay. I understood. It wanted me to follow.

The figure's gaze seemed to pull at something deep within me, something I didn't want to acknowledge. It was an invitation, one that carried a silent warning: If I stayed, I would never escape the dark pull of whatever waited in that cellar. But if I followed... what would I find?

The figure didn't move, its dark eyes never leaving mine. I took a step forward down the stairs, the floor creaking beneath my feet, and then another, my heart racing. As I neared the cellar entrance, the temperature dropped sharply. Then, without warning, the figure slowly stepped back, its movements jerky, like a puppet being pulled by invisible strings. It was guiding me.

I stood at the threshold, paralyzed by fear. The figure radiated an unsettling presence, as if it pulsed with a life of its own, drawing me into the darkness that seemed to consume everything around it. Slowly, it melded into the corner, disappearing from view, but I knew it was still there, watching.

Then, the door slammed shut above me.

I stood in the dimly lit cellar, unsure of where the faint light was coming from. It wasn't from any visible source—no bulb, no lantern—just a strange, ambient glow that seemed to emanate from the very air itself. The shadows stretched and twisted unnaturally, their edges almost alive, writhing like silent whispers in the gloom.

In the center of the room stood a table, its wood warped and cracked, as though it had borne the weight of centuries. Perched on top of it was a barn owl, its feathers shimmering faintly in the eerie light. Its piercing yellow eyes bore into me, unblinking, as if it could see right through my thoughts.

My heart skipped a beat as I caught sight of another

almond-eyed figure emerging from the shadows. Its tear-drop shaped head was barely visible at first, blending with the shadows. It didn't move closer—not yet—but simply watched, its presence oppressive and alien.

A voice called out to me, soft and faint, yet somehow echoing in my mind. "Wake up," it whispered. The words sent a shiver through me, their meaning unclear but urgent, as if they carried a warning.

The figure, still watching, began to move. It approached the table, its pale form almost blending into the cellar's faint glow. Reaching out with a long, slender hand, it placed a small, smooth stone on the table beside the owl.

The moment the stone touched the wood, the owl let out an ear-piercing screech, a sound so sharp and primal it felt as though the very air vibrated with its intensity. The figure froze, its form jerking slightly as if startled. Without making another sound, it stepped back, disappearing into the shadowed corner from which it had emerged.

Then, it was gone.

The owl shifted its gaze to me, its eyes now seeming to glow brighter. I realized the stone was pulsing faintly. I stared at the pulsing stone on the table, mesmerized by the faint, rhythmic glow it emitted. The barn owl tilted its head sharply, its yellow eyes narrowing as it fixed its gaze on the stone. It let out another sharp screech, its wings flaring wide, casting jagged shadows against the walls. The light in the room dimmed even more, as though the owl's cry had drawn the shadows closer, thickening them into something almost tangible.

I turned to glance at the corner where the figure had disappeared, half-expecting it to reemerge, but the space remained empty—or so I thought. A soft, guttural clicking sound echoed from the shadows.

Then, the whisper came again, this time louder, more insistent.

"Wake up," it urged.

My legs felt rooted to the spot, my body unwilling to move even as every instinct screamed at me to run. The cellar door creaked above me, a slow, deliberate groan, but I didn't dare turn around.

Suddenly, the owl lifted off the table, its wings brushing against my shoulder as it soared into the darkness above. Its departure left a deafening silence in its wake. The cellar then seemed darker, the light from the stone barely illuminating the table, leaving the rest of the room cloaked in shadow. I took a cautious step forward, my gaze locked on the glowing stone. As I reached out, my hand trembling, the whispers came again—but this time, they weren't just in my mind. The sound echoed from all directions.

"Wake up.

The warning came too late. My fingertips grazed the surface of the stone, and the world around me shifted. What I had thought was just an oval-shaped stone was actually something entirely different—a gear, a cog, to be exact. As soon as my fingers made contact, a soft, almost imperceptible click echoed through the room. The stone shifted slightly beneath my touch, and I realized with a shock that it wasn't just a stone—it was a key. I had unknowingly triggered something waiting for me to find it. And now, with the turn of this key, I was about to unlock whatever it was.

Suddenly, a memory flashed before me. I remembered being in the garden with Mother, standing between the shed and the greenhouse. There, in the wall, was a loose brick. Beneath it, I had discovered a small box, its surface marked with a symbol of a cog etched into its surface. Could it be the key? A way to open it without damaging the delicate contents inside? My heart raced as I realized the connection. This could be the key to unlocking that box, a secret I had forgotten until now. I hadn't understood its significance back then, but now, standing in the dim cellar, it felt as if the pieces of a much larger puzzle were finally falling into place.

THE NEXT DAY

The ink blurs as I write these final entries in my diary, my hand unsteady from all I've endured. The weight of everything presses down on me, making each word a battle to inscribe. I don't know if anyone will ever discover this diary—or if they'll believe its contents if they do. Perhaps it's best if they don't. Some truths are too perilous to unearth, too terrifying to confront.

I read through my previous entry, the words feeling foreign yet unsettlingly familiar. I don't remember writing any of it, and yet, the events described linger in my mind as though they happened in a blurred, almost unreal dream.

The morning light was still weak, casting a hazy glow over the yard as I stood there, holding the cog. My thoughts were a whirlwind, the puzzle pieces of the past few days coming together in strange, unnerving ways. I couldn't wait any longer. I had to know what was inside.

I heard the sound of my parents in the kitchen, their voices muffled but unmistakable. I couldn't face them yet—not until I knew more, not until I could make sense of the bizarre discoveries I had made. I needed to do this alone.

I quietly stepped outside, the cool air biting at my skin as I walked toward the shed. It loomed ahead, the same one I had passed countless times, yet now, with the strange cog shaped gear in my hands, it felt different. There was a shift in the air. It felt like I was truly immersed in solving a mystery. Each step I took brought me closer to unlocking something long hidden.

I approached the wall where I'd noticed the odd markings before—the ones that had haunted me. My heart pounded in excitement as I carefully traced my fingers over the brickwork, searching for the loose brick I had seen in my memory. I found it quickly, just as I had recalled, its edge slightly raised from the others. I dug my fingers into the crack, feeling the dirt and mortar give way as I pried it loose. The brick came free with a soft, unsettling scrape, revealing a dark space behind it.

There it was—the wooden box with the gear-shaped keyhole. I don't know why someone would create such a key, but somehow, it worked.

I swallowed hard, the weight of what I was doing pressing down on me like a stone lodged in my chest. My hand trembled as I placed the cog into the indentation on the box. The moment it clicked into place, I felt a strange hum reverberate through my fingers. A soft creak of wood echoed through the stillness as the box sprang open, revealing something I hadn't anticipated—a journal. The cover embossed with the same symbol as the box—the same intricate cog design. The words on the cover were faded, but legible.

It read; The Story of: No Name.

I read further. It seemed to be written by someone who had lived here before—someone who knew about the dark history of this house and the twisted forces that had lurked within it. What had I stumbled upon? And why was this box hidden beneath the wall of the shed?

My parents' voices grew louder in the distance, their conversation drifting closer as if they were searching for me. But I couldn't tear my eyes away from the journal nestled inside the box. Its aged leather cover felt warm against my fingertips, the embossed cog symbol almost glowing in the pale morning light. The truth, it seemed, was finally within reach. My heart raced as I opened the cover, the pages inside brittle and yellowed with time. The first entry was written in a spidery, elegant script, the ink faded but still legible:

"For those who find this, know that what you hold is more than a journal—it is a warning."

Whatever I was about to uncover, it wasn't just a story; it was something that had been hidden for a reason.

"Dawn?" my mother's voice called out, startling me.

I quickly snapped the journal shut and looked toward the house. With trembling hands, I tucked the journal back into the box and slid it into the hollow in the wall, covering it hastily with the brick. For now, the truth would have to wait.

Once breakfast was finished, I decided a walk would clear my head. I needed to escape the walls of the house, away from the prying eyes of my parents. I stepped outside and made my way toward the edge of the property. The scent of damp earth mixed with the lingering spring chill, the world around me feeling quieter than usual. When I reached the edge of the woods, I stopped. A strange pull urged me to enter, but hesitation gripped me. The Wendigo. I recalled the chilling experience that Prosperity and I had witnessed. I stood there, looking at the dark expanse of trees stretching before me.

Were Wendigos native to South Dakota, or did they wander everywhere? I shook the thought from my mind, determined not to scare myself. I didn't want to walk through the woods today anyway; I saw no point in doing so.

Later, as the sun dipped below the horizon, painting the sky in deep hues of amber and violet, I sat alone in my room. The faint glow of my bedside lamp cast a comforting light across the space.

I noticed I only have a few pages left to write in this diary. It felt as though the end was approaching, not just for the diary, but for whatever was unfolding around me. There was still so much left unsaid, so many questions unanswered, but I was running out of writing space.

I quietly stepped outside and made my way to the garden, determined to retrieve the journal from the box hidden in the wall of the shed. I carefully pulled the loose brick free, revealing the small wooden box tucked inside. There it was, untouched and safe. A wave of relief washed over me—my parents hadn't suspected a thing, allowing me the freedom to uncover the secrets that lay hidden within the pages of that journal.

I steadied my hands as I turned the pages, revealing fragmented entries, strange diagrams, and hastily scrawled symbols that mirrored the cog on the box. The writer's words grew more frantic with each page, detailing events that felt eerily familiar—shadows that lingered too long, whispers in the dark, and a warning:

"To unlock the truth is to invite the watchers."

The words struck me like a blow. Watchers. The ones with the almond shaped eyes. The pieces began to fall into place, but they formed a picture I couldn't fully understand, not yet.

I came across an odd entry, its ink smeared and chaotic:

"I thought it had ended, but it was merely the beginning. The key unlocks more than doors; it stirs what should remain entombed. If this journal has reached your hands, tread carefully. They are always watching."

The room seemed to grow colder, the shadows around me shifting subtly, as though the very walls were leaning in to listen. A soft knock broke through the silence, startling me. Three steady raps on my bedroom window. My heart leapt into my throat. Slowly, I turned to face the glass.

There it was. A figure with almond shaped eyes.

Its pale, teardrop head tilted ever so slightly, its inky black eyes unblinking, unrelenting. I gasped as it raised one long, thin finger to the glass and tapped once more. And then, it was gone.

Behind me, I heard the pages of the journal flutter, the whisper of paper slicing through the silence, despite the absolute stillness of the room. When I turned, the pages went still as if caught in the act.

The words on the last page had changed—new ink bleeding into the paper, the letters dark and deliberate, as though scrawled by an unseen hand:

"Do not trust what you see."

Beneath the warning, a symbol I had never seen before took shape—what appeared to be a constellation, its stars connected by delicate, glowing lines, forming an intricate, celestial pattern that pulsed faintly as if alive. Curious, my fingers hovered over the ink, yet I didn't dare touch it. The air around me felt charged, heavy—like the tense stillness before a storm breaks.

As I reached the end of this diary, my hands trembled with a growing unease. My pulse drummed in my ears. I am about to open the journal and read the Story of No Name. Deep down, I knew—this wasn't over.

Not by a long shot.

ABOUT THE AUTHOR

Nick Downs has always been captivated by the mysterious and the unexplained. Growing up in Lincoln Nebraska, he found inspiration in local legends, eerie tales, and the quiet allure of late-night storytelling. When not writing, Nick Downs enjoys exploring abandoned places, researching folklore, and discovering new ways to unravel the unknown.

With a passion for crafting suspenseful narratives that blur the line between reality and fiction, Nick Downs aims to create stories that resonate with readers long after the final page is turned. *The Diary of Dawn McWarlick* marks his debut novel and serves as the first installment in what is set to become a spine-chilling series of mysteries.

Nick Downs is the founder of Paranormal L.I.G.H.T.S, a dedicated group exploring the mysteries of the unknown and investigating reports of the paranormal. With years of experience delving into haunted locations and uncovering eerie phenomena, Nick has built a reputation for seeking the truth where others fear to tread.

This book began as a personal project in 2005, inspired by Nick Downs' own experiences and the eyewitness accounts of others who had encountered the unexplainable. Over time, it evolved into a deeply compelling narrative, rooted in true events from the case files of Paranormal L.I.G.H.T.S. (Lincoln Investigations of Ghost Hauntings and The Supernatural).

Nick Downs, also the author of *A Guide to the Paranormal Side*, brings his expertise and unique perspective to this work, offering readers an immersive glimpse into the mysterious and otherworldly.